THE SOHO KILLER

An absolutely gripping crime mystery with a massive twist

BIBA PEARCE

Detective Rob Miller Mysteries Book 6

Joffe Books, London
www.joffebooks.com

First published in Great Britain in 2022

© Biba Pearce

This book is a work of fiction. Names, characters, businesses, organizations, places and events are either the product of the author's imagination or are used fictitiously. Any resemblance to actual persons, living or dead, events or locales is entirely coincidental. The spelling used is British English except where fidelity to the author's rendering of accent or dialect supersedes this. The right of Biba Pearce to be identified as author of this work has been asserted in accordance with the Copyright, Designs and Patents Act 1988.

Cover art by Nebojša Zorić

ISBN: 978-1-80405-562-5

PROLOGUE

Twenty years ago . . .

The club was pumping. Human bodies moving together, gyrating to a techno beat. Mostly male, but also some female couples, scantily dressed, showing off to each other. It was an elaborate mating ritual. They were sizing each other up, testing the waters, pheromones swirling. Eye contact, a flirtatious smile, a flutter of eyelashes.

Would you like to dance?

Moving around each other, then touching, maybe a kiss. Done deal. *Your place or mine?*

He shuddered as he made his way through the crowd. Every fibre of his being wanted out of here, but it was necessary for what he had to do.

There could be only one winner. Him.

He spotted the man at the bar, drinking a cocktail. Lonely, forlorn, upset. Perfect.

The killer went up to him and smiled. "Hello again."

"Oh, it's you." A spark of recognition. The blue eyes lifted. "I didn't know you came here."

"Don't usually." He'd never stepped foot in the place before. "But I was in the area and I felt like a drink. Didn't want to be alone."

A knowing grunt.

"Mind if I join you?"

The man hesitated, then gave a nod. "Sure. Why not?"

Smiling, the killer eased into the seat next to him. "What are you drinking?"

"Mojitos, they do a good one here."

"Great, I'll join you."

He flagged down the barman. "Two more, please."

"Do you come here often, then?" the killer asked, feigning interest.

"Sometimes. My partner and I like to dance. We're both so busy, it helps us let off steam."

"I totally get it." He didn't. He'd never liked dancing. What possessed people to bounce around like idiots to boring, repetitive music in a confined space until they were sweaty and red-faced? Ballroom dancing, yes. Swirling elegantly to classical crescendos. Tuxedos and ball gowns. He could understand that. But not this type of dancing. "My job is fairly stressful, so I like to let off steam too."

"What do you do?"

"I'm in banking. Asset management." The crisp white shirt and tailored trousers he was wearing backed up his story. As did the flashy Rolex on his wrist. A knock-off, but the man wouldn't know that. It was a very good fake. "How about you?"

"I'm a psychologist. I'm between jobs, actually."

"A psychologist, wow." The killer's sheepish grin belied the tension in his shoulders. "What can you tell about me?"

A chuckle. "Not much, since we haven't known each other very long. I know you like photography."

A mutual hobby. That's where they'd met. The local adult community college. The killer had been surprised by how much he'd enjoyed it. He might even keep it up after all this was over.

Once he'd won.

"Anything else?"

"You're outgoing, fairly impulsive, and you don't like being alone."

The killer laughed. "Not bad."

Totally incorrect. If the man was any good at all, he should've been able to tell he was more introverted than extroverted, planned everything to the finest detail and loved being alone.

"Where's your partner tonight?" the killer asked, even though he knew. Mind games. He was better at them than the shrink.

A flicker of an eyelid. A sore point. "He's away on business."

"That's a shame. You didn't want to go with him?"

"It's not that kind of trip. He's in sales. This is a big conference somewhere up north. Partners aren't welcome."

"Well, his loss is my gain." He flashed a naughty grin.

The man's gaze lingered on his face. "You know, I didn't realise you were . . ."

"Appearances can be deceiving. I don't broadcast it."

"Why not? Haven't you come out?"

"It's not that." He didn't need his head read. "It's just with my work . . ." He shrugged. "I think it's better if people don't know. None of their business anyway, right?"

"Right." The man hesitated, as if unsure whether to continue. Finally, he said, "If you ever want to talk . . ."

The killer was getting bored with this conversation. Time to move on to the next step in his plan. "Thanks, I'll keep that in mind."

A shared smile. Eye contact, more than was appropriate.

"Hey, do you want to dance?" the killer asked.

"Sure."

They finished their drinks and moved to the dance floor. The killer had only so many practised moves, but it wouldn't take long. Any minute now . . .

The man stumbled, clutching his arm.

"You okay?" the killer asked.

He frowned. "I don't feel so good. Everything's spinning."

"God, I didn't realise you'd drunk that much."

"I didn't. I—"

He stopped, closing his eyes and teetering to the side.

The killer put an arm around his waist. "Okay, mate. Enough for you. Let's get you home." He shot an apologetic smile at the other revellers, most of whom nodded sympathetically. They'd all been there.

The killer led the man out of the club. "My car's nearby. I'll give you a lift home."

"Thanks. I don't know . . . I can't . . . Oh, God . . ." His words ran into one another.

The killer kept his head down on the way out, just in case of security cameras. Half lugging, half dragging the seemingly inebriated man down the street, he rounded a corner and came to his car. With some effort, he heaved the legless man inside and closed the door.

The man lived a few streets away — within walking distance, but not within stumbling distance. Too many cameras, too many potential eyewitnesses. The grey GTi was far less conspicuous as it slunk down the street, keeping well below the speed limit.

Less than five minutes later, the killer pulled up outside the man's house. He glanced over his shoulder. The man was out cold in the back, drooling all over the seat.

Charming. Still, it was exactly as he'd planned. So far, everything was working out perfectly.

The killer pulled a black hoodie over his white shirt, so he'd blend into the shadows. Then he took a pair of latex gloves out of the glove compartment and put them on. Finally, he wrapped two plastic bags around his shoes and tied them at the ankle, to prevent any prints or other trace evidence. You couldn't be too careful these days.

Making sure there were no dark heads watching from lit windows, he heaved the drugged man into the house. It was easy enough to rummage through the man's pockets for his keys, and as he already knew from his previous reconnaissance, there was no burglar alarm.

It was a split-level apartment with the living room and kitchen downstairs, and a double bedroom and bathroom upstairs. Brown carpets, paisley wallpaper, dark wood furniture. The place was stuck in the seventies.

The killer laid the man down on the carpet. At least the stains wouldn't show.

He returned to his car, opened the boot and took out a length of rope and a rucksack which, as well as some cleaning products and a few other bits and pieces, contained an outfit he'd bought months ago from a fetish shop in Amsterdam. The police would never think to look that far afield. He smiled to himself as he stripped the man and dressed him in the bondage gear. Poor fool wouldn't know what had hit him.

Dressing a semi-conscious man was hard work, and the killer was lathered in sweat by the time he'd finished.

"Let's get on with it," he muttered to himself. The longer he stayed here, the more chance there was of leaving evidence behind.

He tied the rope around the man's neck and secured it at the back with a slipknot. He gave it a firm pull. That wasn't going to budge. Then, taking the other end of the rope, he climbed up the stairs to the top level.

Now for the hard part.

Like a sailor at the mast, the killer hauled the rope until the man began to move. He must have weighed at least seventy kilograms, so it was hard work, but eventually he had him upright. The noose had tightened but it wasn't strangling him yet. That would come.

He hoisted the man up, using the banister as leverage, until the man's feet were off the ground. Another few inches would do it.

Christ, he was heavy.

The man suddenly woke up. Lack of air, most probably. He grunted, then began flailing his arms around, trying to clutch onto something, anything, to stop the noose from tightening further.

"It's futile," whispered the killer, watching from above.

There was a disgusting gurgling sound as the man's air supply was cut off. His legs kicked back and forth, making him sway. The noose would just get tighter the more he struggled.

Eventually, the man grew still. The gurgling stopped and his limbs ceased flailing about.

Was he dead?

The killer secured the rope around the banister, keeping it taut. To be believable, the man's feet should be a good few inches off the ground. If he wasn't dead, he would be soon.

Job done. For there could only be one winner.

All that was left for the killer to do was pack up his rucksack and get out of there. He left via the front door, closing it gently behind him. Not once did he turn back to look at the victim's face.

CHAPTER 1

Present day

DCI Rob Miller sank down on the couch and switched on the television. The last few bars of the news jingle faded out and the presenter appeared, straight-backed and professional, as if steeling herself for the task ahead. She was serious, speaking in a clipped tone, her made-up face carefully devoid of expression.

Protests by an environmental activist group had brought London to a standstill, with traffic chaos in Westminster, crowding on Waterloo Bridge, pop-up stalls and surges of people bringing the tourism industry to a halt. The Metropolitan Police were out in full force, but even they couldn't contain the exuberant protesters. A woman in tie-dyed leggings and dreadlocks held up a placard sporting the slogan *TELL THE TRUTH*. Another said *ACT NOW*.

He was glad he had the weekend off.

Trigger wandered in and lay down, resting his furry head on Rob's foot. Comforted, Rob leaned over and gave the golden Labrador a pat. Trigger had adjusted to the new addition to the family incredibly well. At first, he hadn't known what to make of the baby, but now he adored Jack and followed him everywhere.

The house was quiet. Jo was upstairs putting Jack down after a day of frenzied activity. A walk in the park, home for lunch and then a friend's birthday party, not that a bunch of one-year-olds could do much, other than crawl around and giggle. The soft-play centre had been a hit though. He'd never been to one of those before — hadn't had that type of upbringing.

Rob gave a loud yawn. Domesticity was surprisingly tiring. In a way, it was easier working on a murder case than looking after a baby, not to mention socialising with other new parents, endlessly discussing nappy changes, sleep routines and developmental milestones. At one point this afternoon he'd looked across at Jo and seen her eyes glaze over. She was as bored as he was.

He was glad she'd gone back to work, even if it was just a desk job, as she put it. Jo needed that intellectual stimulation, just like he did. Not that being a parent wasn't satisfying. It was, just in a different way. He'd seen a spark come back into her over the last few months that she'd lost for a while in the endless repetitive routine of crying, feeding and sleeping. Things were getting back to normal.

"He's out cold." Jo padded barefoot into the living room. She was still wearing her summer dress, her blonde hair slightly dishevelled.

"After a day like that, I'm not surprised." He was exhausted, and it was only six thirty.

She collapsed beside him, curling her legs underneath her on the couch. "I'm in the office tomorrow. You okay to handle the morning shift?"

"Of course."

They were getting into a routine. Jo worked three days a week at the MI5 offices in Millbank, and the remaining two from home. Tanya, who they'd initially hired to clean the house, had turned out to be an excellent babysitter, so they now employed her to look after Jack in the daytime rather than send him to a crèche.

Jo laid her head on his shoulder. Soft hair caressed his neck. He put an arm around her and they snuggled for a while. The news presenter had moved on to local politics, and Raza Ashraf, the London mayor, appeared, standing in front of a rough housing estate in South London. He was smiling and pointing to the austere brick block behind him, one of many identical blocks on the estate.

"How's Mike doing?" Jo asked, her eyes on the screen.

Detective Sergeant Mike Manner had left the Major Investigation Team at the end of last year to run a youth scheme on just such an estate. It had been the Mayor's brainchild, a way to get kids back into school and provide them with the skills they needed to find work and not have to resort to crime. It was a good idea in principle, although from what he'd seen, it was yet to take off. The Beaufort Estate where Mike worked had a trickle of youths in the programme, mostly teenage girls. The boys had been slower to get involved. Hopefully, it would improve.

"Good." Rob smiled. "He popped in the other day. I think he's enjoying the change."

"Think he'll ever come back to the force?"

"Maybe." Mike had been a good cop, if a tad intense. But then weren't they all when an investigation became personal? Mike had been shot last year in a sting operation that had gone bad. Two major drug dealers had escaped, but they'd apprehended a couple of minor ones and shut down a child exploitation ring. That was something. One had to applaud the small victories when they arose.

He knew she was thinking about work, about how much she'd missed it. "You got a busy week ahead?"

"I expect so. It's always busy." She didn't elaborate, but he got the gist. As an intelligence analyst, she coordinated teams on the ground, processed intel, forwarded it to the powers that be. MI5 had several thousand people under surveillance at any given time, huge watch lists of potential terrorists, known associates, activists and other agitators. They did what they could, but it was like shaving off the tip of an iceberg. Most frightening was what you didn't see.

"You okay?"

"Yeah, just tired. You?"

"Same."

They sat together for a while, enjoying the silence, while the news gave way to the weather. A heatwave ahead. Temperatures expected of up to thirty-five degrees.

"Blimey," murmured Jo. "I'm glad my office has air conditioning."

So did the squad room, but crime always went up when the weather got warmer. Tempers flared along with the temperature. Domestic violence, gang-related crime, pub brawls — they all spiked in hot weather.

Rob felt his eyes grow heavy. Trigger was breathing deeply and evenly at his feet, and Jo had her arm draped over his chest. Contentment was something he'd never experienced before. Not this kind, when everything seemed right with the world.

A high-pitched peel jarred Rob awake. Jo groaned. Trigger raised his head and looked at him as if to say, "Thanks for killing the mood."

"Sorry," he mumbled. What time was it? Glancing at the screen, he saw it was almost nine. He'd been asleep for hours.

The phone kept ringing angrily in his hand. Rob didn't recognise the number. He was tempted to leave it, but even though he wasn't on call, he was a DCI, and if another unit needed his help, he ought to be available. "Yeah?"

There was a loud crackle as static echoed in his ear. Strange. Was this an overseas call? "Hello?"

Eventually, the line cleared and a tinny male voice said, "Robert, is that you?"

His heart skipped a beat.

It couldn't be. Not after all this time.

Dread swept over him, making his skin prickle.

"What?" mouthed Jo.

Rob felt like someone was walking over his grave.

He took a deep breath. "Hello, Dad."

CHAPTER 2

The main entrance to Charing Cross Police Station was in Agar Street. Once a hospital, it was a large, square classical building overlooking Victoria Embankment. Recently refurbished, it was one of the biggest and busiest police stations in London.

Usually, Rob felt a sense of awe as he walked under the Palladian pillars into the centuries-old building. It was a far cry from the modern glass-and-brick office block in Putney where the Major Investigation Team was located.

Tonight, however, his thoughts were centred on one person. His father. Picked up for God only knew what.

The phone call had been hurried, garbled. His old man hadn't made much sense. All Rob had managed to hear was: *Soho . . . They've taken the money off me . . . I'm a dead man.*

Tempted to leave him there to rot — what had the old bastard ever done for him? — Rob had wrestled with his conscience, finally got dressed and driven to the Strand. Jo had said he'd regret it if he didn't. She was probably right.

The forty-minute journey had given him plenty of time to think, to form answers to the multitude of questions swimming around in his head.

Arrested for possession? Nah, his dad was many things but not a drug dealer. Antisocial behaviour? More likely, but that didn't make sense given his mention of money. Disrupting the peace? Possibly. He did have a temper on him. Rob had felt the brunt of that many times when his father had had a few too many down the Nags Head.

He showed his ID card to the duty sergeant and was ushered through the revolving doors into the inner workings of the police station. It was larger than any other station he'd ever been in, the ceilings double the height of the corridors in his office block and twice as wide. They were devoid of pictures, furniture or carpeting. Fluorescent downlighting illuminated the nothingness.

He squinted, tiredness prickling behind his eyes. The beige walls seemed to unfurl around him as he walked the width of the building to the custody suite, where his father was being held. By the time he got there, he was feeling vaguely nauseous.

"I'm here to see Mr Ronnie Miller." He showed the female officer behind the desk his ID badge. "I'm from the Major Investigation Team."

He purposely didn't mention his name so she wouldn't make the connection. Tired and overworked, she barely glanced at his ID card before giving a brief nod. "DS Abrahams has been assigned to his case."

"Have they seen him yet?"

"Not yet, no."

"So the suspect hasn't been arrested?"

She looked surprised. "No. He was found with twenty thousand pounds on his person. The police officer who did the stop-and-search brought him in for questioning."

Twenty thousand pounds? Christ. What was Ronnie up to? "Did he say where he got it?"

"No, sir."

"Right, I see. I'll interview him."

"You will?" Her eyebrows shot up in surprise.

"Yeah, he may have information pertaining to a case I'm working on. I'll handle the interrogation from here on."

"Okay, if you're sure, sir. I'll have him brought through to Interview Room Seven, just down the hall."

"Thank you."

Rob walked to the room, the sick feeling building in the pit of his stomach. It was always this way with his father. Nothing that Ronnie was involved in turned out to be good. Rob wasn't even sure why he'd come. Ronnie was nothing to him. Not anymore. If he was in trouble, then it was up to him to get himself out of it. Rob took a seat and waited for the custody officer to bring Ronnie in.

Footsteps in the corridor. Rob stiffened. As they drew nearer, he got to his feet. The door opened and in walked his father.

At first, Rob didn't recognise the man standing in front of him. Untidy grey hair, a paunch and a scraggly beard, he was nothing like the image of his father Rob had had in his head. That man was younger, stronger, angrier. Furious at the world for giving him the raw end of the stick. A dead wife, a child to raise on his own, a job that barely paid the rent. Rob had seen one of his payslips once and had been shocked at how little mechanics earned.

Still, his dad was a grease monkey through and through. Always had been and always would be. Even now, his fingernails were black with oil and there were grease stains on his clothing. His only other passion was gambling. Rob bet that was where the twenty grand came in.

"Hello, Dad."

The old guy surveyed him for a long moment. What he was thinking, Rob had no idea.

He shuffled across the room. "Didn't think you were gonna come."

No "*How are you? How have the last sixteen years of your life been?*" But Ronnie Miller had never been one for small talk.

"I wasn't going to." He stopped. How could he begin to explain why he wasn't going to come? Because he didn't give a shit? Because he hated his father? Because pretending Ronnie was dead had been better than the alternative?

A grunt. "You look well."

"Let's cut the crap. I'm going to have to caution you. This is an official interview."

"You're kidding?"

"Would you rather I leave and DS Abrahams take over?"

Ronnie sat down. He moved slowly, his movements considered and cautious.

Rob cautioned Ronnie since he'd been brought in under suspicion of committing an offence. If his responses implicated him in any way, the interview might well result in an arrest. Rob wasn't above arresting his father, if it came to that. Although to save confusion it would be easier to hand him over to DS Abrahams at that point.

"What are you doing here, Dad?"

Just for a second, Rob thought he saw regret pass over Ronnie's features, but then it was gone.

"I got caught."

"Caught doing what?"

A sigh. "I took money from my place of work."

"Took? You mean you stole it?"

"No, it's a loan." Ronnie clasped his hands in his lap, refusing to look at his son. "I was going to return it as soon as I could."

Rob surveyed the man he'd grown up with. His face was nearly as wrinkled as his clothes. The years hadn't been kind, but then they never were to people whose major pastimes were booze and cards.

"I need it, all right? I owe this guy. If I don't pay up, he's gonna come after me."

Now they were getting somewhere.

"You borrowed money? Was it to pay a gambling debt? Except you couldn't pay it back, so you stole it from your employer?"

The look on his dad's face told him he was right.

Rob sucked in a breath. "Jesus, Dad."

The old man spread his hands. "What would you have me do? The guy's an animal."

"You shouldn't have borrowed from him in the first place." Rob tried not to sound sanctimonious but failed.

A snort. "All right for you to say. You don't spend all day in a garage getting paid peanuts."

Here we go, thought Rob.

"After all I've done for you, the least you could do is get me out of here."

"All you've done?" Rob scoffed, trying not to lose his temper. "You'll have to remind me what that is some day." His training meant he didn't go off the boil like he once might have done. He was used to dealing with cantankerous suspects, people who thought the law didn't apply to them, and those who blatantly disregarded it.

"Who is this guy?"

His father stared sullenly at him.

"Who did you borrow from?"

"Magnus Olsen."

The name didn't mean anything to Rob, but then he didn't know many loan sharks.

Ronnie scowled. "Are you going to help me or not?"

"I haven't decided yet." It felt good having the upper hand. Petty, he knew, but his old man deserved it. "How much did you take?" Even though he knew the answer, he wanted to hear it from his father.

"Twenty grand."

Rob pursed his lips. "That's not pocket change."

"I know. The bastards took it off me."

"It'll be evidence now," Rob said. "Nothing I can do about that."

Ronnie thumped his fist down on the table. "It's my money. They've no right to take it."

Rob spluttered. "You serious?"

"Okay, but I need it back."

Rob leaned forward. "Ronnie, I don't think you understand how much trouble you're in. You were caught with twenty grand that you can't account for. You're going to be arrested and charged with theft."

"Can't you do something?"

Rob pursed his lips. "If you can prove that you obtained this money legally, then I can give it back to you and you can go on your way. If not . . ." He shrugged.

Ronnie glared at his hands.

"Who did you take it from?" Rob chose his words carefully. He wasn't about to break the law for his father.

"The scooter shop where I work."

"What's it called?"

"Rex's Scooters. In Marshall Street, off Carnaby."

"Soho?"

"Yeah, I was walking home, just past Soho Square, when I was stopped and searched." He shook his head.

"And your boss, Rex. Will he confirm that he loaned you the money?"

"You mean you're gonna call him?" Ronnie's eyes widened.

"Yes, that's what I'm going to do. If he's okay with you taking the money, then we're good. If not, you're going to jail."

Ronnie swallowed. "Bloody hell, Rob. You're gonna cost me my job, and it's a good one. I'm the store manager."

What idiot put Ronnie — a man with a drinking problem and an addiction to gambling — in charge?

"*You* cost you your job, and I can't help that."

Heaving a sigh, Ronnie nodded. "Okay, call him."

Rob got up. "Wait here."

* * *

A short time later, Rob had roused a groggy-sounding Rex on the phone and explained the situation. "If you can confirm you lent Ronnie the twenty grand, I can get him out of here. Obviously, he'll be giving the money back."

"When?"

"Right now. You can collect it at Charing Cross Police Station. Obviously, Ronnie will resign with immediate effect."

Rex sighed. "He was a good mechanic. Nothing he couldn't fix."

"I know."

Once again, Ronnie had screwed up, but that wasn't Rob's problem.

Eventually, Rex agreed to make a statement saying he'd loaned Ronnie Miller, an employee, twenty thousand pounds with the understanding that it would be paid back in full in the very near future.

Breathing a sigh of relief, Rob spoke to the custody sergeant and Ronnie was released.

"Did you get the money back?" was the first thing that came out of his mouth as they walked out of the custody suite and back through the main reception.

"I did."

"Well, where is it?"

"Rex has it."

Ronnie stopped walking. "You gave it back to him?"

"Yeah, what did you expect? It's his money. Now you don't have to pay it back."

"But what about Magnus?"

They walked down the street to Rob's Skoda hatchback. It was an unmarked pool car, not a pursuit vehicle and not very cool. He saw his father's eyebrow rise as he clocked it.

"Get in."

"What?" Ronnie halted on the pavement. "I'm not coming with you."

"Oh yes you are. We're going to see this loan shark."

"Fuck that." His old man turned away, but Rob grabbed him by the arm. It felt thin under his fingers.

"You're going to agree to pay him back in instalments. I can't have them sending the heavies round with a baseball bat."

Scorn furrowed Ronnie's brow. "Magnus will never go for that."

"Magnus will have no choice," Rob countered.

Ronnie's eyes lit up. He'd obviously forgotten his son was a police detective. "Okay," he murmured. "But he's not gonna like it."

"I don't care. Tell me where he is."

"You wanna go there now?" He glanced at the cheap Casio on his wrist. It had started drizzling, a light spritz of a rainfall that felt more like moisture hanging in the air than actual rain. Even so, Rob didn't feel like getting wet.

"Yeah, now. I'm sure he'll still be awake." The sarcasm was biting.

Ronnie sighed. "Horizons Casino. Leicester Square." Reluctantly, the old man got in. "You're out of your mind," he said. "They'll kill me if I don't pay up."

"I doubt that," Rob muttered. "They'd never get their money if they killed you. They might beat you to a pulp, but they'll let you live." He slammed the door and jumped in the other side.

Ronnie stared at him. "You've changed."

"You haven't. Belt up, let's go." He put the car in gear and drove towards Leicester Square.

Rob wasn't sure why he gave a shit. Perhaps because at the end of the day, Ronnie might be a crook and a gambler, but he was still his father.

CHAPTER 3

They crawled down Lisle Street toward a bustling Leicester Square. Neon lights flickered off the damp tarmac, while revellers and theatregoers darted across the streets, weaving between cars and buses. Rob gritted his teeth while a street-sweeper meandered along the road in front of them, sucking litter from the gutters.

Horizons Casino was housed in a cream-coloured baroque building next door to the Empire Cinema. Understated, the name was printed in black letters on a silver background above the door, and a red carpet beckoned them inside. Rob parked as close as he could get. The Metropolitan Police's Homicide and Serious Crime Command permit on his dashboard would ward off any overzealous traffic cop. He climbed out of the car and headed towards the red carpet. "Come on, then."

Ronnie followed slowly, reluctant to confront his nemesis.

Rob showed the receptionist his warrant card. Two burly bouncers in black T-shirts and trousers cast worried looks at each other. "I'm not here to cause trouble," Rob said. "I just want to talk to someone."

The receptionist gave an uncertain nod, while one of the bouncers touched his earpiece. A heads-up to the boss, no doubt, to give those VIP customers time to make hasty trips to the men's room, while high-stakes backroom poker games would be put on hold.

"He works from the lounge." Ronnie straightened his shirt. It didn't do any good. It still looked like he'd pulled it straight out of a washing machine and put it on. Interesting, though, to see his father nervous. Life had clearly knocked him down a few pegs. Served the bastard right. Rob wasn't a great believer in karma, but it seemed that his old man had got what was coming to him.

They passed a chaos of slot machines frantically beeping and tinkling. The room widened and Rob spotted baccarat, blackjack and three-card poker. Players murmured, glasses clinked and roulette wheels spun. Occasionally there was a gasp of victory, but more often it was moans of dejection as gamblers saw their money thrown away.

"That's him."

Magnus Olsen was a giant of a man with pale skin, a trimmed beard and dusky-brown hair pulled back in a ponytail. He sat in a red leather-backed booth, his laptop open in front of him. The steel-grey suit he was wearing fit him like it was custom made. Flawless lines, tailored to perfection. There was nobody else at the table, only a fresh glass of beer fizzing in front of him.

Rob approached, followed by a shuffling Ronnie.

Magnus looked up. "Can I help you?" His eyes flitted to the side, where a buff guy in a badly fitting suit hovered. The henchman took a step closer.

Rob held up his ID card. "DCI Miller, Major Investigation Team. Could I have a word?"

Magnus held up a hand and the henchman froze.

"Ronnie Miller." Curious arctic-blue eyes roamed over the reprobate gambler behind Rob. "Father, I presume?"

Astute too. "Correct. I'm here to arrange a payment schedule for what he owes you."

"And here was I thinking you were going to cover it for him."

Rob managed a thin smile. "You thought wrong."

The giant's gaze flickered from Rob to Ronnie and back again. He was irritated by the intrusion but hid it well. "What do you propose?"

"Twelve months," Rob said. Ronnie opened his mouth to object, but Rob silenced him with a look. "Twelve months of regular payments until the debt is cleared. And under no circumstances should you lend him any more money. Not if you want to get it back."

Ronnie scowled at the floor.

Magnus studied Rob, stroking his beard. "I can work with that."

Rob nodded curtly. There was no contract, no handshake — just the man's word. Rob had no choice but to accept it. It was quite possible that the hovering henchman would still beat Ronnie to a pulp, but that was out of his control. He'd done what he could. If Ronnie chose not to honour the agreement, he would have to suffer the consequences.

They left the forced gaiety of the casino behind them and stepped out into the night. Rob took a deep breath of muggy air. Despite the dampness, it was a warm evening.

"Now you can go." Rob turned to his father, whose bushy eyebrows rose in surprise.

"You're going to leave me here, in Leicester Square?"

"Yeah. That's where they found you, wasn't it?"

"That was Soho Square. I was cutting through to get the Northern Line from Tottenham Court Road. I live in Camberwell."

Rob had thought he was still in North London. Apparently not.

"Sorry, I can't take you home. I've got to get back." He stared at his old man, unsure what to do next. A hug was out of the question, a handshake inappropriate under the circumstances, and a pat on the back seemed condescending. Would it be another ten years before they saw each other again? Shoving his hands into his pockets, he took a step backwards. "Keep well, Dad."

Ronnie gave a gruff nod. "I suppose I owe you one for getting me out of jail."

Rob shrugged. "Glad I could help."

What would have been an awkward moment was saved by his phone ringing. He answered it, turning away. "Miller."

"This is Control. Could you specify your location?"

Heart sinking, he told the operator where he was. She'd be able to see via the tracker on his vehicle anyway. He knew what this meant. There'd been a major incident nearby and he was closest. He'd have to respond.

"Could you get to Soho, DCI Miller? A body's been reported in Soho Square."

"Soho Square?" He frowned. That was where Ronnie had been picked up with his bag of cash.

"Yes, that's the location we've been given. Multiple phone-ins. The HAT team is on its way, but you're already in the area. Could you contain the scene until they get there?"

"Isn't there anyone local?" Come to think of it, he hadn't noticed any uniformed officers patrolling the West End, which was unusual.

"They've been relocated due to the protest," she told him.

Ah, right. The environmental rebellion protest in Waterloo and Westminster.

He took a deep breath. "Okay, I'm on my way."

When he turned back, his father had gone.

CHAPTER 4

Rob fought his way through the crowd that had gathered in Soho Square. Shocked stares and low murmurings told him it was bad. Some people even had their hands over their mouths.

He elbowed his way to the front, bracing himself for what he was about to see. The first sighting of a dead body was never easy. The unnaturalness of it seemed to grab you by the throat and squeeze, making it hard to breathe. Then your brain overrode the impulse and rationalised it. This was the victim of a crime, a human being. It was his job to be here, to find out what had happened, and to preserve the crime scene so that Forensics could gather as much information from it as possible.

Still, he inhaled sharply as he set eyes on the man. *Bloody hell.*

The victim lay in the foetal position on the wet grass to the left of the statue of King Charles II. The ruler's old, stone eyes stared down unmoved, while the onlookers murmured with horror and righteous indignation.

Rob moved closer. What on earth was he wearing? It looked like some sort of sadomasochistic outfit. Black rubber shorts — if you could call them that — exposed hairy legs and a bloated stomach. A leather collar coiled around his neck, the studs gleaming in the glow of the street lamp. His arms were wrenched back, secured by wrist restraints, and connected to a chain that ran from the collar to the wristbands. He'd been whipped too. The raised welts were clearly visible on his bare back.

It was impossible to see what he looked like, since a black latex mask with cutouts for the eyes and mouth covered his face. Rob stared, unable to look away. What was that red thing in his mouth? Shit, it was some sort of ball gag. An adult toy found in many of the Soho sex shops. But it wasn't the outfit or the gag that got to him, it was the look of sheer terror in the dead man's eyes. Still open, they bulged with shock and panic.

He suppressed a shudder. Was this a sex game gone wrong? Some sort of bondage practice that had got out of control? But why here? He looked around the square. It was lit by a series of bright street lamps that made the grass appear unnaturally green. Behind the body was a tiny Tudor hut, locked and unused. He'd heard that it hid an electricity substation. He bent down. The grass around the body was undisturbed. No scuffs or striations to suggest a fight.

"Is he dead?" called a voice in the crowd.

Rob glanced up. He knew from experience that some perpetrators returned to the scene of the crime, particularly when the body was first discovered. Still, he didn't know the cause of death yet. It could have been an accident, it could have been a heart attack. He couldn't see past the bondage outfit and the terrified eyes.

The speaker was a burly, bearded man in his thirties dressed in black jeans and a leather jacket. A club bouncer of some sort, perhaps? The look on his face was one of genuine concern.

"Could everybody take a few steps back, please?" Rob shouted.

They didn't respond.

The bearded man turned around and yelled, "Get back!"

The onlookers shuffled backwards a few feet.

"Thanks." Rob nodded to the helpful onlooker. "If you could keep them back, I'll grab some police tape."

The man nodded and spread his arms. "You heard the officer — keep back."

The crime scene was probably ruined anyway. Thousands of people traipsed through here every day. They'd be lucky to find anything they could use.

He strode to his vehicle, which he'd parked at the side of the square, and took a roll of police tape out of the boot. He proceeded to cordon off the area around the body. Statue, hut, oak tree. An obtuse triangle designated by red tape. *POLICE INNER CORDON*, it read. *DO NOT CROSS*. It wasn't a large area, but it was enough to keep the onlookers from trampling all over the crime scene.

Sirens screeched and an incident response vehicle along with an ambulance ramped onto the grass. The crowd parted like the red sea, letting them through. High beams illuminated the body, giving it a stark, seedy appearance.

Two plain-clothed detectives climbed out and ducked under the cordon. Rob recognised the female officer from Southwark Police Station on the other side of the river. He didn't know the man with her.

"DS Gillian Tremayne." She offered her hand.

"I know." He shook it. "We've met once before."

Recognition registered in her face. "Oh, yes. You're a long way from home."

He shrugged. "I was passing through when I got the call."

She nodded. "This is my colleague, DS Chakrabarti."

They shook hands.

"What have we got?" Tremayne took a look at the body. "Oh, God."

Yeah, he'd had that reaction too.

"Is that a BDSM outfit?"

"Looks like it." He waved to the cordon. "I can't determine the cause of death. We'll have to wait for SOCO to get here."

"They're on their way," she said, her gaze fixed on the dead man. She shuddered and wrapped her arms around herself. Chakrabarti shifted from foot to foot, clearly unnerved. Rob took a deep breath. Death was never pretty.

A paramedic rushed up, medical backpack slung over one shoulder, defibrillator in his other hand. "Where is he?" His gaze fell on the victim, and he came to an abrupt halt. "Oh, right."

"I think he's dead," Tremayne said. "But you'd better do your thing."

The paramedic checked for signs of life, then looked up at the detectives. "Nothing," he confirmed.

"Stick around," Rob said. "We might need transportation. Everyone else is tied up with the protest." The paramedic nodded and went back to the ambulance to wait.

A white BMW bounced up onto the kerb beside the police vehicle. Liz Kramer, uber-efficient Home Office pathologist, got out, hauling her enormous metal case with her. Around her neck hung a Canon EOS camera.

She looked at Rob. "Fancy seeing you here." There was no humour in her voice.

"Hello, Liz." He nodded toward her car. "You've upgraded."

"It was time." As one of London's premier pathologists, Liz had done extremely well for herself. Given the insane hours she worked, she deserved it.

Rob made the introductions. "DI Tremayne and DS Chakrabarti."

They nodded at one another.

"Where is he, then?" Liz asked, impatient.

"Over here."

She rounded the vehicles and took her first look at the body. Such was her professionalism that she didn't flicker an eyelid. "Does anyone know him?" She put her case down and lifted the camera.

"It doesn't look like it." No one had come forward. The helpful bearded man had left after the two other detectives arrived. "Can't see his features with that ball gag thing in his mouth."

Just the eyes.

Liz took several photographs of the body in situ. "I'll get suited up." She crouched down and pulled a paper forensic suit out of her case, along with a pair of gloves and shoe coverings. It took her less than five minutes to put them on. "Public place like this." She shook her head. "Awful for Forensics."

"I know. Do what you can."

Kitted out, she ducked under the cordon and knelt beside the victim. Starting at the head, she worked her way down, taking photographs as she went. She showed none of the emotion captured in the dead man's terrified stare. Hugely impressed, Rob wondered how she did it, looking at death day after day. Yet Liz was one of the sanest people he knew.

"See the faint blood pooling here." She pointed to the victim's upper back. Lividity suggests he was lying in a supine position shortly after death. There are also a lot of foreign fibres, hairs, grease and the like, on his back. I'd say he was placed somewhere dirty before being dumped here."

"Like a gutter? Or a pavement?" Rob asked.

She nodded.

He watched as she shot a few close-ups of the victim's hands bound behind his back, the welts where he'd been whipped, the studded harness and the neck collar. When she was done shooting, she carefully unbuckled the strap holding the mouth gag in place, slipped it into an evidence bag and put it in her case. Weirdly, the mouth remained open, stretched in a macabre grimace.

"The death grin," she muttered. "Rigor mortis is setting in."

It was now close to eleven o'clock. Tremayne and Chakrabarti had split up and were working the crowd, taking down the names of the onlookers, asking if anyone had seen anything. He admired their initiative, but then he remembered being impressed by DI Tremayne before, when he'd come looking for Cranshaw. She'd been a DS back then. They'd compare notes later. Right now, he wanted to hear what Liz had to say.

"Call one of those paramedics over," she said. "I'm going to need some help. The SOCO team is stuck on the South Circular."

Rob did as requested and the same paramedic came over, still wearing his mask and gloves. Liz threw him a pair of shoe coverings. "Once you've got those on, come and help me turn him onto his side."

She unbuckled the victim's wrist restraints but his arms were frozen in place. Gently, she lifted them back into a more normal position.

The paramedic ducked under the police tape and knelt on the other side of the body. "Ready when you are."

"Now."

Together, they rolled him over.

"Let's remove the mask."

Rob held his breath. They peeled the mask off, once again bagging it for analysis. The man underneath appeared startlingly normal.

Rob exhaled. Slightly disappointed, he realised he'd been expecting some sort of monster. But he looked like a normal fifty-something guy: thinning hair, pale skin, an unremarkable face. Slightly jowly, with no scars or piercings or anything of significance. Beside him, the paramedic heaved a soft sigh of relief.

With nothing interesting to see, the crowd began to disperse. Without the mask and gag, the victim was just another dead guy. A statistic.

Liz inspected the skin around his eyes. "Petechial haemorrhaging," she said. "I can't give you a definitive cause of death yet, but I'd say he died of asphyxia."

"Autoerotic?" Tremayne had come back.

Rob glanced at her, surprised. She coloured slightly.

"Not with his hands tied behind his back. But judging by what he's wearing, it could have been some sort of sex game gone wrong." Liz checked his hands. "No defensive marks that I can see. At first glance, there doesn't appear to be any skin or hair under his fingernails, although he is dirty. That could be contamination from the wet ground or wherever he was lying before he was brought here."

"He could have been drugged," said Rob.

Liz frowned. "It's possible. I'll know more after the tox screen."

"Time of death?" Rob asked.

"Not long. Two to four hours at the most."

"It was called in just before ten," Rob remembered, glancing at his Apple Watch, a Christmas present from Jo. It had a mindboggling array of functions, and he had yet to figure them all out. "If he died between nine and ten, the timing fits."

"He may have died elsewhere," Tremayne pointed out. "And his body dumped here."

"That is certainly a possibility." Liz looked around. "There isn't much to suggest he died here in the square."

"SOCO will be able to confirm that," Rob said. "If they ever get here."

It started drizzling again. "This isn't going to help," Liz muttered. "Let's get him back to the lab."

Rob gestured to the paramedics, who came over, carrying a stretcher. Liz closed her case and got to her feet. They lifted the body onto the stretcher and were about to wheel it away when she frowned. "Wait."

They paused.

"What is it?" asked Tremayne.

Something had caught Liz's eye, and she bent over the body to inspect the neck. He heard her suck in a breath.

"What?" Rob knew that look. She'd found something significant.

"Bruising on the neck," she murmured, feeling along the trachea. "I didn't see it at first, as it was hidden by the collar."

"Bruising? As in a rope or tie?" Tremayne asked.

"Looks like it. I suspect the hyoid bone is fractured. An x-ray will confirm." She stood up again. "I'm not going to investigate any further here. Let's get him back to the centre. Tomorrow will be soon enough."

Now the adrenalin had worn off, Rob felt the familiar pricking behind his eyes. He stifled a yawn. It had been a hell of a day.

As the paramedics loaded the victim into the waiting ambulance, Liz pulled him aside. "I didn't want to say anything in front of your colleagues, in case I'm wrong, but the bruising around his neck could indicate your man was strangled." Rob knew from experience that she was hardly ever wrong. "I'll know more once I see the x-ray."

"You don't think it's a sex game gone wrong?" Rob had heard that strangulation could heighten pleasure. Something to do with the lack of oxygen. "The bruising could have been from the neck collar."

She was shaking her head before he'd even finished his sentence. "Those marks were made by some sort of chain. Whoever bound and gagged this man wanted to harm him. No, Rob. Unfortunately, I think you're looking at cold-blooded murder."

CHAPTER 5

Hearing his alarm go off, Rob groaned. He turned over, wrapped an arm around Jo and lay there absorbing her warmth, not wanting to get up. They snuggled for a few minutes, then she squeezed his hand and threw back the covers.

Monday.

Jo worked at the MI5 offices three days a week. With Jack nearly ten months old, the flexible work schedule suited her perfectly. It took thirty minutes by train into Vauxhall from Richmond, and then there was a short walk across Vauxhall Bridge to Millbank.

Jo padded into the bathroom, and a short while later, Rob heard the shower running. He switched on the bedside lamp, even though sunlight was beating against the closed blinds. No rain today. Loud snuffling could be heard at the bedroom door. He smiled to himself. Trigger had come to say hello.

Rob called the dog's name. After a few seconds of frantic pawing, the flimsy latch released and the bedroom door flew open. The Lab bounded in, his mouth open in a wide pant, and proceeded to shove his snout into Rob's face.

"There's a good boy." He fondled the dog's ears. Opening the door was something Trigger had learned to do after Jack was born, when his exhausted owners had started falling asleep at odd hours and he didn't get the attention he was used to. Jo didn't like to encourage it, because it left scratches on the door, but the house was a Victorian end-of-terrace and the doors all needed replacing anyway.

On cue, he heard gurgling on the baby monitor. They slept with it in their bedroom so they could hear Jack if he woke in the night. Trigger's ears cocked, and he sniffed the device, confused.

Time to get up. Trigger at his side, Rob walked through to his son's room. "Morning, little man."

Jack gurgled up at him and said something that at a push could have been "Dad". He was getting there. A few more days and he'd have it.

Jack raised his arms, so Rob leaned in and picked him up. Trigger danced around his feet, excited to have his playmate back. The Lab slept downstairs in the living room, on a round cushioned bed that was quite comfortable — at least Jack thought so.

Rob changed his son's nappy, then took him downstairs for breakfast. Trigger followed, his breath hot on his heels. As was his routine, Rob opened the French doors and let Trigger out into the garden. It was a glorious day, and he stood there for a moment, Jack in his arms, enjoying the feel of the sun on his face.

The baby began to wriggle, and Rob turned to put him in his highchair. Then Trigger was back, looking pleadingly up at him.

"Yeah, okay, okay."

He fed the dog, then set about making himself and Jo a coffee. He'd finally got to grips with the Nespresso machine and could now make himself a half-decent espresso. Jo preferred a normal coffee with milk.

Upstairs, he could hear her singing to herself. She liked to put the radio on when she got dressed. The days she worked in town, he was on baby duty until their sitter,

Tanya, arrived. Every time he handed Jack over to her, he thanked his lucky stars that they'd met.

Tanya had cleaned for a woman called Judith Walker, who'd been brutally murdered in her house at Box Hill early last year. Having only been in the country a few months, Tanya hadn't had any other work, so Rob had employed her. At first it was just once a week to keep the house tidy, but she'd proved so helpful they now employed her three days a week as a nanny. Somehow, she still managed to find the time to straighten up the house when Jack was napping. Quite honestly, he didn't know what they'd do without her.

Taking a welcome gulp of his coffee, Rob set about feeding Jack. Baby porridge mixed with a little fruit puree. He'd only just gone onto solids. In the corner, Trigger crunched and slobbered his way through the bowl of dog food. It was a domestic scene, and Rob gave a little shake of his head. Who would have thought he'd be lucky enough to have this? One thing he knew was that he'd protect his little family at all costs. Nothing was more important than them.

You're a dead man.

The words of a convict. Rob suppressed a shiver. Had the dirty copper and organised crime boss been serious? Or had he just intended Rob to spend the rest of his life looking over his shoulder? If it was the latter, he'd succeeded.

His family needed him alive. Jo didn't know about the threat — he hadn't wanted to worry her — and at this point, there didn't seem to be any reason to. He wasn't even sure if Cranshaw had been bluffing. A convicted man will say anything to hit back at the police officer responsible.

But if that changed, if at any point he thought he was being followed, or an attempt was made on his life, he'd come clean.

After the fire last year, he'd replaced the downstairs windows with ones that had multiple locking mechanisms. He'd also put in toughened glass and triple glazing. No one was getting through those once they were locked.

The French doors leading out to the garden now had a sliding security gate over them. Trigger wasn't happy about this but had learned to whine when he wanted to go out. If it was a warm day like today, Tanya would leave him in the garden for a while, but she was under strict instructions to keep the gate locked at all times when she was alone in the house with the baby. Given what had happened to her previous employer, she was more than happy to oblige.

"I've got five minutes before I have to go." Jo came downstairs in a navy-blue work suit over a cream silk blouse, her hair in a ponytail with tendrils already escaping. She looked so damn good, he had to fight the urge to take her straight back upstairs again.

"Don't forget your coffee."

"Ah, thanks." She took a grateful gulp, then looked at him. "I want to hear all about what happened with your dad." The incident with his father had faded in significance considering what had transpired afterwards. The studded leather harness, the red gag. Such vivid visuals, hard to suppress.

"Later. It's a long story."

She raised an eyebrow. "Now I definitely want to hear. Where was he arrested?"

"Soho Square."

The same square where the body had been found. He paused, spoon halfway to Jack's mouth. It hadn't been confirmed, but the time of death was probably between eight and nine o'clock. Ronnie had been wandering around Soho with his bag of stolen cash around that time. It was just possible his old man had seen something. He'd have been on the lookout for the cops and would have been hyper alert. A criminal's paranoia.

Not that he wanted to speak to his father again.

"What's wrong?" Jo studied him, her head cocked to the side.

"Oh, nothing. I was called to a crime scene after the business with my father. I was just wondering if he'd seen anything."

She frowned. "A homicide?"

"Looks like it." He didn't go into detail. There wasn't time.

"Was it bad?"

She had a way of reading him, which he liked. They picked up on each other's emotions. He kissed her on the lips and took the half-empty coffee cup from her hand. "Yes, it was, and I promise I'll tell you about it later. You'd better go, or you'll miss your train."

She glanced at the clock on the wall. "Crap, thanks. I'll see you later." And with a tinkling of keys, she was out the door.

Trigger stared forlornly after her. He hated it when anyone left the house. "It's okay, boy. Tanya will be here soon."

The Labrador perked up. He liked Tanya, she gave him lots of pats.

As soon as she arrived, Rob handed a fed and happy Jack to her and went upstairs to shower and change for work. Sun streamed in through the now open blinds, warming the room.

Last night was over. The Soho homicide wasn't his case. He felt a pang of something. It wasn't regret. Granted, it was an intriguing case, but he had more than enough on his plate. DS Tremayne and her colleague would work it and hopefully find out what had happened to the victim. Someone would have seen something. A body in a bondage outfit had been dumped in busy Soho on a humid July evening. There were bound to be witnesses, they just had to find them.

* * *

"Morning, guv." DS Will Freemont poked his head above his laptop as Rob walked into the Major Investigation Team's office in Putney with a newspaper under his arm. "Boss wants to see you."

Mayhew. More accurately, Superintendent Felicity Mayhew. No longer Acting. After successfully closing the child exploitation case last year, she'd been promoted, cementing her place at the Metropolitan Police's Homicide and Serious Crime Command. She was here to stay.

At first, Rob hadn't liked her. He didn't approve of the way she'd slept with the previous superintendent's husband to rattle her and bring on a breakdown of sorts, thereby sweeping in to take her position. She was certainly ambitious, he'd give her that much. She liked to schmooze with the powers that be and was on lunching terms with the Deputy Commissioner, who considered her something of a protégée. That meant she was able to keep them at arm's length, and for the most part, out of the office and out of their business.

While other CIDs were having budget cuts and excessive amounts of red tape to get through to solve basic cases, they were left to their own devices, so long as they didn't step too far over the line. That was Mayhew's doing, and he respected that.

He hadn't told anyone about the ruthless manipulation she'd engaged in to get the position. That was a nugget he was keeping to himself for now. But she had something on him too. The phone.

When his mentor and friend Sam Lawrence had been gunned down in cold blood, Rob had "confiscated" his phone, neglecting to admit it into evidence, thereby compromising the entire investigation. It had been a calculated move, and luckily no one had found out, but Mayhew had suspected. She'd called him out on it, but he'd played dumb. Had he convinced her? Not by a long shot. With a mind as devious as hers, she wouldn't be giving him the benefit of the doubt.

Still, like him, she hadn't pursued it. Perhaps she was also sitting on it until a time when it might prove useful — like when she wanted to get rid of him. For that's what it would mean. The end of his career. Catching Sam's killer had been worth it though, and if he had the choice again, he'd do the same thing.

"Thanks," he told Will. "I'll go and see her now."

He knew exactly what she wanted to speak to him about.

SOHO SEX SLAYING screamed the *Sun*. It was all over the newspapers. The entire community was up in arms. He'd caught sight of the article on the way up in the lift. Amateur photographs of the victim were plastered all over the front page. Well, it wasn't his fault. He'd just done as he was told and secured the scene until the local CID could get there.

Mayhew's office was in the far corner of the open-plan squad room, a frigid glass bubble overlooking the floor. Lawrence had kept his door open, preferring to be part of the team, but Mayhew kept hers firmly shut. Her blinds were up, however, so she could spy on the investigation teams, of which there were four working on this floor, each with a separate DCI.

He knocked and waited to be granted entry.

"Come in," she called.

"Morning, Superintendent." Rob always felt a bit like a schoolboy summoned to the headmistress's office when he came in here. His skin puckered as he entered. It was freezing. She must have had the air conditioning on full tilt.

"I heard you had an eventful night?"

He arched an eyebrow. "Bad news travels fast."

She scoffed. "Especially when it's bound and gagged and dumped in the centre of Soho on a Sunday night."

"It could have been an accident," Rob pointed out, even though Liz had suspected otherwise.

"It wasn't. I spoke to Liz Kramer this morning. The victim, a gay man, was strangled. It's now a murder inquiry."

Rob wasn't surprised. Liz must have had another look at the markings around the victim's neck. There was no way she'd have done the post-mortem already. "Southwark CID were at the scene. If it's a suspicious death, it's their case."

"Not anymore."

He looked up. "What?"

"DCI Burrows doesn't want it. They're inundated right now, and Soho isn't in their jurisdiction. It's Charing Cross, but they're dealing with an influx of arrests from the protest yesterday, so it's been given to us."

"Why us? Surely Central's closer."

She gave him a look. "You were the first responder."

"I know, but it's even further out of our jurisdiction."

"Doesn't matter. The case is ours. You were there, you have first-hand knowledge of the crime scene. Plus, you know Liz. It makes sense."

It did.

"How do you know he was gay?" he asked. "Did Liz ID the body?"

"Yes, and I've forwarded you a copy of her preliminary report."

Her eyes sparkled. The press coverage. That's why Mayhew wanted this case. If her team solved this one, she would be in every newspaper in the country.

"It's not going to be an easy one," he warned her. "Chances of closing it won't be good."

She pursed her lips. That wasn't what she wanted to hear. "It was crowded. Someone will have seen something."

His thoughts exactly. "Agreed, but getting them to come forward is going to be near impossible. No one respects the police anymore."

"You think I don't know that?" She leaned back in her chair. "Trust. That's what we must work to restore. And we're going to do it by finding out who murdered—" she glanced down at her notes — "Michael Bennett."

Rob arched an eyebrow. "I take it he was in the system." It's the only way they'd have got an ID so quickly.

"He used to be a civil servant. Lived in Hampstead with his husband."

"Really?"

"Yes, so let's start by looking into the victim." Her tone was matter-of-fact. "That might give us a clue as to who'd want him dead." She smiled, reminding Rob of the snake in the *Jungle Book*, the story he'd been reading to Jack last night. "But you don't need me to do your job for you."

He'd forgotten to add *passive aggressive* to her list of attributes.

"No, ma'am."

"Good. I expect you to brief the team and get moving on this. The Mayor wants someone's head on a block, and we're going to get it for him."

He might have known Raza Ashraf was the driving force behind the urgency of the investigation. The Mayor didn't want bondage victims turning up dead in his front yard. It didn't make for good headlines. He couldn't afford to be seen to be losing control, not so soon after being elected. And he needed the LGBT vote.

Rob got up. "I'll get right on it, ma'am."

"Good."

Mayhew didn't look up, so she didn't notice the glint in his eye as he left her office.

CHAPTER 6

"Briefing!" called Rob, standing up from his desk. For the last hour, he'd been reading Liz Kramer's preliminary report and digging up what information he could on the victim.

Surprised, his team glanced up. "Have we got a new case?" asked Will.

"Yup, let's go. You too, Celeste."

Everyone, including the young, dark-haired DC, got to their feet.

DS Jenny Bird followed him into the incident room. She took a seat, putting her iPad on the table in front of her. It was more of a boardroom than an incident room, a change they'd made a couple of years back during the refurb. Rob preferred it this way. It was easier discussing a case around a table, heads together, than having him standing at the front spouting information while his team stood and listened.

His management style was relaxed, democratic. He wanted each member of the team to do their bit. They were all smart, skilled detectives and he valued the opinions of each of them. They'd been through a lot together over the last few years.

DS Will Freemont came in next and sat down beside Jenny. He had an iPad too, although his was kitted out with a detachable keyboard. Most of the team used a device of some sort. It seemed Rob was the only one who used a notepad and pen these days. That's what came of being the oldest.

"Morning," said DS Harry Malhotra, bounding in. "How is everyone today?"

The most exuberant member of the team, Harry was a fast thinker whose brain always fired on all cylinders. He'd told them once that he had mild ADHD but had learned to manage the condition. If anything, it gave him more energy than the rest of the team combined. He was also something of a budding thespian.

"Good, thanks." Jenny smiled at him. "Can I spill the beans?"

He grinned. "Sure, most people know anyway."

"Know what?" Rob frowned. "Don't tell me you're leaving too."

He laughed. "No, nothing like that."

Since Mike Manner had gone to work on the community project for the Mayor, they had been a man down. Mayhew was pressing him to recruit someone else, but theirs was a tight-knit team and he didn't want someone new coming in and ruining their dynamic.

Celeste came in, her face flushed. "You want me on the case?"

"Yes, you're officially part of the team. Take a seat."

She beamed. "Thank you, guv."

Celeste had been the general office dogsbody, jumping from team to team whenever they needed administrative work done, documents scrutinised or reports filed, but she'd proved highly competent, and she worked well with the rest of the members of his murder squad. Promoting Celeste to the team would save him from having to hire someone else. He'd clear it with Mayhew later.

Celeste slipped into a chair next to Harry, putting her phone, which was almost as big as an iPad, down on the table. "Congrats," she whispered.

"What's going on?" Rob asked.

Jenny grinned, her eyes sparkling. "Harry got a part in *EastEnders*." It was clear she was delighted for him, as were the others.

"Congratulations." He didn't watch *EastEnders*. Soaps weren't his thing, though his ex-wife, Yvette, had loved them. Never missed an episode. "You'll have to let us know when it airs."

"Thanks, guv." He gave a wry grin. "It's only a small part. I play a copper who—"

Rob held up his hand. "Sorry, Harry, you'll have to fill us in later. We've got work to do."

The sergeant fell silent.

Rob took a deep breath. "Okay, this is a bizarre and rather sudden case that's fallen into our lap. I was meeting someone in the West End last night when I got a call from Dispatch. A body was discovered in Soho Square." He filled them in on the timings.

"Soho's not really our jurisdiction, is it?" Jenny asked. They did cover most of West London, but the West End was usually Central's remit.

"No, but Central's overloaded from the protests, Southwark CID were there but they also have their hands full south of the river, so it's fallen to us. As expected, Mayor Ashraf's been on the phone to Mayhew. He wants it solved ASAP."

Harry rolled his eyes. "Doesn't look good for him," he muttered. There were several murmurs of agreement.

"Indeed." Rob was glad they all felt the same way. "Anyway, on the bright side, it means the post-mortem will be fast-tracked. Liz Kramer was at the crime scene last night and filed a preliminary report this morning. I've just read it. He was murdered."

"What about SOCO?" asked Jenny, always one step ahead.

"The forensics will take a bit longer. They were still processing the scene when I left last night." The scenes-of-crime officers often took several days to analyse a scene.

"I'll chase up on that," offered Celeste.

"How did he die?" Will asked.

"Asphyxiation," Rob reported. He opened the folder he'd brought with him and placed the crime scene photos on the table. "Possibly erotic, possibly strangulation."

They pored over it.

"What on earth is he wearing?" asked Will.

"A leather harness, along with a ball gag, I believe."

"Well, I guess it is Soho." Jenny rubbed her forehead, her gaze fixed on the unfortunate victim. "And no one saw anything?"

"No one's come forward." Rob put his hands flat on the table. "Even though the body was reported around ten o'clock on a Sunday evening in one of the busiest areas of London."

"They won't though, will they?" Harry blurted out. "No one's going to get involved in a police inquiry if they don't have to."

Unfortunately, Harry was right. People had to be coerced to come forward these days. The Good Samaritan no longer existed. No one wanted to be considered a witness, a suspect or a person of interest in a police investigation.

In his opinion, the Met needed a massive public relations overhaul. Recent events had tarred them all with the same brush, and now they came across as the bad guys. One or two bad apples, and they had all suffered the consequences. He used to be proud of being a copper. Now, he didn't volunteer the information. It was cooler being a villain than being in law enforcement these days. Nevertheless, they had a job to do and lamenting the force's PR problems wasn't going to help.

"We must canvass the area, particularly the shops and bars near the square, but first, let's focus on the victim. Liz Kramer identified the body from his fingerprints. He's forty-seven-year-old Michael Bennett from Hampstead. A retired civil servant, he lives with his partner of eighteen years — they were among the first same-sex couples to get legally married in 2014. Something of an artist, from what I can make out online."

Harry frowned. "Could this be a hate crime?"

"At this point, we don't know. It's possible, but we need to follow procedure. The press is already up in arms, as you may have noticed, as is the LGBT community. We need to handle this one with kid gloves."

"Must be a good artist if he lives in Hampstead," murmured Will.

"House is owned by the husband, a banker."

"Ah." Will gave a knowing nod.

"We need to speak to him. Harry, why don't you come with me on this one?" Somehow the extroverted officer with his snazzy suits and coiffed hair seemed a better fit in the gay community than any of the other team members, himself included. Harry could charm the knickers off a nun, and he had a feeling they'd need a bit of charm where they were going. "Will, Jenny and Celeste, see what you can dig up here. We need to paint a thorough picture of this guy. Partner, kids, work life, social life, you name it. We're looking for a motive."

He didn't need to tell them how to do their job either. They nodded eagerly.

"Right, let's get to work. Harry, you ready?"

"Sure, guv."

"Okay, let's go."

* * *

Tudor Crescent was on the border of Hampstead and Belsize Park, in a wide leafy avenue dotted with SUVs and other top-of-the-range cars. As they cruised down the street, Rob spotted several Mercedes, two Teslas and a Maserati baking in the midday sun.

"There's 115," Harry pointed out as they reached the south end. Rob pulled over and parked on the street outside a detached Victorian townhouse.

"Wow." He gave a low whistle.

It was impressive. The front facade shone white in the midday sun, while fuchsia blooms exploded from slate-grey urns outside the glossy black front door. Rob lifted the enormous brass knocker. The sound reverberated through the house.

They waited. Eventually they heard footsteps in the hall, and a moment later the door swung open. "Can I help you?"

A middle-aged man with thick grey hair and red-rimmed eyes stared back at them. His clothes were crumpled, and he was in his socks. Grief radiated off him. This wasn't going to be an easy visit.

"My name is DCI Miller from the Major Investigation Team. This is my colleague, DS Malhotra. Are you Ralph Keaton?"

The man blinked. "Yes."

"Mr Keaton, would it be all right if we had a word? It's about your partner, Michael Bennett."

In response, Keaton turned away and walked back down the hallway, leaving the door open behind him. Harry glanced at Rob, shrugged, and they followed him in.

"Is it right to assume Michael Bennett lived here?" Harry asked.

The man nodded but kept walking. Shoulders stooped, head bowed, socks soundless on the black-and-white marble tiles. "Mikey is . . . was my husband."

"I'm sorry for your loss," Harry said.

Rob followed, letting his younger sergeant take the lead. Modern art hung on either side of the high-ceilinged hallway, softly lit by angled spotlights. Rob glanced up at the swirling colours: heavy reds, unforgiving purples and bilious yellows. He didn't get modern art. Give him a rolling landscape or a peaceful watercolour any day.

At the end of the hallway stood a bust on a pedestal. Striking and masculine. A real focal point. Keaton walked past it unseeing. He turned into a spacious living room with roller blinds halfway up, sunbeams angling onto the cream carpet, pooling into rectangles. Wordlessly, Keaton sank onto a leather sofa, indicating for them to take seats.

"Thank you." Harry sat on an armchair that immediately swallowed him up. He shuffled forward, so as not to lose his air of authority. Rob preferred to stand.

"I'm sorry to have to do this," Harry began, "but where was your husband last night?"

Keaton just shook his head. "Here, I thought. I don't understand it at all."

"You didn't know he was out?"

Forlorn eyes stared up at them. The man was devastated, that was easy to see. "No. I was at a work function and got back around ten. Mikey wasn't here. I figured he was just out with a friend and hadn't told me, but that's so unlike him. I finally called him around midnight, but there was no answer. I was worried, so I called around, but none of our friends had seen him. I even called his mother." His mouth twisted. "She wasn't impressed."

"So what did you do?" Harry asked.

"Nothing." A shrug. "What could I do? I didn't know anything was wrong then. It wasn't until—" He took a shuddering breath.

"What happened?"

"I kept calling, trying everyone we knew. Then I got a text from Gunther. He was heading home from a jam evening and heard that . . . that a man had been found in Soho Square. He passes that way to get home, so he went and had a look. Everyone was talking about it. He got there around the same time as the emergency services, and saw the man's face. It was Mikey." His voice faltered and his head fell forward.

Rob swallowed. It was a shocking way to find out your partner had died.

"He saw the man's face clearly, did he?"

"Yes, he sent me this." Keaton fiddled in his pocket and pulled out his mobile phone. Scrolling, he navigated to a message and then a photograph.

"Do you mind?" Rob reached for the phone. Keaton placed it in his hand.

Yup. That was the crime scene all right. The crowded square, the statue of King Charles, the Tudor substation in the background, and in the middle, the man trussed up in a leather holster, hands wrenched behind him, a chain from the cuffs connected to the neck collar at the back.

He scrolled to the left. The next photograph was a close-up. This guy had obviously recognised the victim and pushed to the front of the onlookers. Rob hadn't noticed him at the time, but then his attention had been somewhat diverted.

The victim's face filled the screen, mouth stretched open, the shiny red jawbreaker gag distorting his face, turning him into some sort of freak. No one's mouth could open that wide. It must have been painful, hence the fear in his eyes.

This man knew he was going to die.

CHAPTER 7

"It hardly looks like him," whispered Keaton, pale against the brown leather sofa. Rob noticed his hands were shaking, like an alcoholic who needed a drink. Like his father's had the night before. This wasn't the DTs, though. This was shock.

"You had no idea he was out?" Rob asked.

Keaton shook his head. "He was going to bake brownies for his painting group. They get together every Wednesday."

"Michael didn't work?" Harry used the victim's first name. It was a way to keep the conversation intimate, not to distance the talker.

"He used to," Keaton said. "But he retired five years ago. He wasn't happy and we didn't need the money . . ." He shrugged. "I was fine with it."

Keaton was the breadwinner, then. Rob glanced around the room at the fancy chandelier, the expensive furnishings, more art on the walls. "What is it you do exactly, Mr Keaton?"

"I work in the city. At Goldman, in the engineering department."

Goldman Sachs. The investment bank.

"Are you an engineer?" Rob wondered if Keaton's job had something to do with his partner's death. Perhaps it was a kidnapping gone wrong, an attempt to blackmail Keaton into revealing a trade secret. Okay, he was grasping here, but he had to cover all the bases.

"I manage a team that creates software solutions for our clients. It's exciting work."

He'd have to take Keaton's word for it.

"Mr Keaton, can you think of any reason why someone would want to harm Michael?"

Keaton's eyes grew wide. "Absolutely not. Mikey was a gentle soul. Creative, you know. He liked to paint — he was pretty good, actually. He was a genius in the kitchen. Loved to cook and bake things." His voice broke again. "God, I don't know what I'm going to do without him."

They gave him a moment to compose himself. Keaton sniffed, rubbed his eyes, then looked up. "I don't understand what he was doing in Soho. He wasn't into BDSM. We didn't go in for that sort of thing — fetishes and kinky stuff. We have friends who do, but it wasn't for us." He nodded to the phone, still in Rob's hand. "I don't understand any of this."

"When was the last time you spoke to Michael?" Harry asked. It was a good question. He was trying to establish the last known contact with the victim. Then, if phone data or eyewitness reports proved otherwise, they had something to use against Keaton in an interrogation.

"At breakfast. We ate together, then Mikey went upstairs to paint, and I left for the office. His studio is upstairs at the front of the house. It gets the most light."

"We'd like to see it before we go," Rob said. "If that's okay with you."

Another shrug. Keaton didn't care what they did. Right now, his life had lost all meaning. Nothing mattered. Rob had seen the same reaction in the relatives of other victims. Lethargy set in when they realised their loved one wasn't coming home. Not now. Not ever.

"You didn't speak to him again after that?" Harry pushed. It was important to be clear on this.

A shake of his head. "No, I don't think so."

"Do you want to check your phone, just to be sure?" Rob handed it back to him.

He took it but didn't look down. "I'm sure. I went into the office around nine o'clock. We had a software launch for a client today, which is why we were working at the weekend. I had a work dinner last night. Mikey knew I'd be back late."

They'd check Michael's phone records, just to be sure. It might also pinpoint where he was last night before he wound up dead in Soho Square.

"Mr Keaton, I apologise in advance for this question, but was it possible Michael was having an affair?"

Keaton's lips thinned. "Absolutely not. I'd have known."

That's what they all thought, until they were proved wrong.

"Mikey was a terrible liar. If there was someone else, he wouldn't have been able to keep it from me."

Maybe. "Let's go upstairs," suggested Rob.

Keaton pushed himself out of the sofa and led the way. He moved slowly, like it was an effort to put one foot in front of the other.

Up the plush staircase, across the landing and into a room overlooking the garden. As soon as he opened the door, they were hit by the acrid smell of oil paint.

"Phew." Harry waved a hand in front of his face. Rob tried not to breathe too deeply.

"Sorry, I haven't been in here for a few days." He walked over to the bay window and lifted it up. Immediately, fresh air rushed in and displaced the pungent odour.

Rob surveyed the brightly lit room. Keaton was right, it got a lot of sun. Used canvases were stacked against the wall, some facing forwards, others turned around so only the wooden backs were visible. There were several male nudes, the subjects adopting power poses or reclining on a chaise longue or vintage armchair.

"Does he use models?" Harry clearly knew something about art.

"No, he painted from photographs and cuttings from magazines." Keaton gestured to a canvas on an easel by the window. Pinned to the top right-hand corner was a magazine cutout of a man in Speedos, barefoot and leaning against a rock, a pensive look on his face. Sunlight beat down on his glistening torso.

"That was his current project." Keaton nodded at the canvas. The rough outline was done, with some pencil markings to dictate dimensions. Presumably they'd have been painted over and rubbed out later. The figure was starting to take shape, the man from the magazine coming to life on the canvas.

"Not bad," Harry remarked.

Keaton gazed longingly at the painting, as if it would bring Mikey back.

Rob prowled around the studio, looking for anything that would explain why the artist had been found in a bondage outfit miles away from home. But all he could see were plastic boxes filled with tubes of paint, jars of brushes, turpentine and palettes splattered with dried paint.

"What's this?" He picked up a box file, heavy with clippings.

"That was his 'inspiration', as he called it. Whenever he was about to start a painting, he'd rifle through that and pick out a subject. He liked to study several shots of the same model taken from different angles. It gave him perspective, you see."

Harry wandered over the window and stared down at the garden. "Did Michael take care of the garden too?"

A sad nod.

"I'm afraid it's going to go to shit now. I'm a terrible gardener. Don't have the knack for it."

Harry nodded. "I'm not one for gardening myself."

The man was in pain, that much was obvious.

"Had Michael been acting strangely at all, these last few days?" Rob asked, flicking through the box of pictures.

"No, not that I noticed. I mean, he was a bit upset about last night, but I promised I'd make it up to him." He dropped his gaze.

"You mean because you were going out?" Harry asked.

"It was our anniversary, you see." A sob caught in his throat. "Damn it. I shouldn't have gone. We've been together eighteen years. Can you believe that?"

"That's a long time," murmured Harry.

"Michael was upset that you weren't spending your anniversary together?" Rob said, making sure.

"Yes, but he knew this dinner was a big deal. I'm in line for a promotion, and the company directors took me out for a meal. We'd been working all weekend on this project, it seemed like a good time to celebrate. It wasn't something you could bring a partner to, you understand?"

Rob nodded.

"Did you argue?" Harry asked.

"No, not really. Mikey was disappointed, but he understood."

"Disappointed enough to go out by himself?" asked Rob.

Keaton stiffened. "No! At least, I don't think so." Then, he frowned. "Do you think that's what happened? He was so upset that he went out by himself and got persuaded to go to a fetish party?"

"A fetish party?" asked Rob.

"It's a thing." He shrugged. "For people who want to step out of the realms of social conformity. If you're into kink, fetish or polyamory, there are places you can go. Parties for like-minded people who want to . . . play."

The mind boggled.

"What makes you think he went to one of these fetish parties?" Harry asked.

"What he was wearing," Keaton explained. "Where else would he get an outfit like that?"

"Maybe he had it stashed away," Rob said.

"I told you already, we didn't own anything like that. It wasn't our thing." His tone was clipped.

"Are you sure about that?" Rob took a magazine clipping from the box.

"Of course I'm sure."

Rob held it up. It was a picture of a masked man in a studded leather holster, a ball gag in his mouth.

CHAPTER 8

Ralph Keaton blinked at the image. "Th-That means nothing. He was an artist. It was a subject, that's all."

He was right. It was just a page from a magazine and would never hold any water in court, but it did indicate that Michael Bennett had an interest, even if only an artistic one, in BDSM.

"It looks just like the crime scene," murmured Harry, who'd come over for a closer look.

It did. Except in the picture, the man was lying on a bed, silk sheets crumpled around him, while Michael had been found on the green in Soho Square, next to the statue of King Charles II. Other than that, they were identical. It was as if the killer had re-enacted the magazine shot. The position of the body was the same — on his side, arms wrenched behind his back, bound by leather straps and then connected to the neck collar by a silver chain. The leather holster was the right colour, the ball gag also red, stretching the mouth to obscene proportions.

The only difference was the eyes. This guy was enjoying himself. Michael Bennett had not been.

Rob pulled out his phone to take a photograph. "Do you mind?"

Keaton didn't reply. He'd gone as white as the Farrow & Ball walls.

Rob snapped a few shots anyway, then slipped his mobile back into his jacket pocket. Keaton put a hand against the wall to steady himself. He knew as well as they did that the photograph his friend had sent him was almost identical to the magazine image. It was too similar to be a coincidence, which meant one thing: the killer had been in this house.

"We're going to need a list of names of people who have visited in the last month or so," Rob said.

Keaton pulled himself together. "You don't honestly think one of our friends did this?"

"I don't know," Rob admitted. "That's what we're trying to find out."

Keaton thought for a moment, then he took a breath. "You know what? I think I'd like you to leave now."

Rob's heart sank. He was clamming up. "Mr Keaton, it's important that we find out if Michael knew his attacker."

"I'm not answering any more of your questions. If you don't mind, I'll see you out." He stood at the studio door and waited for them to leave.

There was nothing they could do. They didn't have a warrant to stay and search the premises, and since Ralph Keaton had an alibi for the night in question, it was unlikely they'd get one.

Rob sighed and walked out. "Don't you want to find your husband's killer?"

Keaton didn't respond but led them down the staircase to the front door. He opened it without a word.

"Thank you for your time," Rob said.

Harry handed Keaton a card. "If you think of anything else."

For a moment, it didn't look like Keaton was going to take it, but then he did, shoving it into his pocket without a word.

* * *

"I want to see the phone data for Michael Bennett, as well as that of his partner, Ralph Keaton," Rob said when they got back to the station.

"You don't think he's involved, do you, guv?" Harry sat down at his computer. "The guy was as surprised as we were by the photograph."

"What photograph?" asked Jenny.

"This one."

The printer whirred in the background. Jenny walked over to it and retrieved the piece of paper.

"Good grief," she muttered.

"Exactly. It's identical to how the body was found — other than the bed, of course."

"Where did you get this?"

"In the victim's studio," said Harry. "He's an artist. Not bad, either."

Rob wouldn't know. "We asked his husband for a list of people who'd visited recently, and he shut down."

"You think he knows who did this?" Jenny asked.

"No. I think he realised that his friends and associates were going to be dragged through the mud, so he decided it was in his best interests not to divulge anything further. Unfortunately, it means we could be missing out on finding our killer."

"You're saying the killer must have seen that picture in order to re-enact it?" Will, who'd got up and was peering over Jenny's shoulder, caught on.

Rob nodded.

Will, who was the tech whizz, gave a slow whistle under his breath. "I'll get on those phone records, then. That's the only way we're going to figure out who had recent contact with the victim."

"Thanks. In the meantime—" Rob surveyed his team — "who fancies a trip to Soho?"

"Not you, Detective Chief Inspector," Mayhew's voice rang out from the other side of the squad room. Her Irish lilt was always more pronounced when she was worked up, like she was now. Her flaming red hair bouncing around her shoulders, she strode down the length of the office.

"Ma'am, we're at a crucial point in this investigation." They had to speak to witnesses before memories faded and details became blurred, CCTV footage got wiped, locals moved on with their lives and the body in the park became old news.

She came to a stop. "You have a team of detectives to do that," she reminded him. "I've got the Mayor coming in twenty minutes for an update. I need you here."

Rob ground his teeth in frustration. He was itching to get to Soho and ask around the shops and cafés near the square if anyone had seen anything. He also needed to get hold of Keaton's friend, the one who'd taken the photographs at the crime scene last night, and question him.

"We're on it, guv." Harry stood up. "Jenny and I will go."

Rob grunted. Sometimes he hated being the one in charge. Red tape and politics, that's what it boiled down to at the end of the day, and it wasn't what he'd signed up for. Still, it was part of the job and he had to suck it up.

He angled his body away from Mayhew. "Visit the sex shops. The killer must have got that outfit from somewhere. Maybe someone will recognise it."

"He probably got them online," Will pointed out.

"Yeah, I know, but it's worth a shot."

Jenny nodded. "Gotcha."

"What should I do?" Celeste asked.

"Come with us," said Harry. "We can split up and cover more ground that way."

Rob nodded. The young constable could use the field experience rather than being tied to her desk.

Celeste's brown curls bobbed as she got up. "Great. I'm ready."

He smiled at her enthusiasm. Mayhew spun on her stilettos and sashayed back to her office. "Twenty minutes, DCI Miller," she called over her shoulder.

Rob bit his lip for fear of saying something he'd regret. "Yes, ma'am."

* * *

The teleconference with the Mayor went just about as well as expected. Which is to say, not well at all. It was no secret that there was no love lost between them. The memory of Ashraf's involvement in the Box Hill inquiry was still fresh in Rob's mind, along with his attempted derailing of the South Bank murders case. Ashraf was outspoken in his support of the police. *Working with the Met to keep London safe* was one of his campaign slogans, but only when it served his purpose. As soon as a case infringed on his personal life, or was potentially damaging to his political career, he shut it down. The man was a two-faced hypocrite.

"So, you have no suspects?"

"Not yet, sir. We've only just started the investigation. The body was discovered last night." They weren't miracle workers. Police work took time. It was plodding, they had to trawl through lots of different information — phone records, CCTV footage, witness accounts, door-to-door inquiries, and that was the tip of the iceberg. Then they had to come back and write it all up, enter it onto the system and send reports to their superiors. All this while Michael Bennett's killer remained at large.

"What about the victim's husband?" Rob could almost hear the distaste echoing down the line.

"We spoke to him today. I don't think he had anything to do with his partner's death."

"But you can't be sure. What evidence do you have to prove that?"

"Keaton has an alibi. He was at a work function in the city last night," Rob couldn't keep the edge from his voice. "Four Goldman Sachs directors saw him there. I have their names if you'd like to contact them." He didn't, but he knew that would shut Ashraf up. The Mayor didn't get involved in police work, it would sully his reputation.

"No, no. You go ahead."

"Thank you, sir. If there's nothing else . . . ?"

"Nothing at present, Detective Chief Inspector."

Titles, that was the other thing he hated. Who cared what rank you were? They all did the same work, all got their hands dirty. It meant nothing. Just a label, and one he could happily do without.

Rob gave Mayhew a stiff nod and left the office.

CHAPTER 9

Before the Superintendent could corner him again, Rob left the building and walked to his car. No way was he going to sit around and push paper. There was someone he wanted to speak to, and he might as well get it out of the way.

The address his father had given when he'd been brought in was in Camberwell. The twenty-five-minute drive took the better part of an hour, thanks to the late-afternoon traffic, so Rob used the time to call Ralph Keaton back. He put the call on speakerphone.

"I'm sorry to disturb you," he began, hoping it would pacify the man who'd shut them down earlier. "But I need to ask you two more things."

A pause.

"What things?" Keaton sounded wary.

"Firstly, we need to account for your whereabouts last night. I know you said you were at a work event, but we have to verify that. It's to clear you from our inquiries, you understand." Rob hesitated. "If you don't want to give us the names of the people you were with, then tell us the name of the restaurant. We'll check with the staff and confirm your alibi."

It was a peace offering. He was giving Keaton a way to save face. His career didn't have to be harmed because of the police investigation.

"It was the Singing Lotus." His voice was breathy, relief evident in his tone. "Near Holborn."

"Great, thanks. The other thing is that we'd like to speak to your friend who took the photographs at the crime scene. There might be evidence on his camera, or he may have seen something that could help us catch Michael's killer."

The pause was longer this time, then he heard Keaton sigh. "I suppose that's okay. His name is Gunther Kershaw. I'll send you his mobile number."

Give and take. That's how it worked.

"Thank you, Mr Keaton. And once again, I'm sorry for your loss."

The phone went dead. Keaton had hung up.

Rob tapped his hand against the steering wheel. At least he'd got what he wanted.

* * *

Camberwell was a multicultural South London neighbourhood made up of sprawling estates, an art college and an eclectic selection of takeaways, bars and tavernas. Sitting in the back-to-back traffic on Camberwell Church Street, Rob counted three ambulances, two police cars and a fire engine as they raced past, zigzagging through the queues of cars.

With easy access to Central London and a bustling local community, it was a cheap and convenient place to live. Ronnie Miller lived up a long, curved road that weaved in and out of two housing estates. His apartment block was somewhere in the middle. Four storeys high, it was a small, purpose-built block in red brick with chunky balconies overlooking the street. Across the road was a park, of sorts — a flash of green in an otherwise grey suburb. From what he could make out, it had some swings, a climbing frame and a cycle path around the edge. A huddle of art students sat in the middle smoking weed. The sweet, pungent odour floated over to him as he got out of the car.

Rob straightened his shoulders, steeling himself. The familiar knot of tension in his stomach was back. He'd forgotten about that. He'd carried it around with him for years, right up until he'd left home. *Here goes.*

He got to a security gate at the bottom of the stairs and pressed the buzzer marked *Flat 4*. There was no reply. He pressed it again, holding his finger down. It was after six. His father should have been back from work by now, unless he'd gone to the pub. Rob could have rung ahead, but he hadn't wanted to give his old man a chance to dodge the meeting. Excuses were second nature to him.

I've got to work late. You sort yourself out.
I get paid by the hour, and raising a kid is expensive.

Meanwhile, he'd been out drinking or gambling. Or both. As Rob grew older, Ronnie didn't even try to disguise it.

Got a big game on tonight. Wish me luck.

One thing Rob knew with the utmost certainty was that there was no such thing as luck. There was only loss and neglect and disinterest, and baked beans on toast because there was nothing else in the house.

He took a sharp breath, pushed the memories aside, and pressed the buzzer a third time.

Eventually a sleepy voice said, "Yeah?"

"It's me — Rob."

A growl. "Fuckin' hell." There was shuffling, then the gate clicked open.

Rob climbed one flight of stairs and walked along a short corridor to Flat 4. The door opened before he got there, and his father stepped out onto the landing. He looked like a crumpled sheet in greasy jeans, a smudged T-shirt with a *Rex's Scooters* logo on the front and holey socks.

"What are you doing here?"

"It's nice to see you too, Dad. Are you going to invite me in?"

With a scowl, his father stood aside. Rob stepped past him into the flat. He nodded to his T-shirt. "You been working?"

"Nah. I lost that job, thanks to you."

Rob wasn't surprised. Rex would have been a fool to take Ronnie back.

His father closed the door. "I haven't cleaned up in a while."

No kidding. The place was a mess. Days-old washing-up piled in the sink, while overflowing ashtrays and empty beer bottles crowded every surface. Rob wrinkled his nose. It stank of stale cigarette smoke and microwave food.

"I need to ask you about the night you were picked up." He was about to sit down, then thought better of it.

"Why d'you wanna know about that?" Ronnie frowned. "I told you everything."

"A man was found dead in Soho Square that night."

"Oh, great." Ronnie threw his hands in the air. "Now my own son thinks I had something to do with a murder."

"I didn't say it was a murder."

Ronnie glared at him. "You didn't say it wasn't, either."

He sighed. "Did you see anything, Dad?"

"No, I bloody didn't. I cut through the square on my way home. I didn't see anyone."

"You must have been on the lookout for the police? You had twenty grand in a bag."

"I kept me head down and stayed in the shadows."

"Except you were stopped and searched anyway."

Ronnie spluttered. "Because an overzealous copper thought I was dodgy. Imagine that?"

Imagine, indeed.

"Besides, I told you why I did it," Ronnie went on. "I'm not a thief, okay? I was desperate. You don't know what it's like to have a man like Magnus Olsen breathing down your neck."

"No, thankfully I don't, but then I don't throw money away at the poker table."

A fragile finger waved in his face. "Poker put you through school, mate. How else was I going to afford to raise a kid on my own?"

Getting a decent job might have been a good start. Rob sighed. "Use whatever excuse you want, I don't care. All I need to know is whether you saw anything unusual on Sunday night."

Ronnie gave him a cold stare. "If all you're going to do is pump me for information, then get out."

"I'm trying to solve a case."

Ronnie shook his head. "I've gotta be somewhere, anyway."

The casino, no doubt. Rob walked back down the threadbare hallway to the front door. "At least think about it. If anything comes to mind, let me know."

Another grunt.

He didn't say goodbye. Ronnie shut the door after him, and Rob kept walking. Along the exposed corridor, down the dirty stairwell, to the car. Why did he always feel unclean after talking to his father? He wasn't going to try to psychoanalyse that one. Rob gulped down the fresh air, feeling better every second he wasn't in that flat.

CHAPTER 10

Rob opened his front door and walked into his nice, clean house. He could hear Jo talking to Jack in the kitchen, the radio was on and Trigger bounded through to greet him.

Magically, the knot in his stomach dissipated. He should have known his father wouldn't help him. When had he ever? Even if he had seen something unusual that night, he wouldn't come out and say it. The coppers were the enemy. His own son was the enemy.

He walked into the kitchen and sat down at the table.

"You look tired," Jo said. Jack waved excitedly while she spooned food into his mouth. "Are you okay?"

"I'm fine now." He smiled, but it came out more as a grimace. "Went to see my father this evening."

"Again?" She shot him a sideways glance.

"Yeah, I thought he might have some information for me about the investigation we're working on."

"The Soho case?"

He nodded. "They've given it to us."

"I read about it in the paper. Nasty business."

That it was. "I don't know why I ever thought he'd tell me anything."

She put the spoon down and gave his shoulder a squeeze. "I'm sorry."

"It's okay. It's to be expected." Rob leaned back, folding his arms across his chest. "You know, I often wonder what would have become of me if I hadn't joined the force."

She continued feeding Jack.

"I mean, I was already getting into trouble as a teenager. It was only a matter of time before I turned to crime."

"Do you think so?" She smiled at him. "Sometimes our parents teach us how not to be. I don't think you'd have become a criminal. You've got too strong a moral compass."

"I didn't always," he mused. "Or at least I don't think I did. Back then I was so lost, I didn't know what I was doing."

"You had no structure, no role model," she said.

"If it wasn't for my uncle . . ." He faded off, momentarily lost in the past.

"He was the one who suggested you join the police, wasn't he?" She spooned the last of the food into Jack's mouth and put the bowl aside. "I remember you telling me once, when we first met."

"Yeah. He suggested the military, but I knew someone who'd joined the force, so I thought that was a better option."

She put the bowl and spoon in the dishwasher, while Jack thumped his chunky hands on the highchair. "Look what you've accomplished. You've put countless bad guys away and made the world a safer place."

He chuckled, feeling the bout of melancholy lift. "I don't know about that, but perhaps a small part of London."

Jo cleaned up the highchair and took Jack out, placing him on the floor. He'd just started standing and trying to walk — he had to hold on to things or else he went sprawling. Trigger, who'd been sniffing at his bowl, came over and sat down at Rob's feet. With a squeal, Jack flopped down next to him.

"Do you think your father saw something on Sunday night?"

"I don't know. He was in Soho an hour before the body was discovered," Rob said. "I thought he might have noticed something when he was skulking around with that bag of money."

"The paper said the victim was dressed in a fetish outfit?"

"Yeah, I've got the crime scene photographs if you'd like to see them. But it's not pretty." Rob often talked through his cases with Jo. It wasn't allowed, of course, but being in law enforcement herself, and having worked with her in the past, he figured it was acceptable in their case. He knew it wouldn't go any further. Jo was as discreet as they came. Besides, he valued her insight.

"Show me." Her blue eyes glittered.

He took out his phone and pulled up the photographs Liz Kramer had taken. The green grass, the body laid out beneath the unseeing eyes of King Charles II, the jawbreaker gag distending his mouth.

Jo stared at it, unblinking. "Wow. That's quite a show."

Rob frowned. "You think the killer staged this?"

"Of course. This is a spectacle, designed to shock. I don't know who the victim was, but the killer wanted to put him on show for the world to see."

Rob gazed at the pictures. "At first, I thought it might have been a sex game taken too far. An innocent mistake. But there was bruising on his neck. Liz thinks it's a chain mark, which means it could be deliberate."

"Again, it could be erotic," Jo pointed out, the same way DI Tremayne had. "But the way the body was left on the green — exposed, visible for all to see." She shook her head. "Why not dump it in a dark alleyway, or a rubbish bin behind a nightclub? Why here, in the middle of the square, in a place it was bound to be found?"

"You have a point." He hadn't considered the relevance of the location before now. "Michael Bennett lived in Hampstead. His partner doesn't know why he was in Soho that night."

"You checked his phone records?"

"We're still waiting for them to come through. Will's looking into that."

Jo nodded. "They might tell you who he was meeting."
He could but hope.

"He's married, you say?" Jo picked up a toy that Jack had dropped, wiped it down with an antibacterial wipe and handed it back to him.

"Yes, his partner works in the city. He had no idea Michael was out that night."

"An affair?" Jo raised an eyebrow.

"Maybe. They seem to have been happy." He shrugged. "But who really knows what goes on behind closed doors."

"That could explain the flamboyant nature of the crime," she said slowly. "The killer could be trying to send a message. Presenting the victim as a . . . I don't know. A loose man. A slut. Someone who doesn't deserve respect. Who deserves to be shown up for what he is. That sort of thing."

Rob stared at her. "You're good at this."

She smiled. "Psychology degree."

"True." He hesitated. "I'm thinking we might need to take a closer look at the husband."

She nodded. "Or the person Michael was having an affair with. He might be teaching the victim a lesson. You never know what goes on in people's heads."

"Scary, isn't it?"

She nodded, stroking Jack's soft blond head. Trigger nudged at her hand, wanting some attention too, so she ruffled his ears. "Sometimes I wonder what we've done, bringing an innocent child into this world."

He'd had that thought in the beginning too, but then they did see a side to the world that not many other people did, or at least not so up close and personal. A black-and-white image in a newspaper, or a few seconds' visual on the news didn't compare with staring at crime scene photographs of butchered victims for hours on end, breaking the news to the grieving relatives or dealing with the scum who committed these offences, hearing their pathetic attempts to lie, coerce or negotiate their way out of harsher sentences.

He thought of Cranshaw, the villain in his last case. A DCI himself, respected in his field. A hypocrite. The worst of the worst. A man of responsibility who had used his position to traffic unaccompanied minors into the country then exploit them for his own criminal enterprise. A member of an organised crime group operating in the London area.

I'm not the only one.

The hairs on Rob's neck stood up. "I wonder how the NCA is getting on with that OCG investigation," he said. Until recently, Jo had worked for the National Crime Agency, but she had left on maternity leave and never returned. Her old boss, Pearson, hadn't wanted her back. They hadn't seen eye to eye. She had challenged him, and he didn't like that. Jo had been only too happy to leave.

"I could put some feelers out," she offered. "You thinking about Cranshaw?"

"Yeah." He still hadn't told her about the threat. Should he?

Jack lifted his arms in the air and Jo picked him up, depositing him on her lap. Tired now, he put his head on her chest and closed his eyes, the toy still in his hand.

Why add an extra layer of stress onto their happy existence? If he could keep the horrors at bay, then that's what he'd do. Besides, it was probably an empty threat. A last-ditch attempt by a condemned man to exact some semblance of revenge on the officer who'd caught him.

He shoved Cranshaw out of his mind. "How's life at MI5?"

"Good. I can't complain. It's not active police work, but it's interesting. And my boss is nice, which makes a change." Her eyes crinkled.

"What's he like, your boss?" Rob asked. She hardly ever spoke about her work. He knew it was confidential and he respected that.

"Ray Humphries. He's a hard taskmaster, but very bright and a good man. Decent, you know?"

Rob nodded.

"He lets me get on with it, doesn't micromanage like Pearson used to. He trusts me to do my job." Jo was used to taking the lead on cases, and she was good at what she did. He had no doubt Humphries recognised that in her.

"Sounds perfect." Pity he couldn't say the same about Mayhew. That woman was constantly on his case. He suspected it was more to do with keeping him where she could see him, rather than because she actually liked him. He was the loose cannon, the DCI that stretched the budget and got the murder squad into the papers. The serial killer catcher — although they hadn't had one of those in a while, thank God.

"I'd better put this little man down." Jo got to her feet, Jack in her arms. "Say goodnight to Daddy."

Rob leaned over and kissed Jack on the cheek. He got a sleepy gurgle in response.

"I'll get supper started," he said. There were two chicken breasts laid out on the counter.

"Thanks. Be right back."

She went upstairs with the sleepy baby, while Trigger snorted at his feet. Rob stroked the dog with his foot. "You've had your supper," he murmured.

Soon, the chicken was in the oven, the potatoes were on the boil, and he'd poured them each a glass of wine. *This is what it's all about*, he thought, as Jo came down and smiled her thanks. *Family.*

Seeing his father had made him realise how lucky he was. It could so easily have been very different. Rob was happy for the first time in his life, and it was a feeling he wanted to hold on to — had to hold on to. This was what he had to protect at all costs. For without this, the horrors would take over and consume him.

CHAPTER 11

Something woke Rob up, he didn't know what. He lay in the dark, listening. Was it a dream? A consequence of his overactive imagination? All he could hear was his heart thumping in his chest, and Jo's gentle, rhythmic breathing beside him.

A low growl. Trigger. It wasn't his imagination. He had heard something.

Slipping out of bed, he grabbed the nearest thing he could find to use as a weapon, which happened to be Jo's cordless hairdryer, and opened the bedroom door.

"What is it?" Jo murmured.

"Nothing," he whispered, hoping that was the case. She gave a soft grunt, rolled over and went back to sleep.

Rob tiptoed along the landing. Trigger was in the kitchen, emitting a low, even growl. He descended the stairs, holding the hairdryer like a hammer, and stood in the hallway and listened without turning on any of the lights. The house was quiet, save for the growling. What was Trigger hearing that he wasn't?

He crept down the hallway into the kitchen. "What is it, boy?" The dog was alert. Fur bristling, ears flattened, eyes fixed on the security gate over the French doors.

Rob heard it. A rustle, like something or someone was sneaking around outside. He peered through the glass, pulse racing, but the garden was in darkness. He couldn't detect any movement.

After a few minutes, Trigger relaxed. Instead of growling, he nudged Rob's leg, happy at the impromptu late-night visit. Whatever it was had gone.

On edge, Rob made a cup of tea and sat in the kitchen drinking it. He didn't put the fluorescent light on, but rather the lamp in the corner. Its dim glow was enough to see what he was doing, but not so bright that he couldn't see outside if he needed to. Not for the first time, he was grateful he'd installed the security gate.

Had Cranshaw sent someone after him? Were they casing the place? Looking for signs of weakness, ways to gain entry? Or perhaps it was just a cat on the prowl that had got Trigger's hackles up.

Not likely. The Lab didn't normally react to a feline presence. But if the intruder was human, how did they get into the garden? It was fenced in on all sides. Mrs Winterbottom on the right and a retired couple on the left. In front of them was a detached house with a messy garden, overgrown and in need of some attention. Perhaps the intruder had come over that way.

Tomorrow, he'd take a look. It was too dark to see now. Maybe they'd left a footprint or something.

"Goodnight, boy," Rob muttered, patting Trigger on the head. He switched off the lamp and waited a further five minutes before he went back to bed. Just in case.

There was no more noise, and Trigger seemed calm.

The threat level was back to normal.

* * *

Jo was working from home, so Rob left the house after breakfast and drove to the Montgomery Centre, where Liz Kramer was performing the post-mortem.

"I'm doing it at nine," she'd told him when she'd rung at eight. "Slotting him in above my other customers. Orders from above."

Rob could guess. Raza Ashraf had been onto Liz too.

Armed with a two-shot coffee from the café across the road, Rob stepped through the automatic doors, which opened with barely a hiss, and entered the Montgomery Centre. Today was hotter than yesterday, and it was a pleasure to get inside the air-conditioned building. It wasn't much to look at from the outside. Flat and squat, it resembled a concrete block with a row of tinted windows overlooking a car park. Rob always thought it looked like it had its eyes shut. Perhaps it didn't want to see what was going on inside.

The interior was a different story. Rob walked across the modern foyer, his heels clicking on the marble tiles. A glossy receptionist slid a book towards him. "Sign in, sir."

He scrawled his name and who he was meeting, and another set of doors wheezed open, allowing him access to the inner sanctum. Silence greeted him. Not even his shoes made a sound as he marched down the carpeted corridor under subtle downlighting and framed photographs of unidentifiable microscopic objects on the walls.

At the back of the building were the labs. This was where the post-mortems took place. He waved to Liz through the glass partition and climbed a short flight of stairs to the viewing gallery. Front-row seats.

Liz glanced up and nodded. The production was about to begin. Rob almost expected the lights to dim and the orchestra to start playing.

Liz's voice echoed around the gallery, thanks to the mic installed in the lab. A pasty-faced technician assisted her, his complexion almost as grey as the corpse on the gurney in front of them. They were both wearing scrubs, gloves and face masks. Liz was a stickler for protocol. A regular expert witness for the prosecution, she'd never risk her evidence being deemed inadmissible — or worse, disregarded in court.

"The victim is a well-nourished male in his late forties," she began, circling the body like an eagle about to swoop down on its prey. "As previously stated, there is significant bruising around his neck. He has a fractured hyoid bone and petechial haemorrhaging consistent with asphyxiation. It looks like this man was strangled."

That's what she'd told him at the crime scene.

"Ligature marks are in a distinct pattern." She nodded to the assistant to take close-ups. The forensic camera snapped away. "They're thick and circular and extend around the front of the throat, lessening at the sides and back. My guess would be a chain of some sort."

"Was he hung?" Rob was concerned by the lack of markings at the back of the neck. "Or strangled?"

"Strangled," she confirmed without hesitation. "The markings would be deeper if the chain had supported his entire body weight. That's not to say he wasn't standing up when it happened, but it's more likely he was attached to a pole or a bedstead."

"The leather bands on his wrists," Rob remembered. "They were tight. He'd tried to get loose. There's evidence that he struggled against them."

Poor sod. It proved his abuser had wanted to hurt him. Had he planned to kill him too, or was that an accident? An unfortunate side effect of the BDSM game they were playing.

Liz inspected his fingernails. "His nails are squeaky clean, almost like they've been scrubbed. I can't find a speck of dirt, which is unusual."

"The killer made sure he couldn't be traced," Rob murmured. That put a different spin on things. It showed forethought. Premeditation.

"You're looking for someone who is forensically aware," Liz said. "He must have cleaned the victim before he dumped him." She swabbed inside the victim's mouth and nose. "I'll take plenty of samples. Let's see if they throw back any DNA."

Rob watched as she put the swab buds into separate evidence bags, sealed them and logged them. Thorough as ever.

"Do you think he's done this before?"

"That would explain how he knew to clean the body." She worked her way down the torso to the thighs. "There isn't a speck on him. Help me turn him over," she said to her assistant. They did so, and she followed the same process as she worked her way down the back of the body.

Rob sipped his coffee.

"There's been anal penetration," she remarked. "Looks forced, judging by the amount of tissue damage. It would have been a large object, made from a hard material. Plastic, most likely."

Rob spluttered his coffee. Why was that so unexpected, especially considering what the victim had been wearing? "A dildo?"

"Possibly, but it could have been anything. I've taken a swab. It might return something we can use to identify the object."

He shuddered involuntarily. He didn't want to think about what this poor guy had been through before he died. Had any of it been consented to? Had he been expecting something else? Or had he been surprised, tied up, raped and strangled? Rob bit his lip. He'd find out. This crime wasn't going to go unpunished.

Liz and her assistant turned the body back over.

"I'm going to open him up now."

She began the incision, carving a Y-shape into the victim's chest. Rob glanced away. He didn't like the slicing and dicing. The evidence was why he was here. Dead bodies spoke to Liz, and he wanted to hear what they said. If he was going to find out who did this, he needed every piece of the puzzle, and this was a big one.

"Yup, hyoid's definitely fractured." She peered into the cavity. "His neck snapped. It was quite sudden."

"Thank God for small mercies," Rob muttered.

"Indeed."

She took blood samples. "I'll have them analysed, but it'll take a few days. I don't think the results will be expedited."

"Okay, thanks. Anything else?" He was keen to get back to the office.

"Not at first glance. I'll forward you my report this afternoon. If there is anything further, it'll be in that."

"Thanks, Liz."

Despite the heat, Rob was glad to get out into the sunshine.

CHAPTER 12

"He was raped and strangled." Rob stood at the foot of the long table in the incident room looking at his team. "It wasn't a sex game gone awry."

There was a shocked murmur. Jenny opened her laptop and flicked to some photographs. "May I?"

"Sure, go ahead." Rob sat down and let her speak.

"We visited several fetish stores in Soho, all of which stock the items the victim was wearing, although nobody recognised him. Apparently, there's a lot more to this than meets the eye . . ."

She hesitated.

"What do you mean?" asked Rob.

Jenny cleared her throat. "Apparently, there is this system of communication in the LGBT community based on colour-coding. It was originally used by gay men in the seventies — the pre-internet era — to signal that they were available. They'd wear a coloured handkerchief in their back pocket. Left meaning dominant, right meaning submissive. The colour system has now extended to other accessories."

Will frowned. "You mean certain colours mean certain things?"

"Yup."

"Like what?" asked Celeste.

"Well, the black hot pants Michael Bennett was wearing are pretty standard, but black meant he was into hardcore S&M."

"Except we know he wasn't," interjected Rob.

"Perhaps someone wants us to think he was," said Harry.

"What about the harness?" Rob asked.

Jenny consulted her notes. "The locked collar means he's taken. No collar would mean he's single."

Celeste's eyes were getting bigger with each passing word. "Since he was wearing a collar, he was in a relationship."

Jenny nodded. "The colour is significant too. Most 'normal'—" she made the quotation signal with her fingers — "fetish harnesses are black with silver or grey studs, like the one Michael Bennett was wearing. According to Jimmy, who works in a fetish shop in Old Compton Street, different colours signify different kinks. Things you're willing to engage in or receive."

"Phew." Will looked rather alarmed. "I had no idea it was so involved."

"Neither did I before we spoke to this guy," said Harry.

Jenny continued. "Obviously, under normal circumstances, everything is done with consent and trust. Jimmy explained to me how there is a certain etiquette among people who engage in bondage practices. Everyone is very polite and respectful. There are fetish parties, where participants get to know one another before they engage in sexual activity."

Rob pursed his lips. Keaton had mentioned these parties too. "Our victim could have met his attacker at one."

"That's what we were thinking," said Harry. "We didn't have time to canvass the whole area, but we'll go back this evening and carry on."

"Yeah, some of the bars and clubs weren't open, and others saw us coming a mile off." Jenny grimaced. "I think we need to go in undercover. They don't want to talk to cops."

Rob gave a reluctant nod. "Okay, if you feel comfortable doing that. If not, talk to SCD9. They'll have various informants working the area." The Human Exploitation and Organised Crime Command, or SCD9 for short, was the rebranded version of the Vice Squad.

Jenny raised an eyebrow. "Maybe we should talk to them anyway. They might be able to point us in the right direction." She glanced at Harry, who nodded.

"I'll get Kat on the phone. She's been in Vice for years."

Rob didn't know who Kat was, but he trusted Harry. "Good, and what came of the house-to-house inquiries?"

"Not much," Celeste admitted. "I visited the few bars and cafés dotted around the square but unsurprisingly nobody saw anything, or if they did, they weren't going to tell me."

"Again, it might be better to go as a paying customer, rather than flashing a badge," Jenny pointed out. "People are more likely to gossip that way."

"I'll leave that with you," Rob said, confident they'd be able to handle it. "In the meantime, I'm going to go to the Singing Lotus, the bar where Michael Bennett's partner was supposedly having dinner on Sunday night. I want to make sure he wasn't lying about his alibi."

"Need one of us to come with you?" Jenny asked.

"No, it's easy enough to check. You guys keep canvassing the area. Someone must have seen something — and we've got to find them."

Jenny gave a firm nod. "We'll do our best."

He knew they would. "Let's reconvene first thing tomorrow." He stretched his back. "I'm also going to talk to the guy who took the crime scene photos and sent them to Keaton."

"Do we have his name?" Jenny asked.

"Yeah, I spoke to Keaton this morning. He gave it to me."

Harry nodded, impressed.

"Where are we on those phone records?" Rob asked Will.

He glanced up. "I've called the phone company several times. The person who pulls the call records from the database is off sick, and nobody else seems to be able to do it. I'll keep on them."

"Please do. It's important."

Will moved on to the next point on his checklist. "Control have been looking at CCTV footage in the area. They haven't been able to pick up the victim or figure out how his body was dumped there."

"There must be something." Rob frowned. "It's in the middle of a square."

"It was drizzling on Sunday night," Will pointed out. "And the protests earlier in the day kept the tourists away."

"That should have made it easier to pick up anomalies."

Will shrugged. "I'll keep chasing them. There's a lot of footage to get through."

Rob nodded. "What about Michael Bennett's bank account?"

"He only had one, and a credit card. Both were paid for by Ralph Keaton. There was no suspicious activity on the accounts. His credit card was always paid off in full, and his bank account was well managed. No large purchases, no loans, no big deposits. In fact, I wish my bank account was that healthy."

"So, Keaton supports him?"

"Yeah, he transfers two grand into his account every month, always on the first. Michael wasn't a big spender. He bought mostly household items, art supplies and food." Will shrugged. "It all seems pretty normal."

Rob drummed his fingers on the table. "We need those phone records. He met someone that night, and we need to find out who. Someone was in that house, saw that picture and recreated the scene."

"There isn't any CCTV in their street, unfortunately," Will said with a grimace. "There is in the next one, which is more of a main thoroughfare, but that doesn't help us much."

"Mayhew will never go for it," Rob said. "We don't even know which time frame we're looking at. What about private security cameras? Anything covering the victim's house?"

"I'm still working on it," Will said.

"Oh, before I forget," Celeste said, turning to Rob, "a man rang demanding to speak to the detective in charge of the Soho investigation. The duty sergeant said he sounded like a crackpot. He was raving about how his partner took his own life twenty years ago."

Rob dismissed it with a wave. This happened all the time with cases that made it into the papers. People called up thinking it was related to their own situation, or it dredged up old memories.

He looked at Jenny and Harry. "Good luck tonight, and I'll see you back here tomorrow morning."

* * *

The Singing Lotus was a Thai restaurant in Fitzrovia, a buzzing Central London district close to the West End. The sign on the door read *Closed*. Rob peered through the front window and saw a man walking around inside, so he gave a hard knock.

The man materialised, murky behind the glass, and pointed to the sign. Rob held up his warrant card.

The door opened. "Is there a problem, officer?" The man frowned, concerned.

"No, no problem. I just need a moment of your time."

"What about?"

"Can I come in?"

The man hesitated. Rob wasn't sure why. Perhaps it was an instinctive distrust of the police — a lot of people had that — or perhaps he didn't want anyone nosing about in his business. Either way, Rob wasn't budging.

"Of course. Come in." He held the door open.

Rob stepped past him into the dimly lit interior. "Are you the manager?"

The man gave a quick nod. "Edward Chang. How can I help you?"

"Mr Chang, I need to check your CCTV footage from Sunday night."

He looked sheepish.

Rob's heart sank. "What?"

"It's not working." He hung his head like he'd been caught doing something wrong.

Rob glanced up at a camera positioned above the reception desk. "Why not?"

"It broke last year and we haven't had it fixed. We get no trouble here." He waved his hands in the air. "Camera's not necessary."

Rob sighed. "What about a reservation book? Do you have one of those?"

"Of course." The man brightened. "This way."

He led Rob over to the reception desk and burrowed under the counter. Eventually, he pulled out a large, flat diary. "Sunday, yeah?" The man's accent was an interesting mix of Thai and London street slang.

Rob watched as he opened the book and thumbed through the pages until he got to last Sunday.

"There!" Rob found the entry, even upside down. Table for four, booked for seven o'clock.

Mr Chang was nodding. "See? All good."

"Do you remember these men?" Rob asked.

Chang's gaze clouded. "Not me. I wasn't here on Sunday night. Weekend off." He grinned. "My cousin, he was working on Sunday night."

"Your cousin?" Rob glanced around. "Is he here?"

"No, he only works Tuesday, Wednesday and Sunday. We close on Monday."

"I see." Rob thought for a moment. So far everything Keaton had said had checked out. He was probably being overcautious. Still, he didn't want to leave any box unchecked. "Will you get your cousin to call me when you see him?" He handed over his card. "It's important I speak to him about these men."

Chang's eyes narrowed. "Is there problem with these customers?"

"No problem." Rob tried a smile but wasn't sure he succeeded. "I need to confirm they were here. That's all."

"Ah, okay. You want an alibi?" He grinned. "Like in the movies?"

This time Rob did smile. "That's exactly right."

Chang pocketed the card. "I'll get the alibi for you. Don't worry."

"Thank you." Rob shook his hand. That had turned out better than he'd expected. He only wished all witnesses were as cooperative.

Next stop was Gunther Kershaw, the man who'd taken the photographs of the crime scene at Soho Square on the night of the murder. According to Keaton, he lived in a one-bedroom apartment above an off-licence on Tottenham Court Road.

Gunther was a big guy, well over six foot, with long sandy-blond hair tied back in a ponytail. He opened the door in torn jeans and mismatched socks. A pair of leather cowboy boots stood to the side, along with a pair of well-worn trainers. No other shoes were visible. His features were also large, in proportion with his body. A big nose, wide eyes, thick lips and a substantial amount of blond stubble. He hadn't shaved in a while, and judging by what he was wearing, didn't work either.

"Gunther Kershaw?"

"Yes." The man seemed curious, rather than suspicious.

"I'm DCI Miller from the Major Investigation Team." He showed his card.

Recognition dawned. "Ah, is this to do with Mikey?"

"Yes, do you mind if we have a chat? I believe you took some photographs of the crime scene."

"Yeah, man." He opened the door to let Rob in. The hallway was narrow, and Rob had to keep moving otherwise he'd have been squashed by Gunther.

"Upstairs," Gunther said.

There was literally nowhere else to go. Rob climbed the creaky staircase to the first floor and went through a door to an open-plan bedsit. They were standing in a living room with a bed at one side and a small kitchenette at the other. It was hard to believe such a big guy could live in such a small flat.

"Now, what can I help you with?"

Rob looked around. There were three guitars resting against the wall, sheet music on the dining room table and a dizzying array of LPs piled on the floor in front of an old-style record player. Rob hadn't seen one of those in decades. He tried not to get distracted. "Ralph Keaton told me you'd sent him some photographs."

"Yeah, hell of a thing." Gunther shook his head. "I couldn't believe it when I saw who it was. I mean, Mikey wasn't into all that kinky shit, you know? Neither was Ralph. They were like an old married couple. They *were* an old married couple. It's insane to think that Mikey was doing that on the side."

"What makes you think he was?"

"Well, how else did he get there?" He shrugged. "And did you see what he was wearing?"

"I did, yes. We're working on the theory that he was coerced." Rob wanted to keep the guy talking. His gut was telling him this man knew a lot about what had gone down in Soho.

"That would make more sense." He smoothed a beefy hand over his ponytail. "Mikey didn't even drink that much. I can't imagine him going to a fetish bar without Ralph, you know? He was kinda shy."

"Yet he ended up dead in the square."

"I know, that's what I can't get my head around." He slumped down in a battered armchair. "Crazy."

"What were you doing there?" Rob asked.

"I play at a jam session at this blues club in Kingly Street every Sunday night. Keeps me young." He grinned. The guy was probably in his early forties. "I'm not even that good, I just love jamming, and I'm good enough to keep the audience happy."

"I see." Rob thought for a moment. "You were on your way home when you came across the body?"

"I saw the crowd first," he said. "There were a group of people standing around gawking, so I went to have a look. I mean, we all do, don't we?"

Rob nodded. It was human nature.

"Anyway, that's when I saw this guy dressed in that leather getup. Bondage gear, you know." He waved a hand in the air. "I don't buy in to all that. Who'd want to be tied up and spanked, right? But some people do, especially in Soho, so who am I to judge?"

Rob gave a slow nod. "That's when you saw it was Mikey?"

"Only when that forensic lady took his mask off. I couldn't believe it. To tell you the truth, I was stunned."

"Yet you took photographs."

"I thought Ralph would want to know. In hindsight, though, it probably wasn't such a good idea."

"What makes you say that?"

"He didn't reply. Not straightaway, at least. He called, totally hysterical, in the early hours of the morning. He'd just seen the message. I wished I hadn't sent them. The guy was beside himself." He shook his head.

It was conceivable that Keaton hadn't seen the message until later, particularly if he'd been out to dinner. Rob scratched his head. Another reason to get that phone data. It would show them what time the message came through, and when Keaton opened it.

"Do you have any other pictures?" Rob asked.

"I've deleted a lot." He reached for his phone. "But I can retrieve them." He fiddled around for a few minutes. "Do you want me to send them to you?"

"If you don't mind."

"What's your number?"

Rob gave it to him. A few seconds later his watch pinged in one long, unbroken note.

"Do you want them all?" Gunther asked.

"Yeah, please. There might be something on them that we missed."

He missed. Tremayne and her colleague had been canvassing the crowd while he'd been talking to Liz.

The Southwark DI had already sent through the list of names, but he hadn't had time to look at them yet. It was unlikely the killer had given his details to the police anyway, although stranger things had happened. Some killers got a kick out of being part of the investigation.

Another long line of pings. "Got them, thanks."

They'd go through the dozens of photographs back at the office, along with the list from Tremayne. Every little detail would be scrutinised, every person looked at — just in case one of them was the killer.

CHAPTER 13

Harry Malhotra walked into Compton's and took a seat at the bar. It was nearly nine o'clock and the place was packed. Thanks to the glorious weather, the customers had spilled outside onto the pavement, drinking and talking. Upbeat music rang out from the hi-tech music system, and there was a lot of finger- and toe-tapping going on. The crowd was warming up. In a couple of hours, the place would be heaving, the back section of the bar having turned into an impromptu dance floor.

Harry had been here before, once, a long time ago. Before he'd become a police officer. Before he'd got that bit part in the soap opera. Before he'd realised that he'd get a lot further in life if people didn't know he was gay.

It felt like home. Everybody was so friendly, so accepting, so like him. Finally, he'd found his tribe, as they say. He loved it here. The music, the chatter, the freedom to be whoever he wanted. Yet he'd never been back.

Not even his parents knew about his sexual orientation. His mother came from a staunch Hindu background, and while she'd rebelled against her parents and married for love, and to a white British man at that, accepting a gay son would be a step too far.

At work, he was known as the "Face of the Force". It wasn't because he was better at public speaking than his guvnor, even though he was. It wasn't because he was younger and better looking, even though he was that too. It was because he ticked all the right boxes. The ethnic-minority detective in the nationally renowned murder squad that everybody had read about in the newspaper.

Imagine what people would say if he came out. What would his team think? He was the charmer, the one with the movie-star good looks, the leading man. They had affectionately nicknamed him "Bollywood" because he had so many lady admirers.

Except he was a fake. A fraud. He lived a lie. Every day he got up and got dressed in masculine clothes that he knew played to his handsome features.

Harry, that tie really brings out the green in your eyes.

A genetic quirk. He had the dark hair of his mother's family, but his father's pale green eyes, which various television directors had told him were "mesmerising".

He drove to work, flirted with the female officers, charmed his superiors and did the best job he could — because he'd been brought up to be a good Indian boy.

You didn't buck the trend. You didn't cause problems. You didn't under any circumstances drop a bombshell on your family, friends and colleagues.

He blinked back the moisture that had sprung into his eyes and reached for his drink. Not tonight. Tonight he had a licence to be who he was. Nobody from the office was here. They'd split up, each taking a different establishment. There was no one to see him, to judge him. He was free to do as he pleased.

A man sat down beside him on an empty bar stool.

"You alone?" A half-smile. Expectant. Hopeful.

"I am. What are you drinking?" He'd buy the guy a beer, flirt for a while, then start asking questions: Do you come here often? I'm looking for a friend of mine. Do you know him?

Callum was in his mid-thirties, maybe slightly older than Harry. Australian originally, now living in London. Short, spiky light-brown hair. A wide, laughing mouth. "I haven't seen you here before," he said.

Once, a long time ago. "Likewise." He was suitably vague. This was an act, after all, and he was an actor.

"What's your name?"

He was supposed to be undercover, but stupidly, he hadn't thought about a name. Good thing he didn't work for the intelligence services. He'd make a terrible spy. In his panic, he used his brother's name.

"Jamie." His mother, still bucking the trend, had been adamant that their kids would have English names. Harry and James. It didn't get more English than that.

"Pleased to meet you, Jamie." They shook hands.

Harry was about to take out his wallet to pay for the drinks, then realised his warrant card was in it, so he used his phone to make a contactless payment instead.

"What do you do, Jamie?"

This, they had discussed. He was in advertising, Jenny worked in finance and Celeste was a political science student. The lie rolled easily off his tongue. He was playing his part to perfection. "How about you?"

"I manage an art gallery in Chelsea."

A fellow creative. "Are you an artist?"

Callum gave an embarrassed laugh. "God no. Can't paint to save my life. It doesn't stop me appreciating it, however." He winked at Harry. "You should come over to the gallery one day and check it out."

Harry smiled. "Sounds good."

Never gonna happen.

This was his opportunity to bring up the victim. "Actually, I recently met an artist from Hampstead," he said.

"Oh yeah? Anyone I'd know?"

"Maybe. You heard of Michael Bennett?"

Callum frowned. "I don't think so. Is he any good?"

"Not bad. Paints portraits, mostly. He has some stunning nudes." It was true, but he wasn't sure why he'd said that.

Callum's eyes sparkled. "Can't say I've heard of him."

"This is the picture on his website." He couldn't very well show Callum the crime scene photographs.

"Nah, mate. Definitely not, but I'll look out for the name."

He wouldn't be painting any more pieces.

Callum excused himself and went to the men's room. Harry ordered another round. "What about you?" he asked the barman. "You know this guy?"

A frown. "He a friend of yours?"

"An artist," Harry said. "I was hoping to bump into him tonight."

The barman looked away. "Yeah, he was here Sunday. I chatted to him for a bit before it got busy. Nice guy, soft-spoken."

Harry's pulse ticked up a notch. They had a lead.

"Was he alone?"

"Yeah, but he did say he was waiting for someone. A client, I think. He mentioned a painting."

"Did the client ever arrive?"

"Yup, he came in about eight thirty. They talked for a few moments and then left."

Harry felt his heart skip a beat. "Together?"

"Yeah. Why all the questions?"

"I was hoping to buy one of his pieces," Harry lied. "I heard he hung out here."

"Nah, never seen him before that night. Or since."

Harry was going to ask what the client looked like, but that might sound suspicious. Too many questions. Besides, the barman had moved away to serve another customer.

Callum returned and spotted the fresh drinks on the bar. "Hey, this was my round." His tone was mildly chastising.

Harry shrugged. "You can get the next one."

There won't be a next one.

Callum grinned. "You got it."

They talked about art and theatre, and what was worth seeing and what wasn't. Callum was extremely knowledgeable, but he had a great sense of humour too. Harry found himself laughing out loud on more than one occasion.

Eventually, they finished their drinks. "My shout." Callum gestured to the bartender.

"Actually, I'm really sorry, but I've got to go." Harry got up.

"But you said—"

"I know, I'm sorry. Wish I could stay but I've got an early start tomorrow."

"Sure I can't convince you to have one more?"

No convincing needed.

"Sorry, I really can't."

The full mouth turned down at the sides. Harry wanted to kiss it. The thought shocked him to his senses. What the hell was he doing? It had been a mistake coming here. The blues bar down the road would have been a better option. Less . . . dangerous. He turned around.

"Can I see you again?" Callum called after him.

Yes.

No.

"I don't come to town very often."

A pause. Callum was studying him, brown eyes probing. Could he see straight through his facade and into his chaotic soul? Eventually, he took out his wallet and handed Harry a business card. "Here's me, anyway. If you do come back, or if you're ever in Chelsea, give me a call. It would be great to see you."

Harry hesitated.

Don't do it. Don't even go there.

"Thanks." He pocketed the card.

Callum grinned. "See ya, Jamie. I hope."

Harry acknowledged him with a tilt of his head, then hurried out of the bar.

CHAPTER 14

"Rob, my office!"

Rolling his eyes at Will, Rob walked down the central aisle of the squad room to Mayhew's sanctuary.

"What are you doing waltzing around Soho? You're a DCI. How many times do I have to remind you that your job is here, not out in the field."

"With all due respect, ma'am, we're a man down since Mike left and we needed more boots on the ground. The team were shattered, so I stepped in to request the CCTV footage from the bar where Michael Bennett was last seen."

She gave an unladylike grunt. "I read DS Malhotra's report. He's an enterprising young sergeant. You should have let him get the footage."

"He didn't want to break his cover, ma'am, and rightly so. We might need him again."

She gazed at Rob for a long moment. He wondered what was going on in that brain of hers. Nothing good, that's for sure. He annoyed her, that much was obvious. She didn't like that he didn't follow protocol, that he was unpredictable. Mayhew was the kind of person who wanted to know what was going on in her department at all times, afraid to take the slightest risk. No fuckups on her watch.

Well, the feeling was mutual. In his opinion, Mayhew was too preoccupied with kissing arse to be an effective superintendent. Sam Lawrence had taught him that your team came first, you had their back, no matter what. You led by example. You earned respect. Mayhew had done none of those things.

Eventually, she let out a slow breath. "Fair enough. View the footage and let's wind this up. If the killer is on there, I want him in cuffs by the end of the day."

"That's the plan," Rob replied with more gusto than he felt. In his experience, these things were seldom that simple.

"Good, that's all."

His cue to leave.

* * *

"You in trouble again?" DCI Galbraith passed Rob on his way back to his desk. Rob had worked with the big Scot on several earlier cases, most notably Sam Lawrence's murder, when they'd combined forces to apprehend the killer.

"So it would seem." Rob rolled his eyes. "You know how it is."

"Aye, I do." Galbraith patted him on the back. "Keep up the good work, mate."

"Thanks, you too."

When he walked in, Will glanced up. "I've got the surveillance footage," he said. "I'm going through it now."

Rob stood beside him, eyes on the screen as Will forwarded the video to the night in question.

"That's Michael Bennett." Rob pointed to the screen. "It's not a great angle."

They could only see the back of Michael's head. The black-and-white picture wasn't the clearest either, and as the bar got busier, the other punters blocked the line of sight.

"The camera is located above the entrance," said Will. "That's why we don't have a clear shot."

Hopefully it would still be enough. The camera would show their faces as they left.

Will let it play in real time. Michael was alone at the bar, a half-drunk beer in front of him. The bartender Harry had spoken to came over and said a few words, then nodded and left to serve another customer. People came and went but nothing else happened.

"Forward to when the stranger comes in," said Rob.

Will sped up the footage, and the images became jerky and frenetic. At a quarter to nine, a man in a long jacket and a cap walked into the bar.

"Hold it," barked Rob.

Will slowed it down again. "We can't see his face."

Bugger. "He knows it's there," muttered Rob.

Hands in pockets, head bowed, loose jacket hiding his shape. He could be skinny or overweight, it was impossible to tell.

The stranger approached Michael, who turned and shook his hand. "They don't know each other, then," Will pointed out.

Rob kept his eyes glued to the screen. "Turn around," he urged, but the stranger kept his head firmly facing forward. He ordered a drink from the other bartender. The bar was busier now, and Rob had to strain to keep his eyes on the stranger. A group of men stood behind him, blocking their view, so all they could see was a hand reaching for the beer and putting it back on the bar again. No jewellery. No noticeable tattoos or scars. Unfortunately, the image was too grainy to blow up.

"It's a man, at least," said Will.

The stance and posture suggested it was a man, but Rob had been fooled by that before. Now he took nothing at face value. "We need to speak to that second bartender," he said. "Get a description. This footage is useless." All it did was confirm that Michael Bennett met someone.

"They're leaving." Will froze as Michael turned around and followed the stranger to the door.

"I can't bloody see him," fumed Rob.

The stranger kept his head down, collar up, and walked out close on the heels of two other men, who blocked the lens.

"Shit. Any CCTV in the street?" snapped Rob.

"Not facing this angle." Will looked downcast. "I've checked the whole street."

Rob threw up his hands. "You think there'd be more coverage in Soho." He stared at the screen. "What's that place across the road? Do they have a surveillance camera?"

"That's a sex shop," said Will. "And no, they 'don't invade their customers' privacy'. That's a direct quote."

Rob just shook his head. So much for having the killer in cuffs by the end of the day. He slumped down at his desk and began to go through his emails. There was one from Liz Kramer with the subject "Lab Results". He opened the attachment. *Please let there be something useful in those.*

Tox screen report for Michael Bennett. His eyes scanned the toxicology report, hoping against hope there was something there.

He caught his breath. There was.

"Have you got something, guv?" Celeste asked.

One of the other SIOs had secured a prosecution and the noise level in the squad room escalated. Rob gestured for the team to follow him into the incident room.

They filed in behind him, Will still disheartened by the failure of the CCTV to ID the killer, Harry tired but expectant. Only Jenny and Celeste had a bounce in their step. They sat down around the table.

"What have you found?" Jenny asked.

"I just got the tox screen back from Liz Kramer. Michael Bennett was drugged."

They stared at him.

"Like, roofied?" asked Harry.

"Yeah, along with the alcohol, he had flunitrazepam in his system, commonly known as Rohypnol."

"How would someone get hold of Rohypnol?" asked Will.

"Black market," said Harry. "Drug dealers. Prescription. Any number of places."

"Get onto SCD9," Rob said. "Find out if they know who's supplying. They might have their eye on someone. Though it's a long shot. He could have got it anywhere."

Harry nodded and took out his phone.

"It's probably a blessing," Jenny murmured. "Given what happened to him."

Rob gave a sombre nod. "I'm not sure it was enough to knock him out, but it would have rendered him unable to fight back."

Harry left the room to make the call.

"What did the surveillance footage reveal?" asked Jenny.

"Nothing. We couldn't bloody see his face. The bastard knew where the camera was. He made sure it didn't capture anything."

"Smart guy." Jenny pursed her lips. "What about the bartender? Can't he give us a description?"

"Don't know. I'm going to go and question him this afternoon. His shift starts at five."

"I'll come with you," Jenny said. "I could do with some time away from my computer." There was so much paperwork these days that some detectives barely left their desks.

Outside, Harry could be heard saying, "Rohypnol. You know, the date-rape drug."

"Yes!" Will punched the air.

"What?" Rob asked.

"The mobile data for Michael and his partner's phone has finally come through."

"Go," said Rob. "Let me know if you find anything."

Will rushed out, sidestepping Harry, who was pacing up and down the corridor.

"I'm worried about him," Jenny said.

"Who? Will?"

"No, Harry. He's not himself. I can't put my finger on it, but he's definitely not his usual bouncy self."

Now that she mentioned it, he did seem more subdued than normal. "Okay, I'll have a word and make sure everything's okay. He could be missing Mike. They were quite close, weren't they?"

"Yeah, it could be that." Jenny smiled. "Thanks, guv. I'd better get on." She left the room, followed by Celeste. Rob sat there for a long moment watching the handsome young sergeant's face as he spoke to his contact in the Vice unit.

"Okay. Thanks, Kat," Harry said. "Appreciate the help."

"Got something?" Rob asked when Harry poked his head back into the room.

"Sort of. My mate in SCD9 gave me the name of a local dealer who might know who's supplying the date-rape drug."

"Be careful," Rob said. "Drug dealers don't like talking to the cops, as you know."

"Then I won't be a cop." He grinned, and his accent changed to rough London slang. "I'm gonna score me some roofies, bruv. I got this peng ting who ain't showing me no love, innit."

Rob was impressed, then he remembered Harry was a part-time actor. "You might be wasted in this job."

Harry scoffed. "Police work is way more exciting than acting. I get to arrest people for real, not just on screen."

He had a point there.

"Okay, but make sure you have backup. Don't meet this guy alone."

"I won't."

"How are you doing otherwise, Harry?" Rob asked, since it was only the two of them left in the room. "I know you and Mike were close."

"I'm okay. We stay in touch."

"That's good." Rob hesitated — subtlety wasn't his strong point. He preferred a more direct approach. "Nothing else bothering you?"

"No, why'd you ask?" Harry fixed worried green eyes on him. "Have I done something wrong?"

"No, nothing like that." Rob was quick to reassure him. "You're doing a great job. Jenny just thought you were a bit quiet, that's all." Damn, now he'd gone and dropped Jenny in it.

Harry shook his head. "It's all good, I swear. Nothing to worry about. Same old me."

"That's good." Rob smiled, relieved, but he didn't miss the crease lines on his sergeant's forehead as Harry walked away.

CHAPTER 15

"Seriously? You expect me to remember a guy who ordered one drink on Sunday night?" The bartender stared incredulously at him.

Busy bar, lots of punters. It was always going to be a long shot.

"This is him." Rob pulled up the photograph he'd taken from the video footage on his phone. His hands were damp with sweat and stuck to the photo. The bartender stared at it, frowning.

"Nah. Sorry, man. I barely look up when it's busy."

Shit. "Okay, thanks anyway."

They walked away, dejected. "I wonder where they went," Jenny said.

They stood outside on the pavement in the blazing sunshine. Christ, it was hot. They could feel the heat rising off the tarmac. It had to be close to thirty degrees out here, and it was forecast to get hotter.

"It had to be close by," mused Rob. "There wasn't time to take him far. His body was discovered just before ten o'clock. That's an hour to drug him, dress him in that outfit, rape him and strangle him."

Jenny fanned herself with her hand. "Don't forget he had to get him to the square, which couldn't have been easy. A dead weight like that."

"He'd have needed a car," said Rob. "He couldn't have carried the body through the streets to the square. There would have been an uproar."

"Unless he lives here." Jenny glanced at him. "What about the apartment blocks surrounding the square?"

It was a possibility. They walked up Frith Street in the direction of Soho Square. A few die-hard locals were sipping coffees in sidewalk cafés, but the majority were inside where there was air conditioning. Soon, the tall trees at the end of the road came into view. Was it his imagination or were they drooping in the heat?

Jenny stopped in front of a lamppost. "There's a CCTV camera here."

The beady eye stared down at them from above. "We've looked at that one. It covers this corner of the square, but not where the body was found."

"And no one crossed its path to get the body there?"

Rob shook his head. "Will would have said. He went through all the council footage in the area."

"Where exactly was the body found?" Jenny asked.

Rob pushed open the wrought iron gate on the south side of the square and jerked his hand away. Bloody hell, it felt like it had been in a furnace. They went through. "Over there, to the left of the statue, almost directly in front of the Tudor hut."

"What is that thing?" Jenny studied the tiny structure.

"It's a statue of King Charles. The Second, I think."

"No, that." She pointed to the hut.

"It's an electricity substation, or so I'm told."

Jenny tried the door, but it was locked. A brass padlock gleamed in the late-afternoon sun. "We should check inside, just in case."

"Good point." The perpetrator could have lured the victim inside and killed him there. Rob kicked himself for not thinking of that before.

Jenny glanced at the gate on the north side of the square. "It's equidistant," she said. "Whichever gate he came in, he'd have had to carry the body at least ten metres to this spot."

"On a Sunday night," added Rob.

"Soho is always busy," Jenny pointed out. "I can't see how he wasn't seen."

The small green was packed with students, tourists and locals enjoying the balmy weather and the shade of the leafy oaks. A pigeon cooed overhead, then flew up to the rafters of a nearby block of flats.

Rob followed it with his eyes. He studied the tall brick buildings with their neat, white-framed windows hiding behind leafy green trees. Michael Bennett could have been raped and murdered in any one of them.

"We can't search them all," he muttered. "Mayhew would never go for that. Besides, the door-to-door inquiries didn't turn up anything."

Jenny wandered over to the north gate and read the attached laminated sign. "It says here the square closes at ten o'clock in the summer."

Rob read the sign, his mind whirling. "The killer must have dumped the body just before the gates were supposed to be locked." No, that wasn't right. "Scrap that. The caretaker would have spotted it."

"Who's to say he didn't?" said Jenny. "Maybe he's the one that called it in?"

Two youths got up from a nearby bench and walked off, so they sat down. It was very close, not much air moving around. Even the leaves on the trees were still. Rob called Dispatch. He asked them to send the recording of the 999 call straight to his mobile phone.

"Let's get a cold drink," he said to Jenny. "I'm melting sitting here."

They left through the north gate. Jenny wrinkled her nose as they walked past an open rubbish bin. "Ugh, it stinks."

"That would be the public urinal." Rob pointed to a booth on the pavement from which a strong, acrid stench wafted.

"Gross." They crossed the street to get away from the smell and went into a small Turkish coffee shop.

"Ah, bliss." Jenny sighed in relief as the air-con hit them. They ordered two coffees and two bottles of water and sat down to wait for the recording to come through. It didn't take long. The waiter had just put their coffee down when Rob's watch pinged.

He took out his phone and pressed play, then reached for his coffee.

"Hello, do you require police, fire service or ambulance?"

"Police." A young voice, panicky, slightly nasal.

"How can we help you?"

"I've just found a body."

"Did you say a body, sir?"

"Yes, in Soho Gardens. He's dressed . . . He's dressed in . . . Oh shit. He's definitely dead."

"Are you there now, sir?"

"Yeah."

"How do you know the victim is dead?"

"I just know. His eyes . . . Oh, Jesus." The line went dead.

"Hello, sir? Are you still there?"

No answer.

Rob looked at Jenny. "Could be the caretaker."

"How are we going to find him?" she asked.

"Call the council tomorrow. They must know who was working the Sunday shift."

She nodded. "We could wait until ten o'clock and see who locks up?"

Rob hesitated. Much as he'd have liked to, he had to get home.

"I'll stay," she offered, sensing his dilemma.

"You sure? It's another three hours."

"That's okay. I'll walk around, grab something to eat. It's a beautiful evening."

"How will you get home?"

She widened her eyes. "I'll take the train."

"It's sweltering."

"Don't worry, I'll be fine."

"Okay, if you're sure." He knew he shouldn't fuss. Jenny was an experienced sergeant. She could look after herself. "Call me if you speak to him."

"Will do."

Rob walked back to Compton's and was about to get into his car when his watch buzzed. Will was calling.

He took out his phone. "Yeah? What's up?"

"I've found something odd in Michael Bennett's phone records. Could be important."

* * *

"The victim received several calls from an unknown burner phone," said Will. "They started a few days before he died."

"You think it could be the killer?" Rob asked, out of breath. He'd blue-lighted back to the Putney office and taken the stairs to the squad room two at a time.

"I don't know, but I checked out the number. The SIM card was brand new. It had never been used before those few calls to Michael's number, and it went offline on Sunday night. In Soho."

"You traced the phone's location to Soho?"

"Yes. I triangulated the signal to the Soho area. I have it down to a three-block radius, but that's as precise as I can get. Every call made from that phone was from the same location in Soho."

"Which means either the caller lives in the area, or he made damn sure he was when he rang Michael."

"That's right," Will said.

"Does Soho Square fall into that radius?" asked Rob.

Will consulted his map. "Yes, it does."

That supported his and Jenny's theory that the killer had an apartment near the square. It was tenuous though. A killer as clever as this one might want them to think that. They couldn't take anything for granted.

"How many calls did Michael receive from that number?" Rob asked.

"Four. The first one was at 11.22 on Tuesday, five days before he died. The next was on Thursday, at 3.07. And a third on Friday, at midday."

"Exactly midday?" asked Rob.

"Yeah, twelve o'clock on the dot."

Interesting. "Nothing on Saturday?"

"Nope."

"I thought you said there were four calls."

"The fourth was on Sunday afternoon at 6.15."

Rob thought for a moment. "Notice how the calls are always when Michael's partner was at work. Apparently, Keaton had some sort of software launch, which was why he was working at the weekend, and his director's dinner was on Sunday night."

"Do you think the killer knew that?" Will asked.

"Could have done. I think the killer posed as a buyer to lure Michael Bennett to Soho. The 6.15 call was probably to confirm the meeting."

"But why didn't he tell his partner?" Will asked. "It's not like anything fishy was going on. He was selling a painting."

"Maybe he did but Keaton forgot to mention it. It's something we should ask him." Rob thought for a moment. "Whatever happened, we know the killer contacted Michael five days before they met. This was a premeditated murder, planned to the last detail. Someone wanted Michael Bennett dead."

CHAPTER 16

Rob was washing the dishes when his phone rang. With Jack upstairs asleep and Jo having a cold shower, the house was quiet. He answered, pressing the speaker button with his little finger. "Hi, Jenny. How'd you get on?"

"I've just spoken to the caretaker," she said. He could hear the faint sound of laughter and music in the background. "He wasn't the one who placed the 999 call."

"He wasn't?"

"No, this guy's, like, sixty and on his last legs. The caller was younger — in his twenties, I'd say."

She was right. The caller had sounded much younger. His hopes of finding a reliable eyewitness went out the window. "Thanks anyway," he said.

"The old guy admitted to falling asleep," she continued. "He didn't lock up at all that night."

"That's why the gates were still open." Rob placed one of Jack's bottles upside down in the draining rack.

"Exactly. And why the body was discovered so quickly."

"Exactly," Jenny said. "Also, I got into that substation. It's filled with electrical equipment. No space to swing a cat, let alone do anything else. It's not the primary crime scene."

She'd been very thorough. "Good work. At least we can rule that out." He heard footsteps and the music faded away.

"I'm going to head home now. See you tomorrow."

Rob finished the dishes and went upstairs. Jo was in bed, scantily clad, reading a magazine.

He grinned. "This is a pleasant surprise."

She chuckled. "Don't get any ideas. It's too bloody hot to move."

It was stifling. All the windows were open but there was no air.

He sat down next to her and kicked off his shoes.

"Any closer to finding the killer?" she asked.

"No, unfortunately not. This guy's got us running around in circles."

They'd talked briefly about the case over supper, in particular how the killer could have dumped the body in the middle of the square unseen. "Sounds like he knows how to play you."

Rob yawned. "He's got the better of me tonight. I'm shattered. Are you working from home tomorrow?"

"I was supposed to, but my boss has got the day off. It's his anniversary." She smiled. "He's put me in charge of the field team."

"That's great. So you're going in?"

"Yeah, I have to. I called Tanya and thankfully she's available, so she'll be round first thing."

He gave a tired nod. Thank God for Tanya.

"Oh, I heard from Kim today."

He glanced across at her. "Tony's Kim?"

"Yes, she called to invite us round for dinner on Saturday night. What do you think?"

"In theory, yes, but anything could happen with this case." Still, it would be good to see his old friend again. And besides, it would be useful to run the whole BDSM thing past Tony. A criminal profiler of some repute, Tony had an in-depth understanding of the criminal mind. He might be able to shed some light.

"Okay, I'll give them a tentative yes. It's been a while since we saw them, so it'll be good to catch up."

Rob had a cool shower, checked on Jack and collapsed into bed beside Jo. He fell asleep almost immediately, dreaming of wrought iron gates, sightless statues and luminous green grass. But when his alarm went off at six thirty the next morning, he had his answer. Sitting up in bed, he stared groggily at the wall in front of him.

"I know how he did it."

* * *

"Jenny, where are those pictures we took in Soho Square?" Rob hadn't even sat down at his desk. His brain was firing on all cylinders.

"Mayhew's been asking for an update," warned Will.

"Let her wait. This is important. I know how he dumped the body in the square."

"Really?" Harry came over and perched at the end of his desk. "How?"

"I need to see those pictures."

"Coming up now." Jenny pressed a button on her keyboard. She clicked through the various ones they'd taken the day before. The lamppost with the CCTV camera on it. The leafy green in the middle of the square, basking under the watchful eye of King Charles II. The two gates. The signpost with the opening hours.

"Stop there," ordered Rob. "Go back one."

She clicked back to the north gate. "What is it?"

In the corner was a huge rubbish bin. On the side was written *COMMERCIAL WASTE COLLECTION*. It was big, double the size of the refuse bins you put your home waste in. More like a tip, really. On wheels, with a lid.

Bingo.

"That's how he got the body in." Rob stared at the photograph.

"In the bin?" Celeste blinked at him.

"Of course," Jenny whispered. "It's brilliant. Nobody would think to look in the bin. He could have wheeled it in in front of everybody."

"Ingenious," muttered Will.

Harry came over. "So, he murders the victim, Michael Bennett. Puts his body in the bin, which presumably he had waiting outside wherever he killed him, wheels him to the green and tips him out on the lawn just before ten o'clock."

"That's about it," said Rob.

Jenny came to her senses first. "Well, we'd better get it swabbed for DNA."

Will grimaced. "Good luck with that."

Rob didn't want to think what sort of things they'd find in a public refuse bin, but they had to try. There might be a strand of Michael's hair, a drop of his blood, an item of his clothing.

"How often are those bins emptied?" Harry asked.

"Weekly, fortnightly? I don't know." He shrugged.

"I'll find out." Jenny took out her phone. Mayhew would complain that it was a waste of their budget. Still, Rob trusted his gut.

"It makes sense," he continued. "This was a showy murder. The killer wanted the body to be found, wanted to send a message. He planned everything else down to the finest details. The phone calls, the meetup at the bar, the outfit. Why not plan this too?"

Jenny got onto the City of Westminster Council and asked to be put through to the right department. Harry was still staring at the picture of the rubbish bin on the screen. "He's very clever, isn't he?"

Rob nodded.

"I can't believe I didn't think of that." Jenny, who was on hold, shot him a sideways glance. "I'm quite annoyed with myself, to be honest."

Rob grinned. "Don't be. It came to me at six thirty this morning."

She shook her head.

Celeste, meanwhile, was helping Will trawl through Ralph Keaton's mobile phone records. "He has a lot of friends," she grumbled, moving her ruler slowly down the page. "I haven't even got to the text messages yet."

Suddenly she gasped.

"What is it?" asked Will.

"Give me a minute." She frowned and searched her desk. "Where are Michael's records?"

"Here." Will handed her a stack of pages stapled together in a neat, diagonal line.

She turned the first page. "I knew it. I knew I recognised it."

"Recognised what?" Will was getting impatient.

"That burner phone, it's on this report too. Ralph Keaton phoned that number on Saturday afternoon."

"What?" Rob jerked his head up.

"What does that mean?" Jenny still had the phone in her hand.

"That Ralph Keaton knew the killer?" suggested Will.

Celeste gasped. "Do you think he hired someone to get rid of his partner?"

We've been together eighteen years.

"It was their anniversary too," Rob murmured.

Will shook his head. "That's cold."

"Hang on." Jenny put the phone down, forgetting she was still on hold. "If Keaton arranged this, why only speak to the killer on Saturday? Surely they'd have got in touch before that?"

"I didn't find any previous contact," said Celeste. "I went back two months."

"Go back further," said Rob. "It may have been months ago."

"Okay." She turned back to her computer.

"Also, remember that photograph in Michael's studio? Keaton could have sent the killer a picture of it, told him to stage the crime scene like that to make a point."

"What point?" asked Harry.

Rob sighed. "I don't know. That's something we'll have to ask him."

"Should we bring him in?" asked Will.

Ralph Keaton didn't have a flat in Soho. Ralph Keaton had an alibi for the night of the murder. "Yeah, let's bring him in. There are too many questions we need answered."

While he was waiting, Rob took a call from Ronald Chang, Edward Chang's cousin.

"You want to ask me about a customer?" the heavily accented voice asked.

"Yes, a man called Ralph Keaton. I believe he was at your restaurant on Sunday night with a party of three others." There had been four people listed in the reservation book.

"Ah, yes. I remember this man. He was here."

Rob nodded to himself. It was as expected. "Okay, thank you for getting back to me."

He was about to hang up when the man said, "But he left early."

"Excuse me?"

"He left at seven thirty. Said he wasn't feeling well."

"Really? Are you sure? We're talking about the same person — middle-aged, grey hair, five foot eleven?" He tried to think of any distinguishing features but couldn't. Keaton resembled every other investment banker out there. It was possible Ronald Chang had the wrong man.

"I'm sure. He left the party early. The other men stayed and finished their meal."

There was a pause as this sunk in.

"This is what you want to know, yes?"

"Yes. Yes, it is." Rob frowned at his computer. Had Keaton really left the restaurant at seven thirty? If so, he'd have had plenty of time to get to Soho, pick up Michael after he'd met the buyer and rape and strangle him.

But why? Why go through all that trouble when he lived with the guy? He could quite easily have killed him at home and made it look like an accident. And what about the phone calls from Soho, the meeting, the proposed sale of the painting? It didn't make sense.

Still, the man had lied to them, and that made him angry.

Harry approached Rob. "Guv, Ralph Keaton's been taken to Putney police station. They're prepping him now."

"Thanks." Putney had a fully kitted-out custody suite, unlike their office block, which was more administrative. Rob gestured to Jenny. "Let's go over and interview him. His alibi doesn't stack up."

Her eyes widened. "Really?"

He told her what he'd just discovered.

She got to her feet. "This changes things."

"You're damn right it does. Ralph Keaton has just jumped to the top of our suspect list."

CHAPTER 17

"Mr Keaton, you've been cautioned. Do you understand your rights?"

A sulky nod. "Why am I here? I've told you everything I know."

Not by a long shot, Rob thought. The heat was stifling in the interview room, but Rob had told them to leave it like that. He wanted Keaton as uncomfortable as possible.

"Did you know where Michael was going on Sunday night?" he asked the sweating, middle-aged man. Even his head was glistening.

"I told you, I didn't even know he was going out. I thought he was at home."

"Do you recognise this number?" Rob placed a piece of paper on the table with the burner number written on it.

Keaton glanced down. "No. Whose is it?"

Rob's eyes narrowed. "We think it belongs to the man Michael met."

"The killer?"

"Possibly."

Keaton's shoulders tensed.

"Michael received several calls from this number in the days leading up to his death. Are you sure you don't know who it is?"

"No, I've no idea." He was adamant. It was a good act. If Rob didn't know differently, he'd probably have believed him.

"Did Michael say anything about selling a painting?"

A frown. "No, but he often sold his work. He was a talented artist."

"Could this number have belonged to a client? Someone who wanted to purchase his artwork?"

The bushy eyebrows rose. "Maybe."

"He didn't mention anything to you about a sale or a commission?"

"No, nothing like that."

"Mr Keaton, how come you dialled this number on Saturday afternoon at 3 p.m.?"

Silence.

Rob let it draw out. Keaton was in a corner, trapped. There was no way out.

"Who did you speak to, Mr Keaton?"

The sulky look was back. "Nobody."

"Yet you dialled the number. Look, the call was made from your mobile at exactly three o'clock." He slid the phone records with the call highlighted across the table.

Keaton didn't look at it. He didn't need to.

"How do you explain that?"

They waited. The sweating got worse. Rob could almost see the cogs spinning in Keaton's brain as he attempted to come up with a feasible excuse.

Finally, he said, "It went to voicemail. I didn't leave a message."

Rob's pulse quickened. The truth, finally. Will had told him the call hadn't been longer than a few seconds. "Why did you call that specific number?"

Keaton threw his hands up. "I wanted to know who was calling Mikey, okay? I knew he was getting calls he hadn't told me about. There was some tension between us because I was going out on our anniversary. He wasn't talking to me, so I snooped. I got his phone and took down the number. Then I rang it on Saturday when Mikey was at the shops."

Rob studied him. Was he lying? He didn't think so. Glancing at Jenny, he raised his eyebrow. She replied with a slight nod. They were in agreement.

Rob moved on. "Previously, you told us you'd been to supper at the Singing Lotus on Sunday night and you got home at around ten o'clock."

"That's right." His eyes were hooded.

"Yet the restaurant manager told us you left early, at seven thirty, because you weren't feeling well."

"What?"

"Is that true?"

"No, of course it's not true. He's mistaken."

"He seemed pretty adamant."

"Well, he's got it wrong. I was there the whole time."

"We checked on the restaurant's CCTV camera," Rob lied. Jenny shot him a surprised look. He was taking a gamble. Keaton wouldn't know it was out of order. "You left early, as Mr Chang said. There is no doubt it was you."

His shoulders slumped.

"Stop lying to us, Mr Keaton."

"I wanted to see who Mikey was meeting," he croaked. "I was curious, that's all. There'd been strange calls, I'd heard him arrange the meeting on Sunday evening, and I wanted to know what he was up to."

"Does Mikey usually hide things from you?"

He dropped his head. "No, never. That's why I was curious."

"Curious?"

"All right — worried, frightened, panicky. I thought this might be the start of an affair, and if it was, I wanted to nip it in the bud. I loved Mikey, I didn't want to lose him."

"So you followed him?"

"Sort of. We can track each other on our phones, so I could see where he was. It was easy enough to catch a cab to Soho and go to the bar."

"Did you?"

"Yeah, I got there at around 8.15 and he was sitting at the bar by himself."

"Did you talk to him?" Rob knew he hadn't, else they would have seen it on the surveillance footage.

"No, I lost my nerve. I didn't want him to know I'd been snooping. As I said, things had been tense between us lately, and admitting I was spying on him would have made the situation worse. I hovered for a bit, but when nobody arrived, I left."

"You didn't stay to see who he was meeting?"

"No. I felt stupid enough already."

They'd clarify that on the surveillance footage from the bar. Rob fired off a text message, knowing Will would be watching the interview from the feed on the server. He got a thumbs up in response.

"You said you called Michael, when he still hadn't come home. Was that true?"

"Yes, I waited a while after I got home, but I was so worried about him. I called his mobile, around midnight, but it was off. It went straight to voicemail. I even called his mother, just in case she'd heard anything, but she hadn't." Rob sent Will a question mark.

Keaton's face crumpled. "I was frantic. I didn't know what to do."

It was a good story. The problem was the evidence was stacking up against Keaton. Unless he could provide an alibi, it didn't look good.

He nodded at Jenny. They'd give it one last push, to see if he broke.

She cleared her throat, glanced down at her notes and looked up, her gaze fixed on Keaton. "Mr Keaton, you admitted you knew about the phone calls your husband was receiving, and you followed him to the bar on the night he died. You suspected he might be having an affair, which gives you motive. You have no alibi for the time he was murdered, and the crime scene looks very much like a photograph Michael had in his studio at your house. You can see how this looks, can't you?"

"I didn't kill him." He looked aghast. "I loved Mikey."

"Are you sure you didn't confront him at the bar after he'd met with whoever was calling him? Perhaps you argued? You decided to get even, to show him up for the adulterer that he was?"

"Of course not." He stood up, his face a mottled pink. "How dare you accuse me of this?"

"Sit down, Mr Keaton." Her voice was hard as steel. "I'm not finished."

"Well, I am." He stormed towards the door, but it was locked. "Let me out of this room."

"I will arrest you if you refuse to answer our questions," Jenny said.

"What's to say you won't arrest me anyway?" he shot back, his hands on his hips. But he was spooked, Rob could tell.

"Nothing. We're trying to ascertain whether you had anything to do with your husband's murder. It will be better for you if you cooperate with us. If you refuse, it looks bad."

"*You're* making it look bad," he insisted. "I left the bar and went home. It was a foolish thing to do, and I don't know what got into me. I should have trusted Mikey. It was a moment of insecurity, and now he's dead!" His shoulders sagged and he let out a ragged sob. "If only I'd stayed, I might have been able to stop whoever did this to him."

He might very well have, but Rob didn't say that. The poor guy was in enough anguish.

His watch vibrated. Will had replied to his question mark with a thumbs up. The midnight call and the conversation with Michael's mother checked out. Either he was a phenomenal actor, or he was telling the truth. Rob's gut was telling him it was the latter.

Keaton slumped in the chair. "What else do you want to know?"

"Do you own or rent any property in Soho Square?" Jenny asked.

"No."

"We will check."

He shrugged. The fight had gone out of him. Rob felt sorry for the guy.

"Is there anyone who can vouch for you on Sunday evening, apart from Michael's mother?"

"No, I don't think so."

His phone vibrated again.

Keaton was at home when he made the calls.

That was midnight, though. He could easily have dumped the body and got home by then. It didn't clear him, unfortunately.

Another text message, this time from Mayhew.

Make the arrest.

Rob passed his phone across the table to Jenny, who gave a brief nod.

"Ralph Keaton, I'm arresting you on suspicion of the murder of your husband, Michael Bennett. You do not have to say anything, but it may harm your defence if you do not mention, when questioned, something which you later rely on in court."

CHAPTER 18

"Congratulations." Mayhew smiled at them as she walked past. The whole team, other than Celeste, who was on a call, was huddled around Rob's desk drinking bad office coffee and dissecting the interview. "I've had the Mayor on the line. He's overjoyed we've made an arrest."

No one said anything.

"What's wrong?" She glanced at them each in turn. "Why do you all look so glum? You did the right thing. You followed the evidence and made an arrest. Even the CPS agreed there was more than enough to charge him."

"It doesn't feel right." Rob wiped a bead of sweat off his forehead. He didn't like it when there were threads left hanging. "Who was the man Michael Bennett met in the bar? Was he really a buyer, or could he have been the murderer? Why did the buyer call to arrange the meeting on an untraceable burner phone? Why didn't he show his face? He seemed to know where the surveillance camera was."

"And where was Michael Bennett killed?" added Harry, who despite the heat looked remarkably cool. "We still haven't found the primary crime scene."

"Keaton doesn't own or rent an apartment in Soho," Jenny pointed out. "I've just checked."

"I'm sure it'll all come to light in court." Mayhew was undeterred.

Rob gave a low grunt. All she cared about was the crime stats. Another case closed, and the Soho Killer put away. That's what the papers would say. The Major Investigation Team's female superintendent would come off looking like a hero. Politics. It always got in the way of police work.

Keaton's anguish had seemed real, his confusion palpable. Rob was willing to bet that he didn't know what had happened to his husband after he'd left the bar any more than they did. Still, there was a chance he was playing them. The timing, the lack of alibi, the call to the burner number, and, of course, the magazine clipping in Michael's studio. It all pointed to the man they had arrested.

"I just hope we're not sending an innocent man to prison," he muttered once Mayhew had sauntered back to her office.

"I'll keep digging," Jenny said. "He may have used a fake name to lease the apartment."

"SOCO has picked up the rubbish bin from the square," Harry said hopefully. "They might find something there."

"We've also got a team searching Keaton's house," Will told him. "I'll let you know if they find anything."

Rob nodded. "Okay. Thanks, guys. Don't stay too late. Keaton's not going anywhere now. We can pick this up tomorrow."

Celeste came over. "Guv, sorry to bother you but that guy is still calling. Name's Felix Hewson. He says it's imperative that he speaks with you."

Rob frowned. "What's it about?"

"He claims his partner was murdered twenty years ago."

"Twenty years ago? What am I supposed to do about that?"

Celeste shrugged.

"Put him onto someone else." He glanced at his watch. "Get them to take his statement and I'll look at it later."

Keaton would be held in the cells until the following day, when he'd be transferred to court and officially charged.

After that, he'd be remanded in custody to await trial. His life was about to implode. He'd lose his freedom, his house, his job. What would those executive directors think of him now, embroiled in this mess? If he was innocent, then a huge miscarriage of justice had been done.

* * *

"We have to be sure," he told Jo later that night while they were making supper. "I can't destroy a man's life without being absolutely certain he's guilty."

She leaned over and kissed him. "That's why I love you," she said softly. "You care."

But did he care enough? He thought of Keaton sitting in a cell right now, not only dealing with the loss of his husband but the loss of his freedom. It was a heavy price to pay if the guy was innocent.

"We can't pick and choose the evidence to suit our own narrative." He was feeling introspective tonight, out of sorts. "We have to consider everything, and there are some things that don't add up."

"The justice system doesn't always work like that," Jo reminded him. "We have to follow the evidence, and in this case, everything you have is pointing to Keaton. It's up to you to disprove that, because he can't."

Rob met her gaze. "I intend to do just that."

"I know you do."

He turned his attention to her. "How did your day go? Did you manage without your boss?"

"Ray? Yes, it went well. Though I had the fan on all day. Bloody hell, it was warm. At least Thames House has air conditioning." Thames House, in Millbank, near Vauxhall, was where the MI5 offices were located.

He grimaced sympathetically. It had cooled down slightly but it was still incredibly humid for this time of night.

"I tried to ring him this evening to give him an update," she continued, "but he didn't answer. That was strange, especially since he asked me to."

"Maybe he takes his anniversaries seriously." Unlike Keaton, who went to a work event on his eighteenth anniversary, and then left early to spy on his partner.

She chuckled. "I suppose that's a good thing. I'll leave him in peace until tomorrow."

* * *

Rob was relaxing in front of the TV, Jo tucked in beside him, Trigger at his feet, when he got a call from one of the Forensics officers.

"DCI Miller? It's Officer Morrison from the SOCO team searching Mr Keaton's residence."

His pulse jumped. "Yes? Did you find anything?"

Jo raised her head off his shoulder.

"We did, sir. I will send through my report, but we found a dildo at the house with Michael Bennett's DNA on it."

Rob sat up straight. "Recent DNA?"

"In the last few days, sir."

"Thanks for letting me know." He leaned back, frowning.

"What is it?" asked Jo. Trigger lifted his head as if he wanted to know too.

"I'm not sure. Michael Bennett was anally raped before he was strangled. A dildo with his DNA on it has just been found at the house." He scratched his chin. "I'm not sure it means anything — I mean, they were in a relationship." But it was another nail in Ralph Keaton's coffin.

"It's circumstantial," Jo agreed. "They'll throw it out of court."

"I hope so." He ground his jaw. "The only problem is that when all the circumstantial evidence stacks up like this, it's hard for a jury to ignore it."

Jo nodded. She knew how it went.

"I feel like I'm fighting a losing battle." He put his arm back around her shoulders.

"You'll get there," she said, with more confidence than he felt. "I know you will."

* * *

The incessant vibration of Rob's watch woke them up in the early hours. He groaned, tempted to ignore it. Galbraith's team was on call, not his.

Jo pulled the pillow over her head. The watch kept buzzing, accompanied by his phone on the bedside table.

"For God's sake." He reached for the device. The time on the screen said 3.20 a.m. "Miller." His voice was croaky.

"Rob, it's Galbraith. We've got a situation that I thought you'd want to know about."

He sat up, rubbing sleep from his eyes. "What is it?"

"We've been called to a townhouse in Pimlico. A man's been murdered, found by his wife a short time ago."

"What's that got to do with me?"

"It's how he was murdered," Galbraith said. There was a heavy pause. "He's wearing some weird fetish outfit and he's tied to the bed with a ball gag in his mouth."

CHAPTER 19

From the outside, the house was elegant and composed. There was no hint — in the pristine white facade, the gently lit Georgian brickwork and the silent pillars at the entrance — of the chaos inside.

The emergency response vehicles had parked across the street, the blue lights bouncing off the two-million-pound Pimlico properties, drawing curious neighbours to the windows. Rob strode up to the front door where Galbraith was standing. "Thanks for the heads-up."

"Looks like it could be related to your last victim." He shook his head. "I have to say, mate, you certainly know how to pick 'em."

A white-faced sergeant walked out of the house, looking like he'd seen a ghost.

"How you doing, Jeff?" Rob shook the officer's hand. He'd worked with DS Clarke on previous cases, including Sam Laurence's murder. The young Yorkshireman had come on a lot in the last few years. He'd proved himself to be conscientious and thorough, qualities that he valued in a sergeant.

"Pretty freaked out, to be honest." He nodded toward the open door. "I've never seen anything like that before."

"Have you called SOCO?" Rob asked the big Scot.

"Aye, they aren't here yet."

"Okay, good. Show me the body."

Galbraith took him into the tiled hallway. White marble floors, recessed lighting, a vase of fake orchids nodding an awkward greeting.

"He's upstairs in the bedroom."

Rob followed the burly Scot, not touching the polished mahogany balustrade, up to the first floor. There was a living room, a study and a bedroom leading off the landing.

"Up one more," Galbraith muttered.

More stairs, lit by a crystal chandelier at the top, flickering merrily. *The stylish house, the expensive features, the plush carpeting — it's luring us into a false sense of security*, thought Rob. Steeling himself, he followed Galbraith into the master bedroom.

"Jesus."

Galbraith gave a slow nod and stood back so Rob could survey the carnage.

A grey-haired man lay spatchcocked on a king-sized four-poster bed, his wrists and ankles strapped to the posts, his middle-aged body stretched beyond what was normal. It looked uncomfortable. There were welts on his back where he'd been whipped.

Rob took a step closer, drawn in by morbid curiosity.

"Careful," warned Galbraith. They weren't wearing protective clothing.

Rob halted. "I need to see his face."

The victim was wearing a studded collar, like Michael Bennett. But where Michael's hands had been wrenched behind his back and chained to the collar, this man had been tied to the bed with studded leather wristbands.

"It's the same," Galbraith murmured. "I've seen your crime scene photos. He's wearing a mask with cutouts for the mouth and eyes. The mouth is wide open, ball gag inserted."

"What about his eyes?" Rob wanted to know. He thought back to Michael's terrified expression.

"Aye. Fuckin' weird. He looks petrified."

Rob nodded. It was the same. "Who found the body?"

"The wife. She was hysterical, we couldn't get any sense out of her. Jeff called her sister, who came to pick her up. You just missed her."

There wouldn't have been any point talking to her in that state.

"What made her suspect there was a problem?" he asked.

Galbraith shrugged. "She was at the country pile, out in Windsor. It's their anniversary today, and when he didn't make their dinner reservation, she got worried. His phone was off, and around midnight, when he hadn't come home, she drove up to this house to check if he was here."

Rob frowned. "Anniversary, you say?"

"Aye, is that relevant?"

"Michael Bennett was killed on his anniversary," he mumbled. "Could be nothing, although it's quite a coincidence."

Galbraith exhaled. "This case gets dafter by the second."

"Do we know who he is?" Rob studied the crumpled sheets, the crusty wounds on his back. It looked like the victim had put up a fight, for all the good it had done him.

"Some city big shot, judging by the look of this place. Apparently, he stayed here during the week. Wife was very well turned-out, if you know what I mean."

"Got a name?"

He nodded. "Raymond Humphries."

Humphries. Rob stared at him as the name filtered through his sleep-deprived brain.

Ray Humphries. Anniversary. City big shot.

"Holy shit," he muttered. "I know who this is."

"You do?"

"Yeah, it's Jo's boss. He works for MI5. Thames House."

It was Galbraith's turn to be shocked. He gazed at Rob, his bushy eyebrows arching into his forehead. "Well, I'll be . . ." He took another look at the body. "That puts a whole different spin on things."

"The Security Service is going to be here any minute," Rob said, rushing his words. "Then we'll be turfed out."

"Bloody hell, I've already given Dispatch the name of the victim."

They had minutes.

Jeff appeared at the top of the stairs. "SOCO is here, guv. Shall I let them in?"

"Hold that thought," Galbraith glanced at Rob. "You've got five minutes at most."

"What's going on?" Jeff glanced from his guvnor to Rob and back again.

"Take photographs," Rob hissed. "Quickly. Anything that might be relevant. We don't have long."

Jeff looked confused.

"Aye, just do it," Galbraith said. "I'll be downstairs to meet the cavalry. I'll hold 'em off as long as I can."

"Thanks." Rob took out his phone. "Jeff, you take the study, living room, kitchen. Photograph anything that looks out of place. We need to collect our own evidence before it's too late."

Jeff had no idea what was going on, but he trusted both DCIs and didn't question the order, just as Rob knew he would.

There was no time to put on protective gear. He'd have to take a rap on the knuckles for that one. Approaching the bed, he snapped as many shots as he could of the victim in situ — the splayed position of the body, the harness, the binding leather straps.

Zooming in, he took close-ups of the victim's bruised wrists and ankles, the whip marks on his back, and the leather neck collar. Heart pounding, Rob shifted position so he could capture the man's face. He was lying with his head facing the wall, his eyes open. Galbraith was right. Petrified was the most appropriate word. He looked like he'd turned to stone in a moment of terror.

Sirens were blaring, racing up the street. Anytime now.

He held the phone in front of the man's face and captured his expression, the ball gag stuffed into his screaming mouth, the dribble running down his chin. There was a gash on his temple, which Rob hadn't noticed before. It was the source of the blood underneath his head. His cheek was resting in it.

Rob stood up and took a deep breath. He could smell it. Bodily fluids, sweat, fear.

A screech as the sirens mounted the pavement outside, ignoring the other parked cars along the street. Rob glanced out of the window. Three vehicles — unmarked black SUVs with tinted windows and official number plates. The Security Service had arrived.

Two suits emerged from the first car and marched up the drive to the front door. Rob heard Galbraith's booming voice, even though he couldn't see him. "Can I help ya?"

There was a bark, a command.

Galbraith argued. This was his crime scene. His team had received the callout. They should contact his superintendent if they wanted to take over. Rob managed a thin smile and took a quick peek out of the upstairs bedroom just in time to see Galbraith throw his hands in the air and storm off. The Scot had put on a good show.

He darted into the adjoining bathroom and snapped a few photographs, just in case there was anything there that warranted closer scrutiny, although nothing seemed out of place.

Something purple caught his eye. He crouched down for a closer look. A dildo lay under the bed. Both he and Galbraith had missed it when they'd first gone in. He took a photograph of it, then a closer one.

Footsteps on the stairs, a cry of, "Everybody out."

He was out of time. Rob straightened up, backtracking to the door.

"Get out." The order came from right behind him.

He turned around. "Excuse me?"

"This is no longer your case."

Rob frowned at the impeccably dressed agent. "I don't understand. DCI Miller, Major Investigations. Who are you?"

"That's not important. Your superior will explain it to you. We're taking over this investigation. I'll show you out."

Rob descended the stairs ahead of him. He joined up with Jeff in the hallway, who gave him a slight nod, barely discernible.

Good. They'd got what they could.

The MI5 agents shepherded them to the door. "You might want to take my shoe prints," Rob said. "I was in the bedroom with the victim."

The officer didn't seem perturbed. "We'll be in touch if we need to. Thank you, Detective. Have a nice night."

They left.

"*Have a nice night*? Seriously?" Rob glanced at Galbraith, who shrugged.

"You were right. It's now a matter of national security. Out of our hands."

"Who is this guy?" asked Jeff, bewildered. "A politician or something?"

"Something like that," Rob replied. "Did you get the photographs?"

"Yeah, I'll email them to you." Jeff glanced at his guvnor. "See you back at the office?"

"Aye," the Scot said. They were still on call, even though this wasn't their problem anymore.

"See you tomorrow." Rob shook both their hands. "Thanks for the backup."

"No problem, mate." Galbraith and Jeff walked back to the HAT vehicle.

Humphries. Shit. What would Jo say?

It would come as a shock. But maybe she could shed some light on who'd done this. Was it work-related? And if so, did Michael Bennett have something to do with Humphries, or a project they were working on?

One thing he knew for sure was that Ralph Keaton was innocent. This proved it.

CHAPTER 20

Jo sat up in bed and gawked at him. "Ray Humphries? Are you sure?"

"Yes. I'm sorry."

She shook her head as if to clear it. "Do you have any photographs?" Despite the obvious shock, she was already thinking like a detective.

"I do. Are you sure you want to see them? It was fairly horrific." Murder was never pleasant, but the way Humphries had died . . . that was the stuff of nightmares.

In response, she took the phone from him.

There were dozens of photographs of the crime scene. Jo looked through them, sucking in her breath when she saw the blood all over the bedsheets. "Good God," she whispered.

Rob put a hand on her shoulder. White-faced, she handed the phone back. "What was the cause of death? I mean, I can see he's been raped, and possibly strangled, but . . ." She faded off. Jo knew as well as he did that the cause of death could be something entirely different to what met the eye.

"We're not sure. The pathologist wasn't there yet, and we were chucked out before they arrived. If I had to guess, I'd say it was asphyxiation like the other victim."

Jo gazed up at him. "You think this is related?"

"I can't see how it's not. Both were dressed in fetish gear, both raped and strangled, both gagged."

"There is one difference, though. Humphries wasn't gay."

Rob pursed his lips. "You sure about that?"

Jo threw back the covers and got out of bed. "Of course I'm sure. I worked with the man. He's happily married. I'd swear he was straight." She put her hand to her mouth. "It was his anniversary yesterday."

"Yeah, that's the other thing . . ." Rob hesitated. "It was the other victim's anniversary too."

Jo stared at him. "What? Are you saying that has something to do with it?"

"I don't know. It could be a coincidence."

"Or someone is targeting middle-aged men on their anniversaries?" She shook her head. "No, scrap that. It's a ridiculous notion."

It was a bit random.

"Who found him?" Jo pulled on her gown and faced him.

"His wife. According to the first responder, she had a meltdown. Her sister was called to take her away. I'll want to speak to her at some point, but it might be worth waiting a day or two."

"You know the Security Service is going to shut you out?" Jo began pacing up and down the room. "They'll close ranks. You won't get near her."

"Sooner rather than later, then." Jo was right. Those agents would make sure no one got near the grieving widow or her family.

"Millie — that's Ray's wife — is pretty highly strung. She'll be too traumatised to speak to you tonight. In fact, they've probably given her something to knock her out. We'll figure out a way to get to her, don't worry."

He liked the way she'd said *we*.

"Jo, was Ray working on anything that could have resulted in this type of crime?"

She stopped pacing, her hands on her hips. "We've been monitoring suspected terrorists, not LGBT protesters or equal rights activists."

"I had to ask. If it's not related to his work, then there must be a connection with Michael Bennett."

"Your first victim?"

"Yeah, although I can't think what it is. Bennett was a happily married gay man living in Hampstead." Rob sighed. "He wasn't into sadomasochism or fetish parties. He didn't even go out much."

"Ray was much the same," Jo said. "Outside of work, he lived a quiet life. The family home was in Windsor, I believe, and he and his wife had been married for at least fifteen or sixteen years. I know that because they have two daughters in secondary school. There's a photograph of them on his desk." She shook her head. "This is going to be hard on them."

Rob nodded. How would Humphries' wife reconcile the way in which he died? She'd question everything. Their marriage, his feelings for her, his sexuality. Another life ruined.

"I wonder if the killer is trying to destroy these men's families," he mused, the thought suddenly occurring to him. "Perhaps it's not enough to murder them."

"That would involve some deep psychological issues," said Jo. "It indicates these killings were personal attacks, not only on the men themselves, but also their loved ones."

"Like he's getting back at them for something. Some deep-seated revenge. Maybe the killer lost everything, and he's making his victims pay because of it. He wants to make them suffer like he did."

"Now you sound like Tony." Jo's phone rang. She glanced at the screen. "That's the office. They're probably going to tell us not to go in."

Trigger could be heard pawing at the door. At the same time, a loud cry emanated from Jack's room. "And that's my cue," he said.

The day had officially begun.

* * *

By the time Rob got to work, all hell had broken loose. "Why have you let Keaton go?" Mayhew demanded. "You know that Forensics found Michael Bennett's DNA in that refuse bin?"

"Did they really?" That wasn't a surprise, if the perpetrator had used the wheelie bin to deposit the body in the square.

"Yes, really." She obviously hadn't read Galbraith's report yet.

Rob felt smug as he took the conversation into her office. "There was an identical murder last night." He watched her eyes widen. "The victim was wearing bondage gear, tied to the bed, raped and strangled. Keaton's innocent. He couldn't have done it."

She threw her hands up. "The two cases might not be related."

"They have to be. The MO is identical."

Hostile blue eyes battled his cool steady ones.

She sniffed, looking away. "I haven't read the report yet."

"There isn't much to read," he told her. "The security services swooped in and took over. We were kicked out."

"What?" Mayhew massaged her forehead. "Who was this guy?"

"Someone in the government. Name's Raymond Humphries." He wasn't sure why he didn't mention the connection to Jo.

"Doesn't ring a bell."

"No. Well, there are other things that don't add up in the Michael Bennett murder. For instance, who did he meet in the bar the night he died? Why did he receive those burner calls? Where was he killed? DS Malhotra was right, we haven't found the primary crime scene. Besides, Keaton doesn't rent or own property in Soho, and finally, he was in police custody last night when the second murder took place."

Mayhew sank down in her chair. "Fuck."

Rob masked a grin. For once they agreed. Not only had they not closed the case, they'd compounded it. The Mayor wouldn't be pleased. In addition, it was only a matter of time before the Security Service called to warn them off the case, and not having access to the second investigation meant it would be a lot harder to solve Michael Bennett's murder.

"Fuck" was about right.

CHAPTER 21

Jenny gave him a hard look. Rob's team had gathered in the incident room so no one could overhear them. They too had resorted to hiking up the air conditioning, just to keep the office at a bearable temperature. "When you say the security services, who exactly are you referring to?"

"MI5."

"How do you know?" Harry whispered.

Galbraith shifted uncomfortably. Jeff, arms crossed in front of him, perched against the table. Neither of them needed to be there, but since they'd been at the original crime scene, Rob had asked them to be present, at least for a while.

He lowered his voice. "This doesn't go any further than this room."

They all nodded. He knew he could trust them. Hell, he had trusted them with much worse. "Raymond Humphries was Jo's boss at Thames House."

Jenny stared at him. "Seriously? I didn't even know she'd gone to work for MI5."

"Not many people do." When he'd mentioned she'd gone back to work, everyone had just assumed she'd returned to the National Crime Agency.

"Did his death have something to do with his work?" asked Will.

"It's unlikely." Rob brought up the photographs they'd hastily taken at the crime scene. "Celeste, get the blinds."

She closed them and they all stared at his laptop screen as he flicked through the photographs.

"Bloody hell," muttered Will, cringing. Harry had gone pale. Celeste, rigid with shock, had her hand over her mouth, while Jenny scrutinised the photographs, her mouth pulled together in a thin line. Only Rob, Galbraith and Jeff didn't flinch. Seeing it in the flesh had been far, far worse.

When he got to the last few shots of the dildo lying under the bed, Celeste asked, "Was he raped?" She swallowed.

"Yeah, same as Michael Bennett." Rob closed the lid. There was a heavy silence.

"Are we assuming it's the same killer?" Harry rasped.

"I think we have to." Rob looked around the group. "What does everyone else think?"

"The MO is similar," Jenny pointed out. "The getup, the restraints, the gag. He's not got his hands bound behind his back, though."

"What is the killer trying to say?" Will scratched his head. "I mean, this is all so flamboyant. So unnecessary. If you want to murder someone, why not just strangle them and be done with it? Why drug them, dress them up in fetish gear, use the gag and the straps, whip them? Is he punishing them for something?"

"All good questions," Rob said. "In fact, I've asked my mate Tony Sanderson to come in this afternoon and give us his take. When it comes to the criminal mind, there's nobody I trust more."

There were various nods around the room. Almost everybody there had worked with Tony on one of their previous cases and respected his professional opinion. Tony had spent his life studying serial offenders and often provided useful insights into the mind of the perpetrators.

"You don't think . . . ?" Jenny bit her lip. Tony Sanderson was famous for dealing with a certain type of criminal. "You're not suggesting that this is a . . ." She couldn't get the words out.

"A serial killer?" Rob said it for her.

She nodded.

"I fucking hope not," Galbraith erupted. "That's the last thing we need. Some idiot going around targeting gay men."

"Humphries wasn't gay," Rob pointed out. "And we don't know if it's a serial offender yet. There have been two deaths, possibly related. That doesn't make it a serial killing."

"One more to go," said Celeste. They all knew a killer had to have three or more victims to earn the title.

Harry pursed his lips. "Just because Humphries was married doesn't mean he wasn't gay."

"Jo seems pretty certain."

Harry gestured to the closed laptop. "So what's going on here?"

"I haven't the foggiest." Rob folded his arms across his chest and leaned back. "That's what we must find out."

"Might I remind you that we've been pulled off this case," Galbraith said.

"I take my orders from Mayhew," Rob replied. "Not some stranger in a suit. They didn't show us any ID, did they?"

Jeff shook his head. "Not that I can recall."

"There you go. They could be anyone. When the Super tells us to step down, I'll consider it."

"That'll be any minute now," Galbraith muttered. "Anyway, Jeff and I have been reassigned, so I'm afraid we won't be able to assist on this one."

Jeff looked disappointed.

"Are they recruiting more detectives to your team?" asked Jenny. First Evan had left, and then Mike. Galbraith was two men down, and since Rob had poached Celeste, he was struggling with the workload.

"Apparently so. I think they're transferring a DC from Barking, but I don't know when."

"I hope it's soon. Thanks for your help yesterday."

The Scot grunted. "You know I'll always do what I can, Rob, but I fear this one might be taken away from you."

"It doesn't mean we can't still investigate Michael Bennett's murder."

"Aye, good luck with that."

"Let us know if you need any help," Jeff said. He followed Galbraith out.

"Thanks, guys." Rob turned to the others. "Right, let's get down to business. We need to look into Humphries' background and search for anything that might be relevant. I believe he was in the military at one point. See if you can obtain his file from the MOD, if it isn't redacted already, and let's figure out who had it in for him."

"On it," called Will.

"Good. Celeste, see if you can find any CCTV in the Humphries' street. There wouldn't have been much traffic at that time of night. Maybe we can pick up the killer's car, or an image of him if he came on foot."

"Yes, guv."

"I'll look into his immediate family," Jenny said. "You said the wife's sister picked her up, so I'll get an address. I presume we'll need to question her."

"If there's time," Rob replied. "The clock's ticking on this one."

"What about me?" Harry's sea-green eyes burned with intensity. "What do you want me to do?"

"You stay on Michael Bennett," Rob said. "We still need to figure out who he met at the bar."

"I'll go through the footage again," Harry said. "Perhaps even go back and have another word with the bartenders that were on duty that night. I know it'll blow my cover, but I think we need to get official on this."

Rob nodded. "Good. That's good. I'm going to have another word with Ralph Keaton. There has to be a link between the two men." He also wanted to call Jo to find out what the latest was at MI5. The internal investigation must have got underway. He was surprised Mayhew hadn't received a call yet. On the other hand, given the scandalous nature of the crime, they might conclude it had nothing to do with Humphries' job at MI5. In which case, they'd shut it down. The Security Service wasn't about to waste resources investigating a sordid sex crime. Not when it didn't have any bearing on national security.

Unfortunately, that meant no follow-up. No evidence. No patterns linking this crime to the first one. They had to move fast, or risk losing everything.

CHAPTER 22

Not even an hour later, two stony-faced men were shown up to the third floor and escorted across the squad room to Superintendent Mayhew's office.

"They're here," mouthed Celeste.

Jenny rolled her eyes. Moments later, Rob got the summons. "Here we go," he muttered.

He walked down the aisle between the rows of desks. The two agents were sitting next to each other on the stylish sofa on the other side of the office, the side with the coffee table and the vase of fake flowers designed to impress just such visitors. Rob had sat there once or twice, but usually it was reserved for the Mayor or the Deputy Commissioner.

Both men were slim with greying hair, fresh shaves, and hard, darting eyes that never settled. Rob nodded a greeting and took a seat on the proffered chair opposite. Mayhew took the remaining chair, cupped like a shell, which she seemed to disappear into.

There was a moment of silence. Rob was waiting for them to speak, but it was clear they expected him to ask what was going on. Maybe they were expecting him to rise. He didn't.

Eventually, the agent on the left cleared his throat. "I'm Mr Smith and this is Mr Johnson," he began.

Sure. Whatever.

"We're from the Security Service."

Rob raised an eyebrow. *Get on with it, then.*

"We understand you were at a crime scene yesterday involving one of our employees."

"Raymond Humphries, yes." The man had a name. They were definitely going to sweep this under the carpet.

"Yes, Humphries." Smith looked like he'd sucked on a lemon. Johnson stared straight ahead at the generic watercolour on the wall. Had he even blinked? "We understand it was a particularly brutal crime scene."

"Not great as far as crime scenes go," Rob said.

Mayhew glared at him.

Smith cut to the chase. "DCI Miller, we're here to inform you that we're taking over the investigation into Humphries' death."

"Murder."

"What?"

"Murder, you mean. Humphries was bound, gagged, whipped, raped and strangled. There's no doubt it was murder."

Mayhew's eyes narrowed.

Smith cleared his throat. "That's what I mean, yes. You're not to continue with this investigation. In addition, we'd like you to hand all your files over to us."

Whoa! Rob's gaze flew to Mayhew, who wouldn't look at him.

"There is a chance this is related to one of our other cases," Rob explained. "The evidence found at this crime scene could help—"

"This is an internal investigation," Smith cut in. "Until we've ascertained whether his death had anything to do with the projects he was working on, everything we discover will be off limits to local law enforcement. I'm sure you understand."

"And if it's not?" Rob asked.

"Excuse me?"

"If it's not related to what he was working on? Then will you hand over the reports to us?"

"That isn't for me to decide," he said, after a pause.

"I'll speak to the Deputy Commissioner," Mayhew interjected in a rare show of solidarity. "Perhaps once you've given the investigation the all-clear, you'll allow us to use what you've discovered in our own investigation?"

Smith gave a small tilt of his head. "By all means . . . but I can't promise."

"If that's all?" Mayhew stood up.

Rob pursed his lips. Turned out Mayhew didn't like being dictated to any more than he did.

"I'll do what I can, Rob," she said, once Smith and Johnson had left. "But for now, shut down the Humphries part of the investigation. Focus on finding Bennett's killer."

"It could be the same person, ma'am."

She shrugged. "Then so be it, but I don't want you poking your nose into the MI5 inquiry. Is that clear?"

"Yes, ma'am."

She shot him a hard look, turned and strode back to her office.

Rob was so irritated that he bypassed his desk and went into the kitchen to make a coffee. It wasn't Nespresso, it wasn't even from a machine. It was instant, but it would have to do. He was *that* annoyed. He'd only just put the kettle on when the rest of the team followed him in.

"What happened?" Jenny wanted to know.

"Are we off the case?" Celeste asked.

He nodded. "Yup. It didn't take them long to shut us down. Also, we're to hand over all our files on the investigation."

Will looked aghast.

"Good thing we haven't started working the case yet," said Harry, with a mischievous grin.

Rob nodded. "Exactly."

"So we're going to keep going?" Celeste asked.

Rob put a heaped spoon of Nescafé into a mug. "No, we'd better play ball for now. Mayhew's going to talk to the

Deputy Commissioner and see what he can do. MI5 want to rule out a work-related killing, which is understandable."

"Can we at least finish what we're working on?" Will asked. He hated leaving anything undone.

"Sure, I think that's fair."

The others went back to their desks, while Jenny got a cup and put a teabag in it. "Pity. I've just found Millie Humphries' sister's address."

"You have?"

"Shall I send it to you?"

He hesitated, but only for a fraction of a second. "Yeah. Go on, then."

Smiling, she poured hot water into both their mugs. "You know what I find strange? There's nothing in today's paper about the Humphries murder. After Bennett, the press went wild, but they must not know about this one."

"It's a press blackout. I'll bet the Home Office have got an injunction to protect whatever Humphries was working on."

"Jo would know, wouldn't she?" Jenny pressed the teabag against the edge of the cup, watching the water darken. "What he was working on, I mean."

"It was something to do with surveilling potential terror suspects." Rob knew Jenny would keep the information to herself. "I can't see his death having anything to do with that."

She shook her head. "Neither can I. Not unless terrorists have taken to BDSM."

He grunted. "We'll have to wait until MI5 come to the same conclusion, then sweep in and take up where we left off."

She narrowed her eyes. "You think they'll hand over their intel?"

Rob snorted. "We'll be lucky if we get a post-mortem report and toxicology screening."

"We could ask Liz," Jenny suggested, stirring in a splash of milk.

"They might use their own pathologist."

"Liz is the best, isn't she?"

He nodded. That she was. Whenever there was an unusual death, Liz was called to the scene, either by the senior investigating officer or the CPS.

"Then they'll ask her."

Rob felt a glimmer of hope. Maybe they would.

* * *

Sandra Baker, Millie's sister, lived in a Victorian terrace house on a narrow street off busy Fulham Palace Road. As Rob pulled up, he saw two armed guards stationed in front of the house. Bugger. His window of opportunity had closed.

They weren't even trying to look inconspicuous — six foot five and nearly as wide, ill-fitting suits, rifles at the ready. Even the pedestrians and dog walkers were crossing over to the other side of the road. And this was keeping it low-key?

Sighing, he drove past, then navigated his way back to Putney Bridge. It would have been useful to have talked to Millie Humphries, though there was no guarantee she'd have opened up to them. Particularly about her husband's sexuality. Not while things were so raw.

It could wait.

As the sun set over the Thames, he drove back home, eager to talk to Jo about what she'd discovered at the office. Hopefully, she'd had more luck than he'd had.

CHAPTER 23

Rob got home to find Jo sitting at the kitchen table staring at a black leather-bound book, an untouched glass of water in front of her.

He gave her a kiss. "What's that?"

"It's Ray's Filofax."

"Filofax?" He glanced at the book. Did people still use those? "How did you get it?"

"I took it from his office."

"Today?" He scratched his head. "I thought you weren't going in?"

"I wasn't going to, but considering what's happened, I thought I'd better see what was going on. You don't hear anything unless you're in the office."

He gave an amused nod. That was Jo all over. Curious, inquisitive, wanting to be part of the action. He sat down opposite her. "So, what was going on?"

She glanced up, pink-cheeked due to the heat. "A lot. And nothing. It was weird, Rob. A team of movers came in and cleared out Ray's office. It's like he was never there."

"But not before you took his Filofax."

"No, I suspected they might do that, so I rifled through his desk and found it. He always had it with him, so it must be important."

"I'm surprised he didn't take it home with him."

"It was his anniversary," Jo said. "Maybe he wanted to leave his work at the office."

"Or he was worried something might happen to him."

She frowned. "Do you think so?"

"It's a possibility. Is there anything in there about who he was meeting the day before he died?"

"I haven't looked yet."

"How come?" It wasn't like Jo to wait on something like this.

"Because if I show it to you, I'm breaking the Official Secrets Act, not to mention wilfully obstructing an official investigation. That's a sackable offense."

He hadn't thought of that. "But there might be something in there that could lead us to his killer."

"I know that." Still, she didn't move.

Rob sat down opposite her. She needed to reconcile this in her head.

"We were questioned today," she said.

"Oh yeah? By whom?"

"These two agents. I'd never seen them before. They talked to us, one at a time, about Ray. When did we last see him? Was he acting strangely? Had we noticed anything unusual about his behaviour? That sort of thing." She paused to take a breath. "Then a man called Charles Hayworth arrived and took over — the new Ray Humphries — and it was business as usual. 'Our surveillance op mustn't be interrupted. We have operatives in play.'" She glanced up. "Two brothers who recently arrived from Northeast Africa. We think they've been training at a Jihadist camp out there."

Rob shivered compulsively. The criminals he dealt with were usually driven by greed, hatred or revenge. At least he didn't have religious fanaticism to contend with. "Was Humphries mentioned at all?"

"Only to say he wouldn't be coming back. No one questioned it. I asked around to see if anyone knew what had happened to him, but nobody did. Rumours are rife, of course.

He's been sacked. He had a breakdown. Not once did I hear a whisper that he might be dead."

"The top brass are keeping it under wraps," Rob murmured.

"It's a dirty little secret." Jo leaned back in her chair, stretching her long legs out in front of her. "They'll do anything to stop this coming out. Can you imagine how embarrassing it would be for the Security Service and the Home Office? I can see the headlines now: *MI5 SECTION CHIEF DIES IN SADOMASOCHISTIC ROMP*. They'd never live it down."

So much for getting that report, Rob thought.

The Filofax was burning a hole in the kitchen table. They were both staring at it. "You could hand it over to the internal investigation team," he said.

Her eyebrow flickered. "Rob, you and I both know that once the internal investigation team have realised his death has nothing to do with national security, they're going to shut it down. You'll never get any of it. Whatever's in there will be lost for ever."

She wasn't wrong. He knew that. Was expecting it.

"That's why I took it. Ray was old school. He didn't like using a calendar app. Didn't want his schedule online."

"Are all spies so paranoid?" he asked.

"Yup." No hesitation. "And he was worse than most."

Rob looked at her. "Jo, we need to look inside."

She gnawed on her lower lip. "Okay, fine. Fuck it. We may as well use it."

Tentatively, Rob reached for the Filofax. It was slightly bigger than his outstretched hand, about the size of a hardback novel. The cover was weathered leather, the pages dogeared. It looked well used.

Keeping it flat on the table, he opened it. Both their eyes fell on the first page. It was blank. No name or address, nothing to link it back to him.

Next page. A yearlong calendar. All the months squeezed into one page, the days in neat little blocks, rigid and unbending. A couple of weeks in August were circled — a holiday, perhaps — but there were no notes.

Rob flipped to the current week in the diary. There was a page per day. Humphries had scribbled across the page in a non-linear fashion. Meetings, lunches, conferences. Dates and times, hurried scrawls. He used initials, instead of names. Rob studied the page before his death.

10.00: Meet with DG
12.30: Lunch with M

"DG?" he asked Jo.

"Director General. Ray reported directly to him. I don't know who M is."

"Sounds like something from a James Bond film."

"We don't have an M at Thames House," she said with a small grin.

There were similar entries on every page. Rob exhaled. "It's going to take ages to decipher all these names."

"I'll know some of them," Jo said. "At the very least I can make an educated guess."

"Great. If you're sure?"

"I want to find out who did this as much as you do. Ray was my boss, and he was a good guy. He didn't deserve to die like this. A shameful secret, his reputation in tatters, his wife reeling because she thinks he's been keeping secrets from her all these years." Her chin jutted out defiantly.

Rob squeezed her hand. "You're the best, you know that."

Her voice was firm. "He deserves justice, Rob."

They spent the rest of the evening going through the Filofax. Jo filled in what names she could, but there were still plenty of gaps. There were several business cards in a plastic folder clipped in at the back. Rob pulled them out one at a time and studied them. Most were people in the organisation. None rang any alarm bells.

"What's this?" There was a white corner sticking out of the back inside cover. He slid it out. It was just another business card. Rob read the name and inhaled sharply.

Jo looked up. "What is it?"

"I think I've found a link." His pulse racing, he laid the card on the table. The name on the front was Michael Bennett.

CHAPTER 24

"They knew each other." Rob gazed triumphantly around the room. Everyone was present except for Harry, who was doing a follow-up at the bar in Soho. "Humphries had Michael Bennett's business card in his Filofax."

"Shit, really?" Jenny stared at him.

"Yes." It was the first real lead they'd had.

"How'd you get hold of his Filofax?" Jenny asked.

"I'd rather not say."

Will shook his head. "I haven't heard that word in decades. I didn't know they still existed."

Rob grinned. "Humphries didn't like having his calendar or contacts online."

"Smart man." Will, for all his technical wizardry, or perhaps because of it, knew the pitfalls of storing your information in 'the cloud'.

"Hang on." Jenny raked her hand through her short bob. "Do we think Humphries and Michael Bennett were acquaintances, friends or something more?"

"We can't be sure," Rob said. "All we know is there's a link. I've looked through the Filofax and there's no scheduled meeting with Bennett or 'MB', as it would appear. He used initials as a form of code," he said in response to Will's raised eyebrow.

"They could have spoken on the phone," Celeste pointed out.

"That is a possibility," Rob agreed. "We won't be able to access Humphries' phone records, but we have Bennett's on file. Let's cross-reference Humphries' mobile number, his home landline, and his work phone."

Celeste gave an eager nod. "I'll get right on it."

Rob thought out loud. "If they had only communicated by phone, how did Humphries get his business card? How did they meet?"

"Humphries could have bought one of Bennett's paintings," Jenny said. "He was an artist, after all."

"His husband might know," Will pointed out.

"Yeah, I'll give him a ring. Let's look at Bennett's history and see if we can find the connection. Humphries is off limits to us, but we can come at this from Bennett's angle."

Will nodded. "I'm on it."

Rob gave Ralph Keaton a call. Understandably, he wasn't very receptive. "I just want to know if Michael ever mentioned a Ray Humphries at all."

"I don't recall hearing that name." There was a pause. "Who is he?"

"It's a lead we're following, that's all. Probably nothing."

"No, sorry. It doesn't ring a bell."

"Did Michael ever have exhibitions?" Rob asked.

"Occasionally, but nothing big. We'd do a showing at the local gallery and invite a few friends, that sort of thing."

"I see. When was the last one?"

"Not for a while. Last April, I think. I can look it up if you like?"

"No, that's okay." It was too long ago to be relevant. "That's all. Thank you, Mr Keaton. I'm sorry to have bothered you."

Keaton hung up without saying goodbye. To be fair, they had arrested and interrogated the man for murder. He had every right to tell them where to shove it.

"He's never heard of Humphries." Rob twirled his pencil around in his fingers. "Yet they must have met."

"Michael Bennett was in recruitment." Will clicked through a website. "He worked for a headhunting firm in London but quit almost eight years ago now. Other than his artwork, he hasn't had a proper job since."

"He was the househusband," Jenny said. "My friend and her hubby have an arrangement like that. She had the better job, so when they had kids, he elected to stay home while she focused on her career."

"We still need to figure out how he knew Humphries," muttered Rob.

"They weren't at school together." Will flicked between several official websites. "Or uni. Bennett studied art at Bristol while Humphries was at Cambridge."

"Naturally," murmured Rob.

"Humphries began working for the Home Office, recruited straight out of university, while Bennett went to work for an employment agency. He had several other jobs in the same field until he got the position at the headhunting firm. Nothing remarkable. Nothing remotely similar to Humphries."

"Could Bennett have recruited Humphries?" asked Jenny.

Rob stared at her. "That could be."

Will was already thumping away on his keyboard. "It's going to take some digging," he said. "There's nothing obvious online."

"Okay, keep going," said Rob. "I'm going to check in with Harry."

* * *

Harry was wearing chinos and a buttoned-up shirt, his warrant badge in his trouser pocket. It felt weird going back to the bar now that he was no longer in disguise. He scoffed.

Come to think of it, it had been the furthest thing from a disguise. For the first time in a long while he'd been his true self. Callum had seen it. He hadn't been able to hide it, not with him. That wide smile flashed into his mind, and he thought about the business card burning a hole in his wallet. *Halston Gallery, Chelsea.* He'd read the card several times. Looked it up, even. Knew where it was on Google Maps.

The big wooden door squeaked as Harry pushed it open, and immediately he was hit by the smell of stale beer, dirty water and varnish. They were mopping the floors and polishing the bar ready for another raucous night.

It was Friday. There was a live act: DJ Foxy Ranger. *Pop, mashups and remixes*, said the signpost that had yet to be placed outside. Looked like fun.

He wouldn't be attending, though. Not tonight. Not ever.

Greg, the bartender, looked up as he approached, gave him the once over and grinned. "Hey, you're back."

"Yeah, I need a few words with you and your mate." He showed them his ID card.

The smile teetered. "You're a cop?"

A nod. "Can you call the other bartender? What's his name? Ricardo. I need to ask you both some questions about that night. And anyone else who was working last Sunday."

The gaze hardened. "Yeah, wait here."

Harry shifted position as he waited for the men to return. Ricardo had been filled in — Harry could feel the distrust radiating off him. Accompanying them was a slim kid about seventeen years old with pimples and the longest lashes Harry had ever seen.

"Eric was here too," said Greg.

"Great. Sorry for the subterfuge," he began, then swallowed his words. Bugger that. He was doing his job. No need to apologise for it. "We need to ID this man. Any of you know who he is?"

Harry showed them a photograph of the stranger's head and shoulders, in the trench coat with the hat on, his hand outstretched over the bar.

"I told your colleague I don't remember him," Ricardo said with a shrug. "It was a busy night. I barely looked up."

"I didn't see him." Greg took a crumpled box of cigarettes out of his pocket. "I remember that guy." He nodded to Bennett sitting on the barstool beside the stranger. "But his friend wasn't there when I spoke to him. Mind if we step out the back for a minute? I need a smoke."

They all went outside to an awning-covered alleyway at the rear of the bar and Greg lit up, inhaling deeply. Eric got his own packet of cigarettes out and did the same.

"What about you?" Harry asked the youngster, who hadn't said anything.

"I can't be sure," he said, not making eye contact. "But I think I saw them leave together."

Harry felt his heart skip a beat. He had to resist the urge to grab the kid's shirt and shake it out of him. *Tell me everything*, he wanted to yell. *Now!* Instead, he calmly said, "So they left on foot?"

"Nah, they got in a car."

Harry blinked several times. "They got into a parked car?" Parking in Soho was almost impossible unless you were a resident.

Greg drew on his cigarette, watching Harry with narrowed eyes. Eric continued speaking. "Yeah, I was on a smoke break when they came around the corner. That guy—" he pointed at Bennett — "was pretty drunk. His mate was helping him along."

That must have been the Rohypnol. "Did you get a look at the one helping him?" Harry found he was holding his breath.

"Nah, not really. He had blond hair, but that's about it. I wasn't really paying attention."

"Blond hair? Are you sure about that?"

"Yeah, pretty sure."

"Was he still wearing the hat?"

"Nah, he was holding it." A trick to confuse anyone looking at CCTV footage outside the club, who would still be looking for a man in a hat.

"Did they look friendly?" Harry asked. "Were they, you know, flirting?" He didn't know how to put it.

"It wasn't a hook-up, if that's what you mean," the kid supplied. "That guy was too drunk. All he wanted was to go home."

"Did you hear him say that?"

"Yeah, he kept saying he wasn't feeling well."

The Rohypnol would have been kicking in at that stage. Harry felt a pang for the poor artist who'd been tricked, drugged, and whose evening was about to get a whole lot worse.

"Tell me about the car," Harry said. "Did you notice the make or model?"

"No, dude. I wasn't paying that much attention. It could have been blue, but don't quote me on that. I was sheltering in the alleyway. It started to rain so I got under cover."

That's right. It had rained that night. Harry remembered the drizzle at the crime scene. "But it was parked around the corner from the bar?"

"Yeah, that's what I said."

Harry exhaled. "Got a street name?"

"Nah, mate. But it's the road next to the Duke."

Winnett Street. He'd go back there now and check for cameras. There might be one they could use.

"Thank you, Eric. You've been really helpful."

The kid looked pleased. "Can I go now?"

"Yeah, if you wouldn't mind writing your details down and leaving them at the bar, just in case we need to verify anything."

"Guess I can do that." Hands in pockets, he skulked back inside. Ricardo shot Harry a hostile look and followed Eric in.

"Got what you need?" asked Greg.

"I think so." Harry couldn't wait to get back to the office and tell the others what he'd discovered. A blue car. A blond man. It was something to go on.

"We going to see you later?" Greg blew a pillar of smoke up into the air.

He hadn't been fooled either. "No, can't. I'm working."

The bartender gave a slow nod, his gaze on Harry's face. Twirls of smoke curled up from his fingers. "Pity. Looked like you were enjoying yourself the other night."

I was.

Harry shrugged.

Greg took one last drag and threw the cigarette onto the pavement. "Maybe one day, eh?"

Harry said nothing as Greg turned and walked back into the bar.

CHAPTER 25

"Let me get this straight." Rob faced Harry, who'd just rushed in and told him what he'd discovered. "Michael Bennett's drink is spiked at the bar. He staggers outside, aided by the killer, who we now think is a blond man. They walk around the corner and get into a car?"

"That's what I've got," Harry said. "The kid didn't know the make of the car, unfortunately. There is one camera in that street, but it's at the other end. We might be able to pick up the vehicle if they drove that way. There's also a Thai restaurant across the road with a surveillance camera mounted outside. I'm going to call them as soon as they open."

"Great work." Rob felt a burst of elation. "We're finally getting somewhere." At least they knew something about who they were looking for now.

"If we can get the vehicle registration, it'll give us something to work with," Will said.

"Notify the CCTV team," Rob said, glancing at the clock on the squad room wall. "I've got to go. I'm meeting Tony in Richmond."

* * *

The Cricketers, situated on the picturesque village green, was one of the oldest pubs in Richmond upon Thames. In summer, it was the ideal place to have a pint outside in the sun and watch the local cricketers, who weren't too shabby as far as interclub leagues went. The night was balmy — twenty-seven degrees according to his snazzy new watch — and most of the punters had opted to sit outside, which meant it was relatively empty inside. Rob walked in to find his old mate, Tony, sitting at a table by the window.

"Hi, nice haircut." Rob grinned as he took his seat. Tony Sanderson was sporting a brand-new brush cut.

He grimaced. "Thanks, it was Kim's idea. She said it would make me look younger."

"It does. Thanks for the drink." There were already two cold pints fizzing on the table.

"You're welcome." Tony smiled. "I was intrigued by your message, especially since you said it couldn't wait for Saturday."

Rob took his laptop out of his rucksack. "I didn't want to talk shop at the dinner table." Even though they always did. "Besides, this one is right up your alley."

Tony leaned forward. "Do tell."

Rob opened his laptop. "Okay. Two murders, similar MOs. You want me to give you some context?"

"Nope, show me the photographs first." Rob knew Tony wouldn't want anything to skew his perspective.

Rob flicked through the first crime scene in Soho Square. Michael Bennett was laid in the foetal position on the glistening lawn, his hands tied behind his back. Studded collar, chain down the back to the wrist straps. Awkward, ungainly. Then the ball gag. The deformed mouth. The terrified eyes.

Tony took everything in, slowly, methodically. He didn't speak, just looked.

"This is the second victim."

Rob clicked on a different folder of images. The master bedroom. Blood staining the sheets, the leather wrist and ankle straps fastening the victim to the bedposts. Same stretched mouth, same terrified eyes.

Rob got to the last photograph and closed the laptop. A couple who'd just walked in shot him a strange look.

"Well?" Rob leaned back in his chair. "What do you think?"

"Two killings?" asked Tony.

"Yep, we think it's the same perpetrator."

"Oh, it's the same person all right." Tony folded his arms. "Unless you've got a copycat who's seen the original crime scene photographs."

Rob shuddered at the thought. "Actually, that is a possibility. Bennett's body was lying in Soho Square for the better part of an hour. There was a crowd of onlookers, and it was in the papers the next morning."

"I saw. Didn't know it was yours." Tony didn't miss a trick when it came to unusual murders. "Still, the nature of the crimes . . . I'd say you're looking at the same offender. A showman. An artist."

"An artist?" Rob stared at him. "The first victim was an artist. He had a magazine clipping in his studio identical to the way he was found."

"Really?" Tony raised his eyebrows. "Can I see it?"

"Yeah, give me a minute." He scrolled through the photos on his phone. "It means the killer must have been in Michael Bennett's house."

"Not necessarily." Tony studied the photo of the clipping. "Your victim could have painted this scene and sold it to the killer. That's one scenario. Another is that the killer commissioned the painting and sent that clipping to the victim."

Both valid points. Why hadn't they thought of that? Surely Ralph Keaton would have mentioned the painting if it existed? Then again, he was at work during the day. Michael Bennett may have painted it, sold it and neglected to mention it to his husband.

"Let's assume it is the same killer." Rob reached for his pint. "Why did he target those two men? Why dress them up in fetish gear and make their deaths look like erotic asphyxiation?"

"He's making a point," Tony said. "He wants them to experience what it feels like to be dominated."

Rob took a thoughtful sip. "Do you think the killer experienced this at some point?"

"Maybe. It's possible he has an abusive background or was mistreated by someone in his past. There are links between childhood abuse — psychological, physical and sexual — and adult sadomasochistic sexual tendencies."

"But why target Bennett and Humphries?" he asked again. "They don't strike me as the type to be involved in BDSM."

"You can't know that for sure," Tony said, with a faint smile. "People are surprising. However, it might not be them, per se. It might be what they represent."

"You mean gay men?"

Tony shrugged.

"We don't know that Humphries was gay. People who worked with him swear he wasn't."

"Some men will do anything rather than let their secret come out," Tony said. "I once met a serial offender who eventually admitted to being gay, but before that, he'd been one of the staunchest homophobes you'll ever meet. Not all is as it seems."

That was definitely the case here. "Something I forgot to mention," Rob said. "Both these men were murdered on their wedding anniversaries. Do you think that's a coincidence, or . . . ?"

Tony was already shaking his head. "No, I don't believe it's a coincidence."

"So it's significant?" Rob scratched his stubbly chin.

"Marriage records are pretty easy to obtain these days," Tony said. "You can do it online."

Rob made a mental note to get Will to look into that.

"It's all about patterns," Tony said. "Serial offenders use patterns, even if they don't realise it at the time."

"You mean like how he finds his victims?"

"Yes, and how he stalks them, how he decides when to strike, how he kills them."

"The same MO," muttered Rob.

"It could also be that an anniversary is a significant day for the perpetrator," Tony continued, warming to his topic. "The day he made his first kill. The day he lost his virginity. The day he was raped, abused, whatever."

Rob frowned. "Psychological significance?"

"Yeah, because he experienced a traumatic event on a certain day, he's going to make sure others do too."

"That's dark." Rob shivered.

"The mind of a killer is a very dark place."

They drank their beers, letting their thoughts settle.

"Of course, it could be a coincidence," Tony said. "This isn't an exact science."

Rob frowned. "I don't—"

"I know," cut in Tony. "Neither do I."

Rob thought about what his friend had said. "If we're looking for a motive, it could be a hate crime. The killer could have something against gay people."

"Adulterous gay people." Tony clicked his fingers. "That would explain the anniversaries."

"We don't know that either of the victims was cheating on their spouse," Rob pointed out.

"True, but you can't rule it out."

"Hmm . . ." Rob wasn't so sure. Bennett had been receiving phone calls that had worried his partner, but that was about a painting, according to the bar staff. He didn't seem to be having an affair. Humphries had been happily married for a decade and a half.

"Except you've only got two bodies," Tony reminded him. "Theoretically speaking, we're not looking at a serial killer yet."

"Yet?"

Another shrug. "Unless the perpetrator had a personal vendetta against these two men, I'd say the likelihood of him striking again is high."

Shit. "How high?"

"Very."

CHAPTER 26

Rob was careful not to wake Jo when he got home. He'd messaged earlier and told her he was going to be late. Tiptoeing into their bedroom, he found her asleep next to Jack, who was spread out like a little starfish. The fan at the front of the room was positioned above their heads, cooling down the ambient temperature. A surge of happiness hit him in the gut. His family.

Trigger was delighted he was home and stood eagerly by his side as he made a sandwich and a cup of tea. Wired after his talk with Tony, Rob knew he wouldn't be able to sleep — there were just too many ideas flying through his head. He picked up Humphries' Filofax, along with Jo's notepad, where she'd written down as many names as she could decipher, and took it into the lounge.

He browsed through it page by page as he ate his sandwich. Jo had given brief explanations of who the people were, which didn't really help much. They had very generalised titles that could mean anything. Operations manager. Department head. Technical analyst.

He focused on the evenings during the week. Dinner dates, late-afternoon meetings, the last entries in the diary for each day. It appeared Humphries worked until six or seven most nights before going to his Pimlico townhouse, where Jo had confirmed he stayed during the week. There didn't appear to be any suspicious entries. Dinner with a department head. Squash with one of the analysts. Drinks with LR and team. LR, according to Jo's notes, worked at the Home Office.

Every Monday morning at nine o'clock, he met the management team in the boardroom, presumably to discuss the ops they were running that week. Every Friday at four o'clock they had another one. A debrief, or a progress report. All things you would expect from someone in Humphries' position.

There was no mention of MB — Michael Bennett. No explanation as to why the artist's business card had been stuffed into the back binding of the Filofax. Rob also couldn't find any references to clandestine or late-night meetings, but if Humphries had been having an affair, he wouldn't have put it in his diary. Not being as paranoid as he was. That kind of secret liaison he'd have kept in his head.

Rob finished his sandwich and started on his tea, thinking. Perhaps he was coming at this from the wrong angle. Maybe he should be looking for gaps in the schedule, things that weren't there, rather than things that were.

Going through the diary again, he focused on the empty evenings — looking for patterns, as Tony would say. Humphries was a busy man but he had most Tuesday evenings free. There was the occasional dinner, which he probably couldn't avoid, but for the most part, Tuesday evenings were blank.

Was this the night he met his lover? Did he come to the Pimlico townhouse, or did they meet somewhere else? A hotel, perhaps?

His vision blurred and he rubbed his eyes. It was late and this wasn't getting him anywhere. Maybe he was looking for something that simply wasn't there. Humphries deserved one night a week to himself. There was nothing suspicious in that.

But then why had he been targeted by a killer who'd made a point of dressing him up in bondage gear and leaving him to be found by his wife?

Ugh. Rob raked a hand through his hair. There must be something, he just hadn't found it yet.

He leaned back on the couch and shut his eyes. Just for a second. The house was silent, except for Trigger snoring softly in his bed. He'd rest his eyes for a minute, then start at the beginning and go through the Filofax again, scrutinising every single page.

A low growl jolted him awake.

Rob sat up, groggy. What time was it?

Glancing at his phone, he saw it was nearly two in the morning. He'd fallen asleep on the couch.

More growling, low and continuous like a finely tuned engine.

Trigger. Where was he? Rob jumped off the sofa.

"Trigger?"

The dog was outside in the hallway.

Rob poked his head cautiously around the door. If there was an intruder, he didn't want to alert them to his presence. "Trigger, what's wrong?" he whispered.

Trigger had his nose to the kitchen door, growling softly. The hair on his back bristled, his lithe body tense and thrusting forward.

Funny, he didn't remember shutting it when he went into the lounge. Could someone be in there?

A loud creak confirmed it.

Shit. Had Cranshaw sent someone for him? Were Jo and the baby all right?

More rustling. Whoever it was, they were still in there.

Heart pounding, Rob looked around for a weapon. Anything heavy that he could use to protect himself. There was nothing. For the first time in his life, he wished he had a firearm.

He darted back into the lounge and picked up the table lamp, wrenching it out of the socket. The base was heavy enough. It would do at a push.

Back at the kitchen door, Trigger was still growling but, strangely, he wasn't going ballistic, as Rob would have expected if there was an intruder who meant them harm. He took a few deep breaths, trying not to overreact. It might not be an organised hit. Perhaps a mouse had got in or something.

You're a dead man.

Cranshaw's words were still fresh in his mind. He could picture the criminal's hostile eyes and that sardonic grin.

I'm not the only one.

Carefully, Rob opened the door. Trigger shoved his nose through first. The growling became more menacing.

"Who's there?" he called.

As soon as the door was wide enough, Trigger bolted through. Rob followed, brandishing the lamp like a sword.

The coolness hit him first, and that distinctive night-air smell. The sliding doors were open. Surprisingly, though, Trigger hadn't gone into attack mode. He was still growling, low and soft, from somewhere in the darkened room.

Rob flicked the light on, bracing himself.

A voice from the kitchen table said, "Hello, son."

"Jesus, Dad!" Rob put a hand against the wall to steady himself. "What the hell are you doing here?" He looked around the room. The doors were indeed open and his state-of-the-art security gate had been concertinaed against the wall. Fat lot of good that was. "How did you get in?"

Trigger, hearing the tone of Rob's voice, glanced back as if to say, "Is this guy all right?"

Rob patted the dog's head. "It's okay, boy."

The growling stopped. Threat neutralised, Trigger wandered over to his bowl and had a sniff, checking to see if any food had miraculously appeared since supper.

Rob collapsed at the table opposite his father, putting down the lamp. He felt shaky now the adrenalin was wearing off — and rather stupid. Of course it wasn't a hired hitman. Cranshaw was full of shit. His threat was nothing but an attempt to intimidate the man who'd caught him and put him away.

Problem was, it was working.

"How'd you get in?" he asked again, as his pulse returned to normal.

"You think that lock was hard to pick?" Ronnie scoffed.

Rob held up a hand. "Actually, I don't want to know. You're lucky the dog didn't go for you."

"Nah, I'm good with animals."

That was a first. They'd never had a pet growing up, Ronnie had never allowed it. It would have been yet another mouth to feed.

Rob glared at his father across the table. "It's two o'clock in the morning. Couldn't you wait until a reasonable hour to come calling?"

"I'm keeping a low profile."

Bloody hell. "Let me guess? Magnus Olsen?"

Ronnie shrugged.

Rob shook his head. "I'm not bailing you out again. If you've gone and got yourself into more debt, that's on you. I've done enough."

"I don't want anything from you." Ronnie looked offended.

"Then why are you here?"

There was a pause. Ronnie's hands were flat on the table as if he were about to push himself up and leave. Then he relaxed. "I came here to help you."

"You did?" Rob stifled a guffaw. Now he'd heard it all. Ronnie had never lifted a finger to help him in his life. He wasn't likely to start now.

"I remembered something."

"You remembered what?" He still wasn't following.

"From that night, in the square."

Rob fell silent. He studied his father. Was he for real? Or was this some ploy to get into his good books so he'd lend him money to pay off his gambling debt? He chastised himself for being so cynical.

Except, this was his father.

"What did you remember?"

"I'd just passed the square." Ronnie's voice was gravelly from too many cigarettes. "I was walking up the street toward Tottenham Court Road when I saw it."

"Saw what?"

"The car." He paused, looking past Rob as he recalled the details. "At first, I thought it was an undercover cop car, the way it was cruising around. Slow and deliberate. Then I realised it wasn't, so I moved on."

"A car?" Rob was aware he was repeating everything his father said, but he wanted to be sure. Could this be the vehicle the blond man had been driving? Had a drugged Michael Bennett been in the passenger seat?

"Did you see who was inside?"

"Two men, but I didn't see their faces. Just dark figures in the car. Dodgy as hell, prowling around like that with the lights dimmed." He shrugged. "Then again, it is Soho."

"Is that why you're here? You saw two men in a car?"

"Hey, I can leave if you'd prefer." Ronnie raised his hands. "You asked if I remembered anything unusual. Well, that was unusual. The car cruised down the road, slow like. I didn't want to be seen so I hid in a doorway so they wouldn't spot me."

His father was good at lurking in shadows.

"What did they do?"

"They drove towards the square. I watched 'em go. At this point I still thought it was the Old Bill."

"What happened?"

"They pulled over outside a block of flats. I heard a thump and a scraping sound, like metal being dragged across the ground. Then nothing. I didn't hang around."

"You didn't see where they went after that?"

"They didn't go anywhere. When I left, they were still parked outside the flat. I figured they must live there."

Questions ricocheted through Rob's mind. Had this been the killer with Michael Bennett in the car? Had he transferred the body from the car to the refuse bin, then wheeled him into the square? Was that the scraping sound

Ronnie had heard? It could have been, but then again, it might have had nothing to do with the murder.

He studied his father across the table. The old man looked pleased with himself. The smell of booze wasn't that strong. Tonight hadn't been a drinking night. Perhaps he was trying to quit, or maybe it was just too hot for the pub. "You left at that point?"

"Yeah, I wasn't going to hang around, was I? I had twenty grand in stolen cash in my bag."

Fair point. "Yet you were picked up shortly after that."

His face clouded over. "I was stopped near Tottenham Court Road and searched by two officers in uniform. Pigs." He pulled a face, then held up a hand. "No offence."

How was that not offensive? Rob let it slide. There were more important things to concentrate on than his father's prejudice. "Could you point the block of flats out to me?"

"Yeah, I think so."

"What about on a map?"

A shrug. "Maybe."

"Okay, great. Let's focus on the car for a second. Do you know what make or model it was? Colour?

Ronnie arched an eyebrow. "You're kidding, right?"

He'd worked as a motor mechanic most of his adult life. If there was one thing Ronnie knew, it was cars. Rob waited for the reveal, his heart thumping in anticipation. "Well?"

"It was a Ford Fiesta. Blue."

CHAPTER 27

As the night eased into morning, Rob got what little sleep he could on the sofa, not wanting to wake Jo or disturb Jack, both of whom were still sleeping soundly on the bed upstairs, oblivious to the break-in.

It was Trigger who woke him, shoving a wet nose into his face at six thirty. *Get up*, he seemed to be saying with his pleading eyes and prodding snout. *I'm hungry*.

"Okay, I'm coming." He got to his feet rubbing the sleep from his eyes. He'd just walked into the kitchen when he heard a cry from upstairs. Jack was awake, and probably also hungry.

A short time later, Jo padded in with Jack on her hip. "Morning." She smiled and gave him a peck on the cheek. "Sorry we hijacked the bed last night. Jack wouldn't go down, it was too hot. I took him in with me so we could have the fan on."

"That's okay." He looped his arm around them and gave them a quick hug. "I had an interesting night myself."

"You did?"

He told her about Ronnie breaking in.

"Holy crap," she blurted out, making Jack giggle. "I thought that security gate was secure."

"Not to a seasoned professional," Rob said. "And before you ask, my father is not a burglar, he's a mechanic. He knows how to get into things."

She gave a small nod. "What did he want?"

"He remembered something about the night Michael Bennett died."

"In Soho?"

"Yeah. Ronnie was there, before he got arrested with his bag of stolen cash."

Jo mixed a scoop of formula into a bottle and gave it to an eagerly awaiting Jack, who shoved it into his mouth with a satisfied gulp. "Anything useful?"

"Possibly. He saw a vehicle cruising the streets. Two men. Suspicious-looking. Then he heard a thud and a scraping sound. I think — and I hope I'm not wrong — that what he heard was Michael's body being transferred to the refuse bin and pulled across the street into the square."

"In plain sight," mused Jo.

"Yup, although there weren't too many people around at that time thanks to the protests earlier in the day, and the drizzle. It could have been the killer's vehicle."

"Did he get a registration number?" Jo raised her eyebrows hopefully.

"No, but he got the make and colour of the car. That gives us somewhere to start. He also indicated where he thought it was parked. I'm going to organise a search of that block as soon as I get in on Monday. I've got to get Mayhew to clear it, and she's not going to like it. It's a tall block. Lots of flats."

Jo sat down, Jack still in her arms. "Have you looked at CCTV footage in the area?"

"On it, although nothing yet."

"It takes a while for them to connect the dots," she said. Jo would know, having worked at the National Crime Agency, where a lot of their work was surveillance-based. "He'll be on various cameras, but they'll have to trawl through the different feeds and look for continuity. It takes time."

Rob grunted. "There's not much we can do on the weekend anyway."

"Have you managed to talk to Millie yet?"

"No, you were right. The Security Service have put an armed guard around her sister's house. We can't get close to her. It can't last for ever though. At some point they'll have to let her move on with her life."

"It's just while the investigation is underway," Jo said. "But if it's urgent, I could try."

She raised the bottle as Jack's sucking got louder. He'd always had a great appetite. Soon he'd be off the formula altogether.

Rob hesitated. "That would be good, but how are you going to get to her? I don't want you to get into trouble."

"I won't. Those agents on guard won't know who I am anyway. I'll pose as a friend of her sister's. Jack can come with me, in the buggy. That'll throw them off. Once I'm inside the house, I'll come clean and tell them who I really am and ask Millie if I can talk to her about her husband."

"You think that'll work?"

"I don't know, but it's worth a shot. What have we got to lose?"

We again. He smiled. "You're great, you know that?"

"I know." She winked at him. "I miss getting out into the field, and this way I'll be helping Ray. He was a good man. I'd hate to see his murder go unpunished."

"I heard Liz Kramer is doing the autopsy," Rob told her. Jenny had messaged him earlier that day with the information.

Jack finished the bottle, pawing at it for more. "That's it, I'm afraid." Jo took it out of his mouth and put it on the table. "I'll give you some water."

Once Jack was settled again, she glanced at Rob. "Liz presiding over the autopsy should make it easier for you to get the report. Unofficially, of course."

He nodded. "Currently, she's not answering my calls."

"Give it a few days," Jo advised. "If I know Liz, she'll be in touch when she's ready."

Rob could only hope.

"When are you going to visit Millie?" he asked.

She looked out of the window at the dappled sunlight dancing on the grass outside. "How about today? It's a beautiful Saturday, and I've got nothing better to do."

"Want me to drive you?"

"No, I'd better go solo. If they clock you, they'll know it's a ploy."

"Okay, but ring me if you need help."

She patted his hand. "Don't worry, I'll be fine."

* * *

Jo parked her racing-green Mini Cooper two houses down from Millie's sister's house in Kensal Rise, North London, and climbed out of the car. She made a big show and dance of getting Jack out of the car seat and putting him in the buggy. It would have been better if he'd fidgeted or cried, creating a distraction, but for once, he was as good as gold.

"Okay, let's go." She locked the car and wheeled the buggy toward the neat white-fronted townhouse. Two imposing black SUVs were parked in the "Permit Holders Only" zone in front. Shiny exteriors, blacked-out windows, official number plates. It wasn't hard to tell they were government vehicles. A show of muscle to ward off nosy strangers.

Well, Jo wasn't deterred, just determined.

She'd dressed carefully that morning, putting on her periwinkle-blue summer dress that matched her eyes. Her blonde hair fanned around her in the welcome breeze, and a plain gold band glinted on her wedding finger. Hopefully, they'd be fooled by the friendly, slightly flustered new mum and her gurgling baby.

She smiled hesitantly as she passed the disapproving guard on the pavement. "I'm here to see Patty." She wiped an errant strand of hair out of her face. "It's Jo, from the Mums and Tums class."

Jo had done her research. Patty McCloud, who was more than a decade younger than her sister Millie, had two children under the age of ten. It wasn't unfeasible that they'd have met at the gym.

The guard swallowed, instantly uncomfortable. "I'm afraid I can't let you through, ma'am. No visitors."

"Oh, I'm not visiting." She flashed her best dimpled smile. "I'm a friend. Practically family. Ask Patty, she'll tell you."

He hesitated, but it was all Jo needed. "Surely she's allowed to see friends? You can't keep her prisoner in her own home."

Jack chose that moment to moan and fidget.

"Okay, darling," Jo murmured. "I'll feed you in a sec." She glanced imploringly at the guard. "He's always hungry."

"Um, okay." He frowned at the writhing baby and stood aside.

Jo smiled. "Thank you so much."

"She can go inside," he told his colleague, who was positioned outside the front door, wearing an earpiece. The man nodded and stood aside.

Jack started crying. He had a set of lungs on him, and the sound reverberated down the quiet street. The guard hastily opened the front door.

Jo waltzed in, only to be confronted by a tired-looking man with hooded eyes and a mouth that wasn't used to smiling. "Can I help you?" He had a broad Scottish accent.

"Hi, Mark, I'm here to see Patty. It's Jo from the Mums and Tums class. I've come to return this." She nodded to a black cardigan she'd pulled out of her wardrobe before leaving and shoved it underneath the buggy. "She left it behind after the last session."

"Oh, right." He scowled. "I'm not sure now's a good time."

"That's okay. Patty told me all about it. Complete nightmare. I won't stay long." And she breezed past Mark. Luckily, she could hear female voices coming from the living room, so she turned off the hallway and knocked on the open door.

The two women looked up. You could tell they were related by their broad, almost manly features. Millie was a robust woman with a messy blonde bob and sturdy frame, although it was currently bent over and withered, like the air had been punched out of her. Her sister had the same wide forehead and large nose, but her hair was up in a no-nonsense bun.

"Hello," Jo breezed, wheeling a squiggling Jack into the room. "I'm so sorry to disturb you. I worked with your husband, Mrs Humphries. I'm terribly sorry for your loss."

Both women stared at her, then at Jack, who was working himself up into a howl. Jo bent under the pram and took out a ready-made bottle, which she shoved into his mouth. Content, he stopped wriggling.

Patty gasped. "Sorry, but who are you?"

"Jo Andersen." She wasn't about to give her real name in case it got back to her new boss. She smiled disarmingly at Millie and ignored the indignant expression on Patty's face. "I worked directly with your husband." She lowered her voice. "I know he wasn't gay."

Millie crumpled, as if the relief of hearing those words was too much for her. "Thank you." It was a soft utterance, barely a whisper, but so heartfelt that Jo wanted to hug her. "Everyone's saying the most awful things. I was beginning to doubt him myself."

"No, Millie." Jo sat down next to her. "I knew Ray. He was devoted to you and the girls."

"God, the girls. They're going through hell." She put her head in her hands.

"I'm going to prove it," Jo said.

Millie looked up. "How? His work isn't interested in what I have to say. I get the feeling they just want the whole ghastly episode to go away."

"That's exactly what they want." Jo took her hand. "But we're not going to let it happen."

"We're not?"

"No." She shook her head. "We're going to make sure the real murderer is caught and put away for a very long time. We're going to clear your husband's name, so that his reputation is safe. So that your children can hold their heads up at university."

Hope flared in her bloodshot eyes. "You can do that?"

"I can. My partner is the leading investigator in your husband's murder. Or he was, until the Security Service took over. You see—" she wasn't supposed to mention this, but she sensed Millie would help her — "your husband isn't the only one."

"What do you mean?" cut in Patty.

Jo kept her gaze on Millie. "Another man died in a similar manner a few days before Raymond. Do you know anyone called Michael Bennett?"

She frowned, her broad features scrunching up. "I don't think so. Is he the man who died?"

"Yes, we think your husband may have known him." She didn't say in what capacity.

"Gosh, I don't ever remember him mentioning that name." A sob. "I'm sorry. I'm being no help, am I?"

"Don't worry, you're doing just fine. What about art? Was your husband interested in art?"

Millie gave her a strange look. "I . . . I don't know. I guess so, but we didn't go to galleries or exhibitions, or anything like that."

"Had he bought anything recently? Any new pieces?"

"No, I would know if he had."

Jo nodded. "Did you ever visit him at the townhouse?"

"Not really. Once in a blue moon, if we went to a play or met friends in town. Then we might stay over there. Otherwise, he always came home on a Friday for the weekend." Her shoulders slumped.

It was the weekend now. Jo could almost see the grief washing over her, sweeping her away in its cold, heartless grip. "When he didn't come home, you went to find him?"

"Yes." She sniffed, rubbing her reddened nose. "It was our anniversary, you see. We had a dinner reservation. When Ray didn't arrive, I called and called, but it sounded like his phone was switched off. That's very unlike him. I didn't know what to do, so I drove into town to look for him."

"That's when you found his body?"

A strangled sob.

"Is it really necessary to rehash the sordid discovery?" Patty interjected, putting a hand on her sister's shoulder.

"I'm afraid it is." Jo turned back to Millie. "Did you notice anything unusual when you arrived?"

"Like what?"

"Like signs of a fight? Was anything in the wrong place? The front door unlocked?"

She took a shuddering breath. "The front door was unlocked, now that you mention it. That was strange. Ray was very security conscious."

"Is the front door on a latch? Does it lock automatically?"

"No, you need a key."

So the killer couldn't lock up behind him when he left because he didn't have the key.

"What about inside the house? Any wine glasses or tumblers lying on the table? Did it look like anyone else had been there besides your husband?"

"I don't . . . I don't know." She frowned. "I called out his name, and when he didn't answer I went upstairs to see if he'd fallen asleep."

"You didn't look in any of the other rooms?"

"I may have stuck my head into the living room, but he wasn't there."

"Any sign of him having made dinner or a drink?"

"No, nothing like that." She bit her lip.

"That's okay. You've been very helpful."

"I have?" Her red-rimmed eyes filled with tears.

"What has this achieved," her sister asked, "other than upsetting Millie?"

"Well, thanks to your sister, we now know that Ray let his killer in, which means he may have known him, but not well enough to have offered him a drink. His attacker probably drugged him, same as the other victim, but he would have used a syringe or tablet to administer the drug since there were no wine glasses or tumblers lying around. We also know the killer left the door unlocked because he didn't have a key."

Patty's mouth hung open. Millie grasped Jo's hand. "If he was drugged, he may not have known what was going on?"

"That's right," Jo lied.

She recalled the expression on Ray's face from the crime scene photographs. The terror in his eyes as he died. He had known exactly what was happening all right, and there had been nothing he could do to prevent it.

CHAPTER 28

Rob took Trigger for a stroll beside the river. The heat of the previous few days had abated somewhat, but the forecasters were warning that the heatwave wasn't over. The tide was low, exposing the pebbled foreshore, sticks, reeds and other flotsam that had fallen into the river or been washed up by the tide. The smell of wet mud drifted up the towpath.

Being a Saturday, the rowing clubs were out in full force. Four- and eight-man boats sliced through the water with a grace that belied their size. Rob could hear the rhythmic thud of oars as they placed them in the catch, and he admired the long, smooth strokes of the rowers as they flew past.

Trigger loved walking along the river. He darted in and out of the undergrowth, sniffing other dogs and peeing against trees. Rob had a lead with him, but the Labrador never strayed very far.

After an hour, they turned off the towpath and into Old Deer Park. As the green fields stretched out in front of them, Rob wondered how Jo was getting on with Millie Humphries. With a bit of luck, she could shed some light on her husband's activities leading up to his death.

He put Trigger on the lead. "Let's go home," he said. He'd walked up quite a sweat. They crossed busy Lower

Richmond and went down Kew Road, where people were emerging from the local supermarket with cold drinks and ice creams.

As soon as he turned into his road, Rob spotted the rear of Liz Kramer's shiny white BMW sticking out of his driveway. He quickened his step. Jo had been right, Liz had come to see him.

As the Home Office pathologist, she couldn't be seen answering his calls about an internal investigation. For all they knew, her phone could be being monitored, as might his. He wouldn't put it past MI5. Snoopy lot.

Liz was sitting in her car, working on her laptop. He tapped on the window, making her jump.

"Sorry," he said, as she got out.

"I was miles away. Glad you're home, Rob. Can we talk?" Her tone was brisk, urgent.

"Yeah, come inside."

He opened the front door and they went into the kitchen. Trigger made a beeline for his bowl and lapped thirstily, while Rob offered Liz a glass of water. She shook her head. He poured one for himself and they sat at the table.

Liz clasped her hands in front of her. "I shouldn't be here," she began, but he didn't miss the sparkle in her eye.

"You weren't. What did you find out?"

"I can't show you anything official," she said, "but there were definite similarities to your first victim. I'd say you're looking at the same perpetrator."

He breathed out. "I thought so."

"This victim was also drugged, although his Rohypnol levels weren't as high as Michael Bennett's."

Rob cringed. "Would he have been fully conscious all the way through?"

"I'd say so." She hesitated. "The item found under the bed was used repeatedly on him. There was a lot of tissue damage."

He didn't want to think about that. "What was the cause of death?"

"Strangulation, just like Bennett. He also had chain marks around his neck, under the leather collar, coupled with the gag in his mouth." She shook her head. "It wouldn't have taken long."

"Do you know when he died?" Rob asked. "His wife found him in the early hours."

"Between ten and eleven o'clock, judging by the rigor and body temperature."

"Anything else? DNA? Fingernails?" His voice was hopeful.

"Afraid not," she said. "The crime scene was remarkably clean. Forensics couldn't find a trace of anything, which, as you know, is very unusual."

He rubbed his forehead. "How is that possible?"

"It's not, usually. It goes against Locard's Exchange Principle, and almost everything we've come to know about processing crime scenes. The body was clean too. Not a fragment of DNA under his fingernails, not a hair, not a bloodstain that wasn't his."

"Shit," muttered Rob. "What does that mean?"

"It means the killer knew what he was doing."

"He's forensically aware."

"Yup." Liz leaned back in her chair. "There's more."

"Oh?"

"A Mr Johnson from the Security Service paid me a visit. He asked for my report, which I gave him. We had a short discussion on the nature of Ray Humphries' death. Johnson asked if there was any sign of foul play."

Rob frowned. "He was strangled."

"Yes. You and I know that it was probably deliberate, based on the first victim, but if you look at this death in isolation—"

"It could have been erotic asphyxiation," Rob finished.

She nodded.

"Let me guess, they're going to shut down the investigation."

She tilted her head to the side. "'A sex game gone wrong' were his words. An unfortunate accident."

He sighed. They weren't interested in the previous murder, in the pattern. All they wanted was to bury the story as soon as possible. It wasn't related to his work, and therefore not important enough to continue with.

"Where does this leave us?" he asked.

"I don't know, but that's why I came by. This poor man was brutalised, and over the space of an hour or so. It wouldn't have been pleasant. And it links up with your previous victim. I can't give you the physical report, but I wanted you to know in case . . . in case it helps."

He managed a small smile. "Thank you. I appreciate it."

She got to her feet. "Catch this bastard, Rob. These are violent crimes. He needs to be stopped."

Rob couldn't agree more.

* * *

"We've got him on camera," Jenny exclaimed as Rob walked through the door on Monday morning. He'd spent a quiet Sunday with his family. A picnic in Richmond Park followed by an afternoon with Jack watching the grand prix on television and trying not to think about the case. That, of course, had proved impossible, but it had given him some downtime, which he sorely needed.

Jo had filled him in on what Millie had told her. Humphries' wife hadn't recognised Michael Bennett, she didn't know who her husband had met that night and was adamant he wasn't a closeted gay man. Nor was he into bondage or kinks of any kind. Their sex life, by all accounts, was completely average, if a little lacklustre after fifteen years of marriage. How Jo had found out that last bit, he had no idea.

"Who?" He took out his laptop and threw his rucksack under his desk.

"The Soho Killer. That's what the papers are calling him." She rolled her eyes. "Will's managed to pick him up on CCTV."

"Actually, Control did," Will interjected. "They've just sent me the feed." He played it for Rob.

"This is from that camera on the lamppost in the southwest corner of the square," Jenny told him.

He recognised the angle. Occasionally, leaves from the overhanging tree brushed the lens, but you could make out a man in overalls, a dirty high-visibility jacket and a cap wheeling a refuse bin across the street. He appeared to be a City of Westminster council worker, and if Control hadn't been told what to look for, they'd never have flagged this as unusual.

The man pushed the large wheelie bin through the open gate of the park. It was slow-going and he walked with a slight limp, but that could have been put on. Head down, shoulders stooped, hands gloved. The refuse man gave nothing away.

"Damn, he's careful," murmured Rob.

"He doesn't look up," Jenny said. "Not once."

They lost sight of him while he wheeled the bin behind the electricity substation. "He knows he's protected there." Rob frowned. "He's sussed this out."

A short time later, the man emerged on the other side of the hut and rolled the wheelie bin to the north gate.

"At that point, we think the body's been tipped into the centre of the park," Jenny concluded. "We can't see it from this angle."

"Any other CCTV cameras?" Rob asked.

"Yeah, there's one on the north side." Will brought it up on his screen. "It's a similar story. We see him leaving the bin outside the gate for collection the following morning, but not what he did with it before that. Then he walks off, head down, hands in his pockets. We can't even see what hair colour he's got, thanks to that cap."

Could it be blond? Nope, impossible to tell. "On a more positive note," said Rob, "I may know where the primary crime scene was."

They all stared at him.

"Where?" asked Jenny.

He told them what his father had said about the parked car and the scraping sound.

"It makes sense. Shall I organise a warrant?" Jenny jumped on it straightaway. "We need to search that block."

"I have to speak to the Super first," Rob said. "It's going to require extra manpower. If she agrees, we'll go in this afternoon."

"Don't you have Cranshaw's trial this afternoon?" Will asked.

"Shit." He was giving testimony on the shooting at Tilbury last year, where he'd taken a bullet. If he hadn't been wearing that vest . . . Bloody Cranshaw.

His watch buzzed. It was a message from Jo. His eyes flickered across the screen. "The Security Service is dropping the case." He glanced at the others. "It's official."

Harry chose that moment to walk in. "Who's dropping what case?"

"MI5 are dropping the Humphries case," Jenny clarified.

"That's good, isn't it?" Harry said. "It'll get them off our backs."

"They won't be happy when we pick up where they left off," muttered Will.

"They won't have a choice." Rob thought about what Liz had said. "This killer needs to be stopped, and it's up to us to catch him."

"And we will," Jenny said. "You speak to Mayhew and get the warrant, and I'll make sure the search happens today."

"You'll have to draft in officers from Putney," Rob warned her.

"Leave it with me. You concentrate on Cranshaw, and we'll keep you posted."

He didn't like letting it go, but he had no choice. He was needed in court.

"Did Tony Sanderson come up with anything?" Jenny asked. The team knew he'd met up with the criminal profiler on Friday night.

"A few points." With everything that had happened, he'd almost forgotten about his discussion with Tony. "He agrees it's the same killer. I showed him the magazine cutting from Bennett's studio, and he came up with a few scenarios we didn't consider. Bennett could have painted the scene and sold the painting to the killer, or — and this is more likely — the killer commissioned the painting and sent Bennett the magazine cutting to copy from."

There was a pause as the team absorbed this.

"That last one makes the most sense," Jenny said. "We know he took commissions. His partner might have known if he'd sold one recently."

"You'd think so," agreed Rob.

"There was nothing in Bennett's bank statement," Will pointed out.

"Maybe he hadn't started it yet," said Celeste.

"Could Humphries have been the one to commission the painting?" Harry said.

They all gazed at him, surprised.

"Hear me out." He held up a hand. "Say, for example, that Humphries commissioned the artwork from Bennett and someone found out about it. Someone who wanted to ruin him."

"You mean someone from his work?" Rob asked. "Someone who wanted his job?"

"Or personally," added Jenny, warming to the idea. "Like his wife. If she found out he'd been having an affair with a man . . ." She left it hanging.

There was a stunned silence.

"If that's the case, it means we're looking at this all wrong," Rob said. "If Humphries was the primary target, Bennett could have been collateral damage. An extra opportunity to link Humphries to a scandal."

"It's a possibility," said Harry.

Jenny exhaled. "I think we need to dig deeper into Humphries. He might be the key."

Rob sighed. It looked like he was going to break his agreement with Mayhew.

CHAPTER 29

Rob sat in the witness box at the Old Bailey and pointedly ignored Cranshaw. The ex-police detective and corrupt, human-trafficking scumbag glared at him the whole time, but Rob refused to look in his direction.

He gave his testimony, explaining how he'd chased Cranshaw all the way to Tilbury, where a fishing boat had been waiting to take him across the Channel. Rob had run toward the boat to stop Cranshaw from leaving when the dirty copper had opened fire. One of the bullets had hit Rob square in the chest, but luckily, he'd been wearing his vest and only had a fractured sternum to show for it.

Attempted murder had been added to the long list of charges.

Would Cranshaw try again? Rob recalled the night Trigger had gone mental — the one before his dad had shown up. Had that been someone trying to get to him? To his family?

Before he'd arrived in court, he'd checked the prison visitor logs. Apart from Cranshaw's solicitor, his soon-to-be ex-wife and the NCA agent looking into Cranshaw's organised crime group, there hadn't been any other visitors. Certainly nobody who'd be able to organise a personal hit.

The judge thanked him and said he could go. Rob exhaled in relief as he left the dock. Job done. It was finally over.

* * *

"You want me to do what?" Jo stared at him. They were in the kitchen making spaghetti bolognese for supper. Jack had already gone down for the night.

"Well, he did benefit from Humphries' death."

"Charles Hayworth did not kill Ray." She stirred the bolognese with vigour.

Rob set a glass of wine down on the counter beside her. "How do you know?"

She paused, reached for it and took a large gulp. "This is insane. I can't go snooping on my boss. Besides, he's a temporary stand-in. I don't think he even wants Ray's job."

Mayhew had been a stand-in, and look what she'd done to get the superintendent position.

"We just need to find out where he was on the nights Bennett and Humphries were murdered," Rob said. "He must have a diary somewhere."

"It's probably online," she said. "I don't have any way of accessing it."

Damn. "Could you ask around?"

"What if I get caught? I could lose my job."

"You won't. You're good at this undercover stuff. I've seen you in action, remember?"

She gave a wry smile. "That was a while ago. A lot has happened since then."

The pasta water boiled over, so Rob took off the lid and turned down the heat. "Okay, forget it. I don't want you getting into trouble."

She gave him a look. "Okay, I'll see what I can find out."

"Thank you." He kissed her on the lips.

"You really think the killer went through all that trouble to discredit Ray?"

"Maybe. I don't know. It can't be his wife — she was at a restaurant in Windsor when he was killed. The manager and waiter both spoke to her. She also has an alibi for last Sunday, when Bennett was murdered. The whole lot of them were at home having a barbecue. I got the family liaison officer to check it out."

"I'm glad she's off the hook," Jo said. "I like Millie. Her sister on the other hand . . ."

"What about her?" Rob cocked his head.

"She's a bit of a firecracker. But still, she'd have no reason to disgrace Humphries, let alone kill him."

"Unless she was protecting her sister?"

"By shaming the entire family?" Jo waved the wooden spoon in the air. "No, I can't see it. Sorry, Rob, I think you're barking up the wrong tree with them. If anything, they'd want to keep his indiscretion a secret, not broadcast it to the world."

"Yeah, you're probably right. I just can't get rid of the feeling that this is about Ray somehow."

"Okay, I admit the job thing is a possible angle. I'll see what I can find out at the office."

He squeezed her hand. "Thanks, you're a star."

She grinned at him. "Don't you forget it."

* * *

Jo got in early. Thames House was quiet, the entrance hall empty except for a solitary receptionist and the security personnel. It felt strange not to have to fight her way through a throng of people to get to her office. Only the agents and analysts on active cases would be working now, and they were usually closeted away at the back of the building, like she was.

"Morning, Zelda," she called. There was always someone in the office, just in case the targets made a move — which they often did at night. Zelda saw far more action than she did, but Jo couldn't work the night shift, nor did she want to. Her current schedule suited her perfectly. Once

Jack was older, perhaps she'd move into a more involved role. That was if she didn't get fired.

She sat at her desk. "I've been asked to set up a meeting," she told Zelda. "Do you know where I can find Charles's calendar?"

The senior analyst shrugged. "Sorry, I have no idea. What meeting?"

"Don't worry, I'll see if he's got a diary on his desk."

Zelda gave her a funny look but made no comment, and Jo got up and walked through to Charles Hayworth's — formerly Ray Humphries' — office. She stood there, looking around. How weird that it still felt like Ray was there, like he'd walk in at any moment and ask for an update on the targets.

Pulling herself together, Jo approached the big mahogany desk. The inbox was overflowing with reports, updates and documents requiring signatures. She rifled through them, looking for anything with a date on it. Nothing.

There was no diary or calendar on the desk, no way of knowing his schedule.

"Since you're here, do you mind if I take off?" Zelda appeared at the office door.

Jo forced a smile, even though her heart was racing. "Sure, that's fine. I'll just grab a coffee and take over the comms." She would be in constant contact with the agents on the ground — a man and a woman, both watching a house in Wembley. If there was any movement, they'd inform her, and she'd call in the mobile agents, who'd take it in turns to follow the targets.

Zelda left and Jo sat at her desk wondering how on earth she could get into Hayworth's calendar. Unlike Ray, Hayworth appeared to keep his schedule online.

Nothing was happening at the targets' house. The agents checked in with a sitrep every hour. It had been ten minutes since the last one, when a young pimply-faced guy walked in holding a clipboard. He couldn't have been older than twenty.

"IT," he said. "We're running an upgrade and I have to set it manually on each computer."

"Go ahead."

She watched him log in to Zelda's computer, an idea forming in her mind. She checked the time: 8.15. Hayworth would be in at around half past.

"My boss will be in soon," she told the IT guy. "You'd better do his before he gets here."

"Oh, sure."

"Let me show you in," Jo said. She kept the comms in her ear, just in case. "He wouldn't want you to be alone in his office."

The IT guy gave a nervous nod.

Jo stood next to the techie as he logged in to Hayworth's computer using an administrative password. He didn't even try to hide it. The username was the IT department email and she obtained the password by watching his fingers hit the keys. She thought she could just about remember it.

He initiated the upgrade, then logged off.

"Thanks, you can do the rest now." She moved to the filing cabinet against the wall. I'll be in here for a few minutes."

"No worries."

He left her alone in Hayworth's office. 8.20. She didn't have much time. Darting back to the computer, she entered the login details and the password, praying she had it right.

Bugger. It failed.

She tried again, taking her time. *Concentrate.*

She keyed in the sequence of numbers. That was it, she was sure of it.

Bingo. The computer screen unlocked. Jo reached for the mouse and navigated to the calendar app. Last Sunday Charles was at the Henley Royal Regatta. That put him firmly out of the picture for Bennett's murder. What was he doing the day Ray was killed?

"Morning," came a booming voice down the corridor. Jo froze. Her boss had arrived. She was out of time.

Thursday. What had he been doing last Thursday? She read through the entries again, forcing herself to focus.

Dinner with the Home Secretary.

Thank God for that. He was in the clear.

Hurriedly, she shut down the calendar app and locked the computer using a keyboard shortcut.

"Zelda?" Charles called.

Jo emerged from his office. "She's gone home."

His eyes narrowed. "How come?"

"I got in early so I told her she could go."

He glanced behind her into his office. "Did you want something?"

"Nope, the IT guy was installing updates on everyone's computer. I didn't think it right to leave him in your office alone."

Hayworth grunted.

The IT guy gave a hasty smile. "I'm done now."

Jo thanked him and sat back at her desk. It was only when Hayworth stalked past her into his office that she realised her hands were shaking.

CHAPTER 30

Rob arrived at work late. He'd had to wait for Tanya to arrive so he could hand Jack over to her. Normally he didn't mind — he enjoyed his time with his son — but today he was eager to get to the office. The search team had found what they thought was the original crime scene.

The search warrant hadn't been granted until late last night, by which time it had been too dark to conduct an effective search, so Jenny had made the decision to go in at dawn. An hour ago, she'd called him at home.

"We've got blood on the floor in one of the apartments on the second floor."

"Really? Do you think that's it?"

"It's a lot of blood, Rob. Something bad happened here. We've locked it down and SOCO is on the way."

"Good, keep me posted." He was dying to get out there.

Mayhew, however, had other ideas. "You're a DCI, Rob, let the professionals handle it. You signed off on the search warrant, you arranged for them to gain entry to the building, that was your job, but it stops there. If they find anything, they'll let you know."

Much as he hated to admit it, Mayhew was right. There were things he had to do here. SOCO would process the scene and send through their report. Jenny would have taken preliminary photographs on her camera phone. He'd just get in the way.

Sometimes it sucked being in charge. He sat down at his desk and got to work. A couple of hours later, he was breaking for lunch when Jo messaged him.

Boss is in the clear. Busy both days.

It wasn't entirely unexpected, but he did feel a slight anticlimax when he read her text. He'd been sure Humphries was the key. Anyway, maybe the apartment in Soho Square would give them a fresh lead. God knows they needed it.

Thank you. I owe you dinner.

He got a heart in response.

A loud bang made him glance up. Mayhew had stormed out of her office and was making a beeline towards him.

"Heads up," muttered Will. "She's on the warpath."

She came to an abrupt halt in front of his desk. Rob tried to think what he'd done to piss her off. Everybody else decided to look busy. He was on his own. "Ma'am?"

She was very pale, her skin almost alabaster in the fluorescent light. "There's been another incident."

"'What?" He stood up. "Where?"

She battled to form the words. "I . . . I've just had a DS Hancock on the line. A man has been found dead at his home in Battersea. Their team responded and are on site. It looks like suicide."

"Suicide?" He frowned. "What's that got to do with us?" And why did Mayhew look like she'd seen a ghost?

"He was dressed in a bondage outfit," she rasped.

Shit. Murder number three.

Rob reached for his rucksack. "Tell Hancock I'm on my way."

* * *

Rob stepped inside the house. "Jesus."

Will, who'd come with him, wrinkled his nose.

"The victim's been here a while," said a blonde woman in a cream trouser suit.

Not the best colour for a crime scene, he thought.

"DCI Miller? I'm Joyce Hancock."

He shook her hand. "This is DS Will Freemont."

Will nodded.

"I'd guess a week or so," she said.

That was clear from the smell. "Who found him?"

"The neighbour, Mr Webb. They're friends, I believe. He hadn't seen him in a few days, so he came round to check he was okay."

"How'd he get in?"

"He didn't. He saw the mail piling up on the floor and called us."

Rob nodded. Fair enough. "Where is he now?"

"He's gone home with a liaison officer. She's taking his statement."

"Okay, good." The correct protocol was being followed. "Do we know who the victim is?"

"Judging by the mail, his name is Felix Hewson." Hancock handed him an envelope.

They walked along the hallway to the stairs. The body was hard to miss, dangling from the banister.

Rob exhaled. It wasn't pretty. The man was swollen and distended, which looked ridiculous, considering he was wearing tight leather shorts and a studded harness. No collar though. No ball gag. But something else was preying on Rob's mind. Felix Hewson . . . where had he heard that name before?

The rope around Hewson's neck was attached to the upper banister. Once the victim had stepped off the landing, there'd have been no way to save himself. A clean break, most likely. It did indeed appear to be a suicide.

SOCO was buzzing around, fingerprinting the front door, the staircase, the banister and everywhere else that a potential perpetrator may have touched. They had to rule out foul play before the court could rule it a suicide.

"Is the pathologist here yet?" Rob asked.

"Not yet." Hancock put her hands on her hips. "He's on his way."

"Could we get Liz Kramer in here?"

"Why?" Hancock frowned.

"It makes sense not to break the chain of continuity." Having done the other PMs, Liz was best placed to decide whether this was suicide or not.

Hancock hesitated. "Fine," she said, after a beat. "It doesn't matter to me. Call her if you like."

"Thanks." He whipped out his phone and dialled Liz's number.

She answered on the first ring. "Please don't tell me you've got another one."

"Looks like it."

"Where?"

"Battersea." He gave her the address.

"Give me twenty minutes. Keep it clean, Rob."

"Will do."

"Everybody out," he yelled once he'd hung up.

Hancock glared at him. "Excuse me. What do you think you're doing?"

"Until we know if this is linked to our case, it's the Major Investigation Team's crime scene," he retorted. "You're welcome to take it up with Superintendent Mayhew."

Hancock thought about this for a moment, then obviously decided it wasn't worth her while. "Fine. You go ahead."

He nodded.

"What if it's not connected?" she asked.

He managed a thin smile. "Then it's all yours."

Hancock turned and strode from the house, leaving him and Will alone with the body. The noose was pulled tight around the victim's neck, causing his head to loll to one side.

"It's a murder, isn't it?" Will came back into the house after ushering out the forensic team and the police officers who'd originally secured the scene. "This is the same killer."

"It looks like it." Rob stared at the victim's face, bloated and disfigured from the effect of gravity. The eyes were open and soulless, unnerving in their blankness.

He glanced away. His sergeant was looking rather pale too. "Will, why don't you check upstairs and see if you can find any evidence of Mr Hewson's sexual orientation? We need to know if he was straight, gay, bi or whatever. It might be important."

Will nodded and took off up the stairs. Rob looked around the entrance hall. He selected one of the piled-up envelopes with his gloved hand. Like Hancock had said, it was addressed to Felix Hewson. The others were all addressed to the same man. No Mrs or another Mr. It seemed Hewson was unmarried.

The carpeted hallway was neat, containing a sideboard on which was a basket for keys, a couple of hooks behind the door to hang his coat and a small shoe rack with three pairs of shoes in it. Work shoes, wellies and a pair of trainers.

Come on, Liz.

"Any sign of forced entry?" he asked a man in a white suit standing outside the front door.

"No, sir. Not that we could determine. The front door was locked from the inside and all the windows were secure."

That played into the suicide theory, unless the killer had locked the door behind him. He inspected the latch. It was one of those that locked automatically when you shut the door.

"Felix Hewson, Felix Hewson," he chanted to himself.

Then an icy chill hit him. Wasn't he the guy who Celeste said had been calling the station?

He pulled out his phone, hands trembling. "Celeste, what was the name of that man who kept calling about his partner's death twenty years ago?"

"One minute."

His heart thudded in his chest.

"Felix Hewson. Why?"

Jesus. "I'm looking at his dead body."

There was silence on the other end of the line.

"For real?"

"Yes, it's him, Celeste."

He stopped speaking as his brain kicked into gear. "Right, I need to know exactly what he was calling about. Everything. Get the tapes of the calls and bring in the duty sergeant he spoke to. I'll be back in a couple of hours and we'll go through them."

"Yes, guv." Her voice was a whisper.

CHAPTER 31

"Liz Kramer doesn't think it's a suicide," Rob told his team, his voice sombre. Mayhew had sat in on the briefing, which was a first. "There were strangulation marks around his neck."

Rob pointed to the photograph of the prone corpse on the whiteboard. It had been taken after they'd cut him down and laid him out on the floor. When the noose had been removed, they'd found chain-like impressions on his skin. "There's no way those were made by the rope."

"Why strangle him if you're going to hang him?" asked Will, confused.

"Maybe the killer wanted to hide the fact he'd been strangled," Celeste said.

"Bit too obvious, isn't it?" said Mayhew.

Celeste shrank back into her chair as if she wished it would swallow her up. Rob turned back to the picture of Hewson. Swollen face, bulging eyes and lips drawn back in a snarl — the death grin, Liz had called it.

Mayhew had regained some of her colour, but still looked pale. This new development had shocked her. Rob was guessing that up until now she'd thought Bennett's and Humphries' deaths were intimately related and there wouldn't be any more.

She didn't have Tony Sanderson as a friend.

"It is." He shot Celeste an apologetic look. "Too obvious. If this is the same killer, he'd know we'd determine that the cause of death was strangulation, not hanging."

"He's toying with us." Mayhew crossed her arms in front of her body.

Rob clenched his jaw. It did feel like it.

"Are we absolutely sure this is the same guy?" Jenny cut in. "I mean, the victim is dressed in a fetish outfit, sure, but there's no ball gag, no hand restraints. It feels different."

"He was strangled in exactly the same way," Rob pointed out. "According to Liz Kramer, the indentations in his neck are identical to the marks on the other two victims."

Mayhew exhaled. "We're sure about that?"

"To the millimetre, ma'am."

Jenny sat back. "Then there's no doubt."

Mayhew nodded. "I'll confirm with DI Hancock. It's our case."

Will met Rob's gaze. It wasn't often the Superintendent backed them up. They were usually rallying against her. This was a pleasant surprise.

Rob continued with the briefing. "The victim had been dead for several days. We're not yet sure how many, but it's possible he was murdered before Humphries."

"Bennett, Hewson, Humphries," muttered Jenny. "Does that change things?"

"It might." Rob glanced around at his team. "We know Bennett and Humphries knew each other because of the business card in Humphries' Filofax. Now we need to find out where Hewson fits in."

Harry stood. "I'll look into his background."

Will raised a hand. "Phone records and bank statements."

Jenny pushed her chair back. "I'll chase up SOCO."

"Hang on," said Rob. "There's more."

They turned to look at him. Only Celeste couldn't meet his gaze.

"Felix Hewson rang this office several times over the last few weeks."

Mayhew sat up straighter. "He did?"

"Yes, ma'am, and I'm sorry to say we ignored his calls."

She frowned. "Why?"

"Because we didn't know they were related."

Jenny and Harry sat down again.

Celeste swallowed. "He first rang last Thursday, asking for DCI Miller. I took the message."

"What did he say?"

Rob nodded to Celeste, who got up and opened the door. In walked a young, lanky sergeant, clutching a laptop.

"This is Sergeant Deeks," Rob said. "Sergeant Deeks, please play the recording."

Deeks set his laptop down, opened the lid and pressed a button. A moment later, the sound of a high-pitched nasal voice filled the air.

"Hello, I'd like to speak to the detective in charge of the Soho murder."

"I'm sorry, which murder is that, sir?" asked the operator.

"The murder that took place in Soho yesterday. I've just seen it in the newspaper."

"The Senior Investigating Officer is DCI Miller. If you'll bear with me, sir, I'll transfer you to his department."

"Thank you."

Ringing as the administrator tried to connect the call.

"I'm sorry," she said. *"DCI Miller is unavailable. Can I take a message?"*

"It's imperative I speak with him." The caller's voice was more urgent now. *"I have information about the case."*

"I'll put you through to someone else in his department."

There was a brief moment of static, and then the call went through to Celeste.

"Major Investigation Team, can I help you?" She was friendly and professional. Rob had no problem with her conduct. It wasn't her fault that they'd ignored the call.

The man on the end of the line spewed out a few hurried sentences, his words falling over one another in his rush to get them out. He was clearly desperate to be heard. The only problem was it came across as slightly unhinged.

"I'm sorry, did you say your partner committed suicide twenty years ago?"

"No, I'm saying he didn't."

"I'm sorry, sir. I'm not sure what you mean. How can we help?"

"He was murdered," the voice hissed. *"But they made it look like suicide."*

"Who?" Celeste asked. *"Who made it look like suicide?"*

"The killer, of course. I got home and found him dead. God, it was horrible. I told the police at the time he'd never take his own life. Alan wasn't like that. He . . . We had too much to live for." A hiccup. *"No one believed me."*

"I'm sorry for your loss, sir," Celeste said diplomatically, *"but how can we help?"*

"You need to find whoever killed him," he urged. *"Please, you've got to get justice for Alan."*

"Um, I think you may have come through to the wrong department, sir. This is the Major Investigation Team. We deal with active cases. If your partner died twenty years ago, you need to speak to—"

"You don't believe me either," he interrupted.

"No, sir, it's not that. It's just—"

"Typical. I don't know why I expected any different. There's no bloody justice in the world and you lot are useless."

He hung up.

"That was the first call," Deeks said.

"I'm sorry," Celeste whispered. "I didn't know it was important."

"None of us did." Rob grimaced. "You relayed the message and I ignored it."

"To be fair, he did sound like a bit of a nutter," Jenny said.

Celeste gnawed on her lower lip.

"Don't worry about it." Rob waved his hand in the air. "I don't think any of us would have taken any further notice of the caller."

Everyone around the table shook their heads except Mayhew. "There's nothing we can do about it now," she said practically. "Is that it?"

"No, ma'am. He called a second time." Deeks played the follow-up call. This time, he'd taken down a statement as per Rob's instructions, but hadn't been particularly enthused by it.

"What you're saying is that you came home and found your partner hanging by his neck from the banister." Deeks sounded tired and irritable.

Everybody's heads shot up.

"Yes." His voice cracked. *"It was awful, just terrible."*

"I see." Deeks didn't have Celeste's telephone manner. It was clear he just wanted to get the statement down and get off the call. *"Where had you been, sir?"*

"Me?" Hewson sounded surprised to be asked. Most witnesses were shocked when the questions were turned on them. *"I'd been in Manchester at a work conference. I worked for a consultancy at the time, so I travelled a lot."*

"What happened next?"

A pause. *"The police concluded he'd taken his own life, but it wasn't true."*

"What makes you think that?"

"Because he was dressed in some sort of sadomasochistic getup with one of those ball gags in his mouth."

Mayhew's eyebrows shot up. Everybody listened intently, glued to the laptop, even though all they could see was the jagged visual representation of sound waves on the screen.

"We didn't own anything like that. I'd never seen the outfit before. It was bizarre."

Deeks didn't respond.

"I'm telling you, he was murdered by the Soho Killer."

Mayhew winced at the term the media had adopted.

Hewson's voice turned up at the end, his desperation audible. *"Just like the guy in the square."*

"When did this happen?" Deeks asked, showing some sign of initiative.

"Twenty years ago."

Another pause.

"Okay, thank you for calling. I'll pass your statement on to DCI Miller."

"Is that it? You don't want to hear more? I have proof—"

"No, sir. I've got all I need for now. If DCI Miller has any questions, he will get back to you."

A ragged breath. *"Fine. He can call me back on this number."*

"Thank you, sir."

The call ended.

Rob was the first to speak. "In light of what's happened to the caller, I suggest we dig up everything we can on his partner's suicide."

Mayhew was nodding. "He said he had proof." She turned an accusatory gaze on Deeks, who shifted uncomfortably. "Pity we never got it."

"If the proof is anywhere, it'll be at his house," said Rob. "I'll head over there and take a look. Celeste, you up for an outing?" Since she'd taken the initial call, he thought he'd give her a chance to get in on the action.

Her face lit up. "Yes, guv."

"Hang on." Jenny shook her head as if to clear it. "Are we assuming that the person who killed Hewson also killed his partner twenty years ago?"

"It's possible," Rob said. "Hewson was killed in the same way as his partner. That's a hell of a coincidence."

"But twenty years?"

Rob shrugged. "There are cases where a killer has been active for decades. Remember the Shepherd?" Several years back, they'd apprehended a serial killer who began his career twenty years ago in the north of England and finished it in Surrey, where he was now serving a life sentence.

"It's unusual, though."

"I'm going to suggest we get Tony Sanderson in as consultant on this one." Rob glanced at Mayhew. "He's expensive, but worth every penny. No one knows the mind of a psychopath like he does."

Mayhew thought about it, then nodded. "Okay, do it. Let's get to the bottom of this as soon as we can. We've had three murders in as many weeks, all by the same perpetrator. Once the press gets wind of it, all hell is going to break loose. We've already got the Security Service breathing down our necks. They're not going to be happy if this makes front-page news."

That was an understatement.

"I know we said we'd leave Humphries out of it," Rob said carefully, "but I don't think we can look at this in isolation anymore."

"Agreed."

They all turned to her in surprise.

"What? It's obvious the murders are connected. I'm not going to ignore that just because the Home Office wants to prevent a scandal. This killer must be stopped. I'll do what I can on my side to smooth the way."

"Thank you, ma'am." Rob broke into a grin. Would wonders never cease?

Mayhew got to her feet. "Let's just catch this bastard."

CHAPTER 32

"What's got into Mayhew?" asked Will once the Super had left the room.

Jenny poked Rob in the ribs. "You must be rubbing off on her, guv."

He shrugged. "We can only hope."

Everyone knew what they had to do, so Rob and Celeste left to go to Felix Hewson's house. SOCO were still there processing the scene. "You take the kitchen and living room. I'll look upstairs," Rob said. They sidestepped the forensic technicians and went their different ways.

An hour later they reconvened on the upstairs landing. This was the balustrade that Hewson had supposedly hung himself from. Every bit of dust and fibre had been collected from the carpet, and the entire span of railing had been fingerprinted. Given the pristineness of the other crime scenes, Rob wasn't hopeful they'd find anything here.

"Nothing," Celeste said. "I couldn't find anything about his partner, Alan Clayton."

"Me neither. Hewson liked to collect things. I've got some old photographs and memorabilia, but nothing about Clayton."

"There's an attic," Celeste pointed up.

Rob surveyed the square panel in the ceiling above the stairs. "We should take a look." He looked around for a loft ladder pole and found it stored behind the bedroom door. Hoisting it above his head, he pulled the hatch open.

"Ladies first." Rob stood back. Celeste climbed up the ladder and stepped into the darkened loft.

"There must be a switch somewhere," called Rob.

"Got it." The loft was flooded with light. "Good heavens, this is the tidiest loft I've ever seen. You should see my mother's, it's like a jumble sale."

Rob snorted and followed her up. Celeste was right. The spacious loft was strangely devoid of dust. A slanting window under the eaves had a roller blind on it, drawn to prevent sunlight from coming in.

He looked around. Everything had a place. On one side old furniture, stacked neatly, on the other, piles of boxes, all clearly labelled. Some had stickers on, reading *This way up*.

Celeste bent over and read the labels. "This one's got Alan Clayton's name on it," she said, excitedly. "Shall I open it?"

"Definitely."

He joined her and they sorted through the box, which contained mostly old clothes, some personal items and a pair of vintage shoes.

"Damn." Rob sat back, defeated. "I was hoping there'd be something in that one."

Celeste straightened up. While Rob replaced the contents of the box, she prowled around the attic. "What about up there on the shelf?"

All he could see were pots of paint, a toolbox and an old bucket.

Celeste took down a worn shoebox. He hadn't seen it behind the paint tins. "It's taped up but not labelled."

"Open it," Rob said.

She ripped the tape off, and then silently stared into the box.

"What is it?" He stood up, feeling his back crack.

"Um . . . I think I've found something." She took out an official-looking document. "It's a coroner's inquest report." Her eyes widened. "It returned a verdict of suicide in the case of Alan Clayton."

"That's it," Rob hissed, taking the box from her. "This could be what he was talking about. The proof must be in here."

The box contained an assortment of papers with yellow Post-it notes stuck on, old photographs held together with rubber bands, receipts, phone records, bank statements. Rob read some of the hand-scrawled notes:

Why didn't they talk to him?
Who is this?
What about the club?

There was also a bunch of press clippings with words circled in red ink. "He was following the case," Rob said. "And when it ended, he began his own investigation."

"This was his evidence box," Celeste whispered.

Rob took a deep breath. "Let's take this back to the station and go through it. Hewson may have just saved us a hell of a lot of work."

* * *

"How's it going?" Will poked his head into the incident room. Celeste, Jenny and Harry were sorting through the contents of Hewson's evidence box, which were spread out over the boardroom table.

"We're still trying to piece it together." Jenny pushed a stray hair off her face. "There's a lot of stuff here."

Rob had printed out a copy of the original police report filed twenty years ago, and was reading through it. His hair stood on end. "The description of the original crime scene matches the current report on Hewson to the letter." He glanced up. "It could be the same report."

"The killer's replicating the original crime scene," Jenny breathed.

That was something he'd have to run past Tony when he got here.

"Hewson insisted it wasn't suicide, even though the inquest ruled that it was. Eventually, he gave up trying to convince them, but he continued his own investigation."

Will sat at the table. "I think I've found something too."

"Oh yeah?" Rob put the file down. "What have you got?"

"Get this: Felix Hewson called Humphries several times in the weeks leading up to his death." He paused to take a breath. "They spoke on three separate occasions. I've also got an incoming call to Hewson from Humphries. It's short, less than a minute."

Rob jumped out of his seat. "They did know each other!"

Jenny clapped. "Well done, Will. Now we have a link between all three victims."

"Perhaps that's how Humphries got Bennett's business card." Rob frowned. "The link could be Hewson. Humphries may not have actually met Bennett."

"You mean he was killed before he could contact him?" Jenny's eyes were huge.

"Or to stop him contacting him," said Harry.

Will exhaled. "We don't know any of this for sure."

"No, but we do know Hewson was looking into his partner's death. He didn't believe it was suicide."

"But this is twenty years later," Will pointed out. "Why contact Humphries now?"

"That I don't know." Rob sat back down in his chair. "But for some reason, the killer decided to target all three of them. Four, if we include Clayton."

"There goes the random hate crime angle," murmured Jenny.

"Not necessarily." Rob thought about what Tony had said. "Three of our victims were gay. It does seem to be a common denominator."

"Humphries must have been in the closet." Harry spread his arms out. "It's the only thing that makes sense."

"It still doesn't tell us how he's targeting them." Jenny pursed her lips. "Bars? Clubs? We know Bennett met the killer in Soho."

Too many questions.

Rob sighed. "Tony's coming in this afternoon. Maybe he can help us make sense of it all."

* * *

Tony Sanderson was shown in by the duty sergeant at the desk downstairs. He cut a fine figure in smart suit trousers, a white shirt and shiny dress shoes. It was too hot for a jacket.

Rob shook his hand. "You didn't need to dress up to come and visit us."

The profiler laughed. "I gave a presentation at Oxford University this morning. I've only just got back to London and came straight here."

"We're honoured."

Tony waved the comment away. "Show me what you've got."

Rob led him into the incident room. The rest of the team followed like eager puppies. No one wanted to miss a thing. Tony whistled when he saw the whiteboard. "You've been busy."

"The killer's been busy."

Tony studied the pictures of all four crime scenes, then pointed to the oldest one. These photos weren't as high-resolution as the more recent ones and the décor in them was dated. "What's this?"

"That is an apparent suicide twenty years ago," Rob said. "The victim was a twenty-seven-year-old man called Alan Clayton. He was found hanging in his split-level apartment by his partner, Felix Hewson."

Tony narrowed his gaze. "What makes you think they're connected?"

"This is Felix Hewson." Rob pointed to the last crime scene photograph showing Hewson hanging from his banister.

"Ah." Tony's gaze flickered between the two.

"Yeah."

Rob pointed to the board. "According to the post-mortem reports, they died in this order. First, Bennett was killed in Soho, followed by Hewson, who was found dead in his house. He'd been there for some time — his body was discovered after Humphries, but in actual fact, he was murdered before. Then, as you know, Humphries was found by his wife in his Pimlico townhouse."

Tony moved closer to the board. "Have you found a link between any of the victims?"

"Sort of." Rob glanced at his team, who were sitting quietly around the table, listening. Tony had a wealth of knowledge on forensic psychology, and they were keen to learn what they could. Profiling had been popular in the States for years, but it was still only used sporadically in the UK.

Tony followed his gaze. "Tell me."

Jenny spoke up. "At first we thought these were homophobic hate crimes. Michael Bennett was an artist and Humphries had his business card. The killer could have targeted them at an art gallery or exhibition or somewhere like that."

"It's feasible." Tony nodded.

"Except then we found Felix Hewson's body," Rob added. "Which scuppered that theory."

Tony frowned. "Why? It's a good theory."

"Well, Clayton died twenty years ago. Now we're wondering if that wasn't where it all began. If he wasn't the first victim."

"I'm not following."

Rob raised his hand. "Hear me out, okay. Let's say, for argument's sake, that Clayton was murdered and didn't commit suicide as the inquest ruled, and his partner, Felix Hewson, figured out who the murderer was."

"Why didn't he come forward?" Tony asked.

"He may not have known who it was back then," Rob argued.

"You're saying he figured it out twenty years later?" Tony scratched his head.

"Yeah, why not? We know he looked into it at the time. We found a box with his research in his loft."

"You did?" Tony raised his eyebrows.

"It was an evidence box with receipts, news clippings, that sort of thing."

"That could also be the actions of a desperate man unable to accept that his partner killed himself," Tony said.

"Could be," admitted Rob. Tony had a point. "But what if it was more than that? What if he was right?"

"Did you find anything in the box to suggest that the first man, his partner, was murdered?"

"No." Jenny's shoulders slumped.

Rob wasn't willing to let it go just yet. His gut was telling him there was something more to this than just random hate crimes. "What if Hewson contacted Bennett and Humphries about the murder — perhaps they knew the victim or the killer? — and the killer silenced them to keep them quiet."

There was a long pause.

Tony glanced around the table. "You're saying that all three men were murdered to prevent them from revealing who the original killer was?"

"In a nutshell, yes." Rob grimaced.

"Do you have any actual evidence that supports this?"

"Only Hewson's mobile phone records," Will said. "We know he contacted Humphries."

"What about the other guy? Bennett."

Will shook his head.

Tony shrugged. "Without definite evidence that he called or met with them both, I'd say it's a long shot. Your biggest and most obvious clue is what they were wearing and how the crime scenes were staged. Let's go back to that for a minute."

Rob pulled out a chair and sat down. His friend was right. Their theory was all supposition. They had no evidence that Hewson had spoken to the other two victims about his partner's death. The phone calls to Humphries could have been about something else entirely.

"The killer is setting the scene." Tony walked up and down, his gaze lingering on each of them in turn. "He wants to portray his victims as subservient, weak and helpless. He's punishing them."

"For being gay?" asked Harry.

"I can't think of another reason." Tony turned to face Rob. "Their reputations are in tatters, their friends and family shocked by their betrayal. This was all intentional. This was planned."

"But we don't know that Humphries was gay," Rob argued.

"Doesn't matter," Tony said. "The point is that the killer thought he was. Correctly or incorrectly."

"Humphries must have been gay," mumbled Jenny. "The killer wouldn't have made that kind of mistake."

"With his job, you can understand why he would have kept it secret," Tony remarked.

Harry glanced down at his hands, while Rob gave a reluctant nod.

Tony took a deep breath. "Do you want my honest opinion?"

"Of course. That's why I asked you here. We need your help on this."

Tony nodded. "Okay, this is what I think. The man you're looking for is sexually confused. He's a closet homosexual but is trying not to be. He sees homosexuality as wrong, as sordid or disgusting. That's probably because he had a strict or religious upbringing. The values are deeply instilled in him, and despite his own inclinations, he can't ignore that. Perhaps he blamed the victims for making him feel things he didn't want to feel."

"You're saying he knew them?" Harry interjected.

"I wouldn't be surprised." Tony fixed his gaze on the handsome detective sergeant. "It could even have started with your first victim — like you said, Rob. What's his name again? Clayton?"

"That's right." Rob turned his gaze back to the grainy crime scene photographs taken in the split-level apartment. The pale, bloated face. The noose digging into the victim's neck. The leather holster and tiny shorts.

"Perhaps," Tony continued, "Clayton was the first man to shame him, or to hit on him. Or the first man he was attracted to. Who knows? Then twenty years later, his partner does the exact same thing. The killer can't bear it, so he murders him, recreating that earlier crime scene."

It did make a twisted kind of sense.

"What about Bennett and Humphries?" Will asked.

"Same thing, except no link to the past. The killer could have met them somewhere — a gallery or a gay bar, say. Perhaps he met them through Hewson. It doesn't matter. The key is that there is a connection between them. A pattern."

"You mean they all made him feel ashamed that he was gay?" Harry raked a hand through his hair.

Tony rubbed his hands together. "I don't know how, but it is possible they knew his guilty secret. A secret that he didn't want coming out."

Harry swallowed. "Because it would affect his career or his personal life in some way?"

"Exactly." Tony gave a sharp nod. "Perhaps he was married, or a celebrity or in politics. Perhaps he just had a lot to lose."

Harry fell silent.

"So, Bennett and Humphries may not have had anything to do with the first murder?" Rob tried to get it straight in his head.

Tony shrugged. "Why dress them up and set the scene like he does just to cover up a murder? No, there's more to this than a cover-up. There's a definite psychological angle. I'd stake my career on it."

CHAPTER 33

Harry stood outside the gallery in Chelsea.

Should he go in?

Come on, he told himself. You've got this far. What's a few more steps? He hadn't told Callum he was coming, just in case he got cold feet at the last minute.

Harry still wasn't sure what he was doing here. The only thing he knew was that he wanted to see the Aussie man again, and this was the easiest way.

I'll pop in and view the art. If he's not there, nobody will know the difference. If he is—

He'd broken out in a cold sweat.

Christ, this was ludicrous. What was he doing? Once he started down this path, there was no turning around. Was that what he wanted?

Yes.

No! What would his mother say? She'd be devastated. His father would never talk to him again. Then there was the police force. How would they view him if they knew he was gay?

Still, that criminal profiler's words were stuck in his brain. He was denying who he was. Harry didn't want to do that. He was tired of hiding his feelings, of depriving himself of human contact, of a relationship, just because he didn't want anyone to know his secret. He craved affection too.

His mother thought he was a player, had too many girlfriends. His colleagues teased him because all the women at his workplace flirted with him. Amazingly, none of them had picked up that he was gay. But then he'd learned how to flirt, how to hold them at bay. Never too close, but close enough to avert suspicion. Had the killer done that too?

Harry sighed. "I can't do this." He turned away.

"Jamie?"

Shit. Harry turned around. Callum was coming across the road with a Diet Coke in his hand. "Is that you?"

"Yeah, um . . . Hi. I was in the neighbourhood, so I thought I'd stop by."

"That's great." Callum grinned. "I'm so glad. Come on in, I'll show you around the gallery."

Harry found himself smiling back. "Okay, thanks. If you're sure you've got the time."

"For you, absolutely."

The gallery viewing was followed by an early supper at the Italian on the corner, during which they didn't stop talking. Harry felt like he had a lifetime of stories to tell, and Callum was interesting and funny. Harry couldn't remember when he'd last enjoyed himself so much.

Eventually, it was time to go home.

"I had a great time." Callum smiled at Harry. Somehow, they were holding hands.

"Me too."

There was so much he wanted to say, to explain, but couldn't.

"Can I see you again?" Callum asked.

"I'd like that." For once, he didn't want to deny himself. This was what dating was meant to be like. Fun, exciting, filled with anticipation and hope.

Callum looked relieved. "Okay, great. I'll call you."

Harry nodded.

There was an awkward moment where they both stared at each other, but then Callum gave his hand a quick squeeze and released it. "See you soon."

"Definitely."

Harry walked back to the tube station on a high. He'd never felt so alive, so filled with anticipation. The fear, the trepidation, the worry — he pushed them aside for now, determined not to think about it. Sooner or later, reality would come crashing down on him, but right now, he wanted to enjoy this moment.

He opted not to take the crowded Piccadilly Line from Green Park but to walk through Trafalgar Square to the new Elizabeth Line that would take him directly home. It was a lovely evening, mild and balmy. The intense heat of the previous week had gone, and the sky was a pale blue, deepening to indigo in the west.

He got to Tottenham Court Road and realised he was very close to Soho Square. That Thai restaurant still hadn't got back to him about the security camera. Their phone number had diverted to voicemail every time he tried calling them. Perhaps he'd see if they were open.

He passed Soho Square, cutting through the gardens where Bennett's body had been found. Spying the refuse bins at the side, he shook his head. Ingenious, really, transporting a body in plain sight like that.

Standing in the centre of the square, Harry looked up at the apartment block where Bennett had been killed, and shivered. Next to him, King Charles II stared vacantly across the lawn. If only he could tell them what he'd seen. "You're no bloody help," Harry muttered.

On he walked, down Old Compton Street into the heart of Soho. There was Compton's, where he'd met Callum for the first time, where Bennett had been drugged and kidnapped. A blue car, a blond man. Around the back and across the street was the Thai restaurant.

Harry walked down a narrow side street into the road behind. There wasn't much on it, not at this end anyway.

Only delivery access points for the bars and restaurants. This was the Thai restaurant's back entrance, where they took out the trash at the end of the night. There was parking for one vehicle, which was empty. The windows were in darkness. He sighed. Perhaps they'd closed permanently.

Walking round to the front of the restaurant, he saw that there was a light on. The door was locked, and the sign said "Closed". He knocked.

Nobody came.

He knocked again, harder this time. *Come on. I know you're in there.*

Eventually, a cross-looking Asian woman in her mid-thirties came to the door and pointed to the sign. "We're closed."

"Open up. Police." He held up his warrant card.

She looked him up and down, suspiciously. He couldn't really blame her. He was in civilian clothes — jeans and a T-shirt. Not very official.

"DS Malhotra, ma'am. Could I come in? I need to ask you a few questions."

"What about?" She didn't move from the door.

"About an incident that occurred outside your restaurant."

"I've been away. I don't know anything about an incident."

"We know, but I noticed you had a camera above your back exit. Does it work?" He held his breath.

She frowned. "Yes, it's connected to my phone so I can see if anyone tries to break in while we are away."

His pulse leaped. "Excellent. Could I see the footage from last Sunday? It's extremely important."

"Last Sunday?"

"Yes, please."

"Um, I suppose so."

"Great, I'll wait for you to retrieve it from your phone." He leaned against the door frame, arms crossed.

Almost angrily, she pulled the phone from her jeans pocket. "I'm busy, you know. I have things to do."

"The Metropolitan Police appreciate your assistance," he said with a smile.

She grunted in response.

"What time on Sunday you want?"

He gave her the specifics and she found it on the app. "Here, you look."

Harry took the phone from her, his pulse racing. Would he see the murderer? Had they finally caught him on camera?

There was no sound, and the image, although in full colour, was not good quality. Up close, it was perfect, but more than a couple of metres from the back door it was blurry as hell. *Dammit*.

At 9.07 the bar boy, Eric, came out for his smoke. It was raining, as he'd said, and he hovered in the alleyway, the glow from his cigarette a moving orange dot in the darkness.

Halfway through his smoke, two men appeared. Harry stiffened. He recognised them from the bar footage. Bennett in the baggy jeans and checked shirt, stumbling, clearly inebriated. The other man, *the killer*, in a beige trench coat, collar pulled up against the rain, hat in his hand. His arm was around Bennett, supporting him.

Harry stared at the screen on the smartphone. It was too unclear to see the man's features. *Bugger*. He ground his teeth. The man was blond, that much was accurate. His hair flopped over his face, a long fringe obscuring his eyes, making it even harder to identify him. He kept his head down beside Bennett's, almost as if he were murmuring in the man's ear. Coaxing him to the car, which was out of shot, parked further down the road.

He saw Eric glance up, toss his cigarette onto the ground and grind it in with his shoe. Without another look, the kid went back to work.

"Can you send me a copy of this?" The tech guys at work might be able to clean up the image a bit. As it stood, it was impossible to make out the killer's features. They were just a hazy blur.

She shrugged. He gave her his email address and she nodded. The large file would take a while to come through.

Harry thanked her and headed back to his car. So close! He'd really thought he was on to something there, but it might turn out to be another frustrating dead end.

It did back up what Eric had said, however. The image might be grainy, but it wasn't nothing. They might still be able to get something from it.

CHAPTER 34

"Great job," Rob told Harry once he'd showed them the footage. "It's a pity it's not clearer, but at least we know we're on the right track."

Harry gave a sigh of relief. "Maybe IT can clean it up."

"Doubtful," said Will, who knew about these things. "The quality of the camera isn't good enough. You can't get a clean image from a bad camera."

"We won't get an ID off it," Jenny agreed, deflated. "Our facial-rec software won't be able to read it."

"Still, it backs up everything we've been told." Rob refused to be dejected. This was confirmation that their eyewitness accounts were correct. The guy at the bar, his father's, they all tied in. Another layer to build on. Another piece of the puzzle.

"Guv, I've got retired DCI Poulson on the phone for you." Celeste waved the receiver from her desk phone in the air. Poulson had been the SIO in the Alan Clayton investigation.

"I'll take it at my desk."

"DCI Poulson, this is DCI Miller," he said, once Celeste had transferred the call.

"*Retired*, son," came the gravelly response. "Nearly fifteen years now. I believe you want to talk about one of my old cases?" The ex-detective got straight to the point.

"Yes, if you have time?"

"I have nothing but time," came the reply.

Rob smiled. "Okay, great. It happened in 2002. A man was found hanged by his partner, a Mr Felix Hewson. I believe it was ruled a suicide?"

There was a pause as Poulson thought back. "The gay couple? Can I say that nowadays?"

"Yes, sir. You can."

"I remember." There was another short hesitation while he gathered his thoughts. Rob gave him time. "It was one of my last cases. The man hung himself from the banister. Hard to believe it would hold his weight, but it did. He was dressed in some weird getup. Studs and the like. Quite a sight, I tell you. I'll never forget it."

"I'm sure." Rob doubted he would either. "What was your impression? Was it suicide?"

"I can't see how it wasn't," Poulson said. "There was no sign of forced entry, the partner was miles away at a work thing, and the man had some sort of tranquilliser in his system."

That was news.

"Tranquilliser?" Rob frowned. "Do you know what kind?"

"No, I don't remember. It'll be in the case files, though."

"I don't recall a tox report."

"No? Well, I'm sure he'd taken something."

"Did you ever consider foul play?" Rob was reluctant to leave it at that.

"Not after the PM. And there was no motive. The man was well liked, bright, ambitious. A real go-getter. That's what made it so strange, but I guess we all have our demons."

Some more so than others. Rob sighed. He didn't know what he'd hoped to find, but this wasn't it. "Well, thank you for your time, DCI Poulson."

"You're welcome, laddie," he said. "If you don't mind my asking, why do you want to know about that old inquiry?"

"We've had a similar death," Rob explained. "We were wondering if it's related."

"Also suicide?"

"Murder."

There was a pause. "Are you saying that my case twenty years ago wasn't a suicide?"

"I don't know," Rob admitted. "That's what I'm trying to find out."

"Well, it certainly looked like it from where I was standing." After a beat. "The victim's boyfriend never believed it though."

"He didn't?"

"No. He was furious when we dropped the case. Kept insisting it was murder. Said his friend would never have topped himself. He had too much to live for. Yes, that's right. He was about to start some new, high-paid job or something."

"Can you remember what?" Rob asked.

"Sorry, laddie. My memory isn't what it was. It might be in the boyfriend's statement. He called several times, unwilling to let it go. He was a bit of a pain, to be honest."

Rob thought about Hewson with his shoebox of evidence. He may have been a pain, but he also might have been onto something.

"Thanks for your help." Rob wound up the call. "Appreciate you talking to me."

"No problem." Poulson cleared his throat. "Keep me posted, won't you? If that suicide turns out to be a homicide, I'd like to know."

Rob promised he would. The search for the truth never left you, no matter how long you'd been gone.

* * *

"It's weird," Jo said when he got home that evening. "Everyone is acting like nothing happened. It's like Humphries never existed."

"What about the new guy, Hayworth?" Rob asked. "What does he say?"

"Nothing, really. I asked if there was any news on Humphries, but he shut me down. Said he couldn't talk about it. I didn't want to push."

"Probably best not to draw too much attention to yourself." Rob grimaced.

Jo scoffed. "Too late for that." She told him how she'd found out her boss's alibi.

"Holy shit, Jo."

"You wanted proof it wasn't him, I got you proof."

"I know." He didn't know what to say. "I'm grateful, but I didn't want you to risk your job."

"It was a calculated risk, and it paid off. Anyway, I won't do it again."

"Do they know I'm your partner?" Rob asked.

She shrugged. "They must do. They vetted me before I joined the agency."

"I hope it's not going to affect your job, me looking into the case. It could be deemed a conflict of interest."

Her eyes widened. "Crap, I didn't think of that."

Rob put his hand on her shoulder. "It might be better if I didn't discuss the case with you. That way you can deny all knowledge of the investigation."

Jo gave a very unladylike snort. "They wouldn't believe me anyway."

She was probably right.

"Tony came into the office today," he told her after they'd put Jack down for the night. He was sleeping soundly. The weather had been more bearable these last few days, although tomorrow was forecast to be the hottest day in living memory. Thirty-eight degrees. He'd believe it when he saw it. This was England, for goodness' sake. It never got that hot.

"Oh yeah? What did he have to say?"

"He seems to think there's more to the killings than a simple cover-up."

"The flamboyant nature of the crimes does suggest a deep-seated psychological issue," she agreed. "Let's face it, there are easier ways to kill someone if your only aim is to shut them up."

"We're looking into cold cases," Rob told her, as they sat down on the couch. Trigger loped in after them and lay down on his bed.

Jo turned to face him. "You think your killer may have been active all this time?"

"Why not? It's happened before." And she would know. It was her sister who'd been the Shepherd's first victim.

"What does Tony think?"

"That it's unlikely the killer took a twenty-year break. If Alan Clayton was his first victim, he's probably been killing since then."

"You just haven't pieced it together yet."

"Yeah." He leaned back and put an arm around her. "This could be the tip of the iceberg."

"He could have been in prison," Jo said. "That would explain why he's been inactive all these years."

Rob sat up straight, causing Trigger to raise his head too. "You might have a point."

He made a mental note to look into it first thing tomorrow morning. Twenty years? With good behaviour, that was about right for a murder rap.

* * *

"Hey, guv." Jenny glanced up from her computer. "I think I've found a possible."

The team had been trawling through cold cases since they'd got in that morning, and it was now lunchtime. So far, they'd had several maybes, but there was always something not quite right. The MO was off, the murder too messy, the details not thought out.

"What you got?" Rob stretched in his chair. He'd been wrong about the weather. It was a blistering thirty-six degrees and climbing, and it was only midday. Thank God they had air conditioning in here. He felt sorry for the elderly and vulnerable who were more susceptible to heatstroke. The news networks had been warning people to stay out of the sun, to keep hydrated and keep the curtains closed to ward off the worst of it.

"Marius Henning, died from autoerotic asphyxiation in his Kensington home in 2007." Jenny's voice tightened. "Henning was found naked in the bathtub with a ball gag in his mouth and his hands cuffed behind his back. A hypodermic needle was sticking out of his arm, and he had given himself a fatal dose of heroin. The word 'cocksucker' was written in lipstick on his stomach." She exhaled. "It was initially ruled a suicide, but after BDSM paraphernalia and sex toys were found in his house, it was changed to death by misadventure."

"Seriously?" asked Harry. "With 'cocksucker' written on his chest?"

She shrugged. "That's what the report says." Her gaze turned to Rob. "What do you think?"

"'It sounds like they were looking for an easy verdict. Let's look into it again,'" he said. "The drug is different — our killer has used Rohypnol on Bennett and Humphries. But it was fifteen years ago. Maybe he's changed his MO."

"They assumed he'd given it to himself." Jenny scanned the report. "Hence the original suicide verdict."

"Was he a user?" asked Harry. It was a good question. If the victim was a junkie, it was unlikely to be murder.

"Um . . . It doesn't say. I'll look into it." She got back to work.

"I've got to eat something," said Rob. His watch had been telling him to stand up for the last two hours. "Let's break for lunch."

"I brought mine in," Celeste said, barely looking up from her screen.

"I'm meeting a friend in the canteen," Harry said. "Thanks anyway."

Jenny didn't budge.

"I could do with a sandwich." Will shut his laptop. "I'll brave the heatwave with you."

Putney High Street was strangely deserted. There were no shoppers, no bustling mothers with buggies, no teenagers heading for the river.

Will wiped perspiration out of his eyes. "Everyone's indoors," he muttered. It was like a furnace outside.

"Probably sensible." Rob narrowed his gaze. It was almost too hot to keep his eyes open. He wished he'd brought his sunglasses with him. The sky, impossibly blue, was criss-crossed with fading vapour trails caused by jets whisking holidaymakers off on their annual vacations. There was no breeze, which didn't help.

"We still haven't found the proof that Hewson mentioned," Will said, inevitably bringing the conversation back to the case.

"I'd pay good money to find out what it was."

"I've been through the contents of that shoebox with a fine-tooth comb," Will grumbled. "The only thing that's a bit strange is a ticket to some bar or club. It's pretty faded, so I've sent it to the tech department to see if they can get anything off it."

Rob remembered Hewson's handwritten note.

What about the club?

"Does it say which club?"

"Can't tell. The name's truncated and the print is too faint. There also might be something scrawled on the back. Hewson liked to notate things."

"Chase it up," Rob said. "There must be a reason why he had it in the shoebox."

"Will do."

They bought a sandwich and a cold drink from a local café and debated staying there to eat it.

"It's too bloody hot." Will had gone quite pink. He had the type of skin that burned easily. "Let's go back to the office."

"Agreed."

Taking their food and drink with them, they walked back along the High Street to the intersection with Upper

Richmond Road. Will pressed the button and they waited to cross.

Rob's watch buzzed, and he glanced down to check who was texting.

The light changed. He stepped into the road, head still bowed, reading his message.

A loud screech made him look up just in time to see a white van run the lights and swerve across the junction.

It was heading straight for them.

CHAPTER 35

Rob had often wondered what he might do in situations such as this, but to his horror, he froze. Couldn't move a muscle. He stood and watched the white van barrel through the intersection in their direction.

It hurtled towards them, apparently out of control. Time seemed to slow down. He heard a shout from behind him, the screech of tyres on the asphalt and the heat of the engine as it bore down on him. Somewhere, a light flashed. Bright, but only for a split-second. The speed camera had gone off.

Then, a hand on his arm, a forceful tug, and he was falling backwards onto the kerb. Will had sprung into action.

"Fucking idiot!" the sergeant yelled, as the van righted itself and sped off, leaving a couple of shocked onlookers in its wake.

Rob sat in the gutter, dazed.

"You okay, guv?" Will, who was somehow still on his feet, offered him a hand.

Rob grabbed it and pulled himself up, his legs wobbling. He took a moment to compose himself, then the anger set in.

"What the hell is wrong with that guy? He could have killed us." Would have — if Will hadn't had his wits about him.

"That was close." Will stared after the fleeing van. "I thought it was the end."

Rob turned to face him. "Thanks, mate. I mean it. You saved my life."

"I got a look at the driver," Will said. "I could have sworn he was aiming for you, guv. That van didn't look like it was out of control to me."

Rob, who'd bent over to pick up his lunch, jerked up his head. "You think it was deliberate?"

Will gave a sombre nod. "He was trying to hit you."

Rob felt the colour drain from his face. Someone had just tried to take him out. In Putney High Street of all places, in the middle of the day.

"Who would do something like that?" Will asked.

Cranshaw.

Nah, too risky. The idiot ran a red light. It wasn't Cranshaw's style. Even the goons he hired were smarter than that.

"The killer." He rubbed his back where he'd hit the kerb. "We must be getting close."

"He's getting desperate," Will surmised.

"The camera went off." Rob's brain kicked into gear. "Let's get back to the office and find out who that bastard was. You said you got a look. Would you be able to ID him?"

"Not really." Will gave an apologetic shrug. "I couldn't see into the van, just his hands on the wheel. He was steering towards you, I swear. Not for a moment did he lose control of that vehicle."

Rob gritted his teeth. "Never mind. With a bit of luck, he'll be on camera."

* * *

Back at the office, the team were horrified to hear what had happened. "You should lay a charge," Jenny said. "If it was deliberate, that's attempted murder."

"Maybe. Let's see what we can find on this guy first."

"I'm logging into the traffic database now." Will's hands were flying over the keyboard.

"Do you think it's our killer?" Celeste studied him with worried eyes.

"Could be."

He didn't mention Cranshaw. The others had viewed the interrogation footage and knew about the threat, but since nothing had materialised, it had faded into insignificance. Besides, the National Crime Agency had taken over the investigation into the organised crime group that Cranshaw professed to be involved in. It was out of their remit.

Mayhew came out of her office. "What happened?"

Will gave her the rundown.

"Holy shit. Are you all right?" She looked genuinely concerned.

"Yes, ma'am. Thanks to DS Freemont's quick thinking." It had been the Superintendent who'd texted him as he'd crossed the road, asking for an update.

"If you need some time . . ."

"I'm fine."

"Okay. Well, when you're ready, come and see me in my office."

He gave a nod. There were some things he had to do first.

"Control sent this through from the CCTV camera outside Putney station." Jenny turned her screen towards him. They watched as the nondescript white van, similar to thousands of other delivery vans on the streets of London, ran the red light and swerved across the junction, narrowly missing Rob and Will.

Celeste gasped when Will grabbed Rob's arm and pulled him out of the way. Rob watched himself fall into the gutter, his phone bouncing across the asphalt. It seemed surreal, almost like an out-of-body experience. Too damn close.

Will was right, however. The driver hadn't lost control of the vehicle. His hands were clearly visible adjusting the steering. First one way, then the other. Skilful. Deliberate.

"I've got the shot from the traffic cam," Will announced. He turned his screen so the others could see.

There it was, a moment frozen in time. The second it took for the camera to flash. They could make out the shadowy form of a person behind the wheel, gloved hands, face unfortunately in darkness. But the number plate was clearly visible.

"Got him," said Will.

Will looked up the car on the DVLA database. "It's registered to an Imran Abboud in Hounslow." He looked up. "Should we pay him a visit?"

"Don't have time," Rob said. "Tell Uniform to bring him in. We'll interview him at Putney."

Will nodded and picked up the phone.

"Ma'am." Rob knocked on Mayhew's office door. It was slightly ajar, which was unusual. "You wanted to see me?"

"Yes, Rob. Come in and sit down. Are you sure you're okay?"

"I'm sure." He took a seat opposite her. As usual, her desk was neat and uncluttered. A glass of something that looked like herbal tea steamed on one side of it while she tapped a notepad with her pencil on the other.

She studied him. "Do you think this was deliberate?"

"We've looked at the CCTV footage," he told her, "and the driver appears to be in control of the vehicle. I don't think it was an accident."

"Do you have a lead?"

"Yes, the plates are visible. We've sent a patrol car round to pick the suspect up."

"Good. That's something, at least."

He waited, sensing there was more to come.

"Is this our guy, Rob? Is this our killer?" Her face was pinched into a frown.

He sighed. "I don't know. It's hard to say. It could be. We are making some headway with the case. The killer might be getting desperate."

"You recently testified at Cranshaw's trial," Mayhew said.

Rob sighed internally. He knew where this was going. The Superintendent had watched the interrogation video too, and nothing escaped her.

"You don't think this is retaliation for that?"

He threw his hands wide. "I suppose it could be. I wouldn't put it past Cranshaw, but it doesn't feel like him. It's too visible, too easily traced. The red light, the camera." He shrugged. "He's not that dumb."

"Neither is our killer."

He couldn't deny she had a point there.

The Superintendent pursed her lips, the pencil still tapping softly, grating on his nerves. "I've had an update from the NCA on the OCG."

Rob was amazed at the different trajectories her brain fired on. The organised crime group was yet another angle. "Oh yeah? Any developments?"

"It seems they're still active."

He frowned. "In what sense?"

"There's been a new shipment of trafficked girls. The police raided a brothel in Bermondsey last night and rounded up six female immigrants all under the age of twenty-one. No passports. Same story as before."

"Christ." He'd never forget the squalid conditions of the makeshift brothel they'd shut down last year. The stench, the deprivation, the hopelessness. It still haunted him.

"Who was running it? Not the same guys?"

"A cousin." Mayhew's mouth formed a thin line. "Recently entered the country. For some reason he wasn't flagged at customs."

"Then it's the same organisation bringing them in."

"The crime agency seem to think so." She sighed. "I'll keep you posted."

Rob got to his feet. "Any news from the Security Service on Humphries?"

"The silence is deafening."

He nodded. It was as they'd assumed. The investigation had been shut down, the scandal swept under the carpet. If the Security Service had anything to do with it, Humphries' killer would never be brought to justice.

Jenny was standing at his desk when he got back. "That guy with the heroin needle in his arm, he was a user. There were also several domestic violence reports on file for him and his partner, a woman named Lila Biggens, whose occupation is listed as 'escort'."

"Have you spoken to her?"

"Yeah, she said she was glad he was dead, but denied having anything to do with his tragic passing. She did call him a cocksucker, though."

"Hmm . . . It's probably not related, then."

"That's what I thought, although I did let the SIO know." She paused. "Anyway, so then I looked at the case from a different angle."

Rob arched his brows. "Oh yeah?"

"Remember during the Surrey Stalker investigation, we made the mistake of not checking crimes where arrests had already been made?"

He nodded. They'd almost missed out on the all-important connection that had led to them solving the case because some other poor sod was serving time for the serial killer's first murder.

"Well, I didn't want to do the same here, so I checked for crimes where the culprit had been put away, and guess what?"

"You found a lead?"

"Silas Baxter beat up a transgender woman outside a bar in Camden five years ago. According to his statement, he said that God doesn't make mistakes and that gender is determined at birth. He called the person confused for thinking they could rewrite God's will, and said they had mental health issues. That they needed help."

"So he beat her up?" Harry, who sat nearby and was listening, shook his head. "That's not ironic at all."

"They got into an argument. The victim told him to eff off, and that's when he lost it."

Rob raised an eyebrow. "Okay, so where is this guy now?"

"He was in Wandsworth," she said. "He was released three weeks ago."

CHAPTER 36

Rob had to fight his way through a barrage of reporters to get to the front entrance the next morning. He'd had next to no sleep, thanks to the bloody heat — not a delayed reaction to his near hit-and-run, as Jo had claimed — and was in a stroppy mood. The only good thing about the day was that the heat had broken and it was now cloudy and wet. The nation as a whole had breathed a collective sigh of relief.

"DCI Miller, can you confirm Raymond Humphries was killed by the Soho Killer?"

"Was Raymond Humphries gay, Detective?"

"When are you going to release a statement about Raymond Humphries?"

Bloody hell. He put his head down and marched into the building. "Can't we contain that lot?" he barked at the duty sergeant in the lobby.

The officer in question stood up, uncertainty etched all over his young face.

Rob waved a hand. "Forget it. Just make sure they can't get in."

He took the stairs two at a time up to the third floor, which housed the four Putney-based major investigation squads. As expected, Mayhew was hopping.

"Who leaked it?" Tension radiated off her like a magnetic field.

"I have no idea." He wasn't in the mood to be conciliatory, and made a beeline for his desk and sat down.

"I've had the bloody Home Secretary on the phone. I told her it wasn't us, but I'm not sure she believed me."

"It wasn't," Rob said. "It was probably the family. They weren't happy it was swept under the carpet."

That gave her pause. "Do you think so?"

"That would be my guess."

"Thank God there aren't any photographs." Mayhew calmed down to a simmer. "Can you imagine if that crime scene was all over the news and social media?"

Rob didn't want to. They had photographs, but they weren't about to give them to the press. The Security Service had photographs too, but they'd probably buried them in a warehouse, never to be seen again.

"Do you think it was the wife?" Harry asked, once Mayhew had stalked back to her office. The young sergeant handed him the *Mail*.

"No idea," Rob admitted. He'd said that as a deflection, but realistically, it could have been. "If it wasn't us, and it wasn't the Security Service, then it could well have been Millie or her sister. They're the only other people who know what happened. Maybe they felt justice wasn't being done."

He remembered what Jo had told him. Millie had been devastated that the truth wouldn't come out. He wouldn't blame her if she had spoken to the press. But it was a nightmare for the Home Office, one of their senior officials embroiled in a sex scandal. *MURDERED*, the headlines screamed. The Soho Killer was mentioned.

In the squad room, the phones were ringing off the hook.

"Don't talk to the media," Rob yelled. Not that they needed telling.

In her office, Mayhew was pacing up and down, the phone glued to her ear. With the blinds up, they could see her storming back and forth, her flaming hair catching the light.

"I'm glad I'm not superintendent," Rob said, with some degree of satisfaction. At least he was free to continue with their investigation.

Jenny chose that moment to come in. "For God's sake," she muttered. "It's mayhem out there. Same at Putney."

"What did Abboud say?" Rob asked.

"Not our man."

His heart sank.

"His van was stolen two days ago from outside his house. He's a delivery driver for Amazon."

"Why didn't he report it missing?" Rob growled. "That would have saved us the trouble."

"His visa's expired." She shrugged. "Now he's got Immigration Services on his back too."

"So we're no closer to finding out who ran me off the road."

"Sorry, guv." Jenny sat down at her desk. "I've also put out an APB on Silas Baxter. Patrol is watching his home and Wandsworth Police are on full alert."

"He's on the run," Rob said. "This could be our killer, guys. We've got to find him."

"I'm running his credit cards as we speak," said Harry.

"I'm triangulating his phone signal," Will added, "but it's currently off. Last known location was Tooting Bec, but that was two days ago."

"It's been off since then?" Rob asked.

"Yeah, looks like it."

That was not good. "Okay, let me know if you find anything."

Rob grabbed a coffee and saw Vicky Bainbridge, the press officer, waiting for him by his desk, so he held his phone to his ear and strode past to the incident room. Once inside, he closed the blinds and sat at the table to drink his coffee.

"You okay, guv?" Jenny popped her head around the door.

"Yeah, just taking five minutes," he replied with a grimace. "And avoiding Vicky. She'll want to issue a press release."

Jenny chuckled and left him to it.

The shoebox was still on the table, the contents now photographed and logged. Rob wondered if they'd heard back from the tech guys about the ticket. He texted Will.

"I've just got it back." Will came into the room. "It says, 'Cascades Nightclub. Admit One.'"

"Cascades?" Rob frowned. "Where's that?"

"I'm not sure. I haven't had a chance to look it up yet. But that's not all — there's a telephone number written on the back." He placed a blown-up photocopy of the ticket on the table. The number was now clearly visible.

"It's a landline." Rob felt his pulse accelerate.

"With an old area code." Will paused. "We'll be lucky if it's still operational."

"Why would Hewson write this phone number on the back of a ticket?" Rob scratched his head.

"He didn't." Will gave a slow grin. "That isn't Hewson's handwriting. It doesn't match the other Post-it notes in the shoebox."

Rob paused. "You mean it could be Clayton's?"

"That's my guess."

Rob dived into the box and pulled out everything written by hand. Eventually, he came to a note on a white slip of paper.

Have a good trip. Didn't mean to sulk. Love you. A x

"Alan Clayton," breathed Rob. He laid the two samples side by side. "It matches."

"There must be a reason why Hewson kept that ticket," said Will. He gasped. "Maybe Alan Clayton met his killer at that club."

Rob stared at him. "Like Michael Bennett."

"Just like Michael Bennett. He meets with the killer and for some reason takes down his phone number. Maybe he likes him, maybe he's tempted."

"Whatever the reason, Clayton calls him the night Hewson goes away on business. The killer comes over, drugs the unsuspecting Clayton and strangles him, making it look like a suicide."

"That works," Rob said.

Will slapped his hand down on the table. "That's why Hewson kept the ticket. That was his proof."

Rob scrambled to his feet, spilling most of his coffee. "That telephone number belonged to our killer."

CHAPTER 37

"The telephone number belongs to a Duncan McGregor." Will glanced up from his laptop. "0171 is the old London area code, but the number is still valid."

Excellent. "Do we have an address?"

"Yeah, it's registered to a residence in Marylebone."

"Marylebone?" Rob frowned. That didn't sound familiar. "Where was Alan Clayton living when he died?"

"Hackney," Jenny supplied. "It's in the original suicide report."

"Not exactly close," said Rob, even though he knew it wasn't relevant. There was nothing that said a serial killer had to kill near to where he lived.

Will scribbled the address onto his notepad and tore off the page.

Rob took it from him. "21 St Margaret Mansions, Balcombe Street. Jenny? Let's go."

* * *

St Margaret Mansions was not an apartment block as they'd assumed, but a row of neatly stacked terraced houses on the south end of Balcombe Street. Narrow but tall, they sported four storeys, a basement and a wrought iron Juliet balcony on the second floor.

"Must be worth a bit," Jenny said, staring up at them. "Especially in this neck of the woods."

"Most have been subdivided." Rob walked along the row. "Not number twenty-one though." He pressed the tarnished buzzer beside the shabby blue door. A voice echoed from somewhere within the house. "Coming!"

A few minutes later the door was pulled open by a slim woman in gym clothes holding a yoga mat under one arm. "Can I help you?"

"Hello. I'm DCI Miller from the Major Investigation Team and this is my colleague, DS Bird. Is Duncan McGregor home?"

She scrutinised them through eyes that were too close together, giving her an intense, worried look. "My father died a long time ago."

Rob felt like he'd been punched in the gut. "I'm sorry to hear that. And you are?"

"I'm Sally Davies, but McGregor's my maiden name. Would you like to speak with my mother?"

Perhaps all was not lost. "Yes, that would be great."

"Come on in." She shot them an apologetic grin. "I must warn you, though, my mother is ninety-four years old. I'm not sure how much help she'll be."

They followed Sally down the threadbare hall. The carpets were worn down, the wallpaper peeling in places. The entire house could have done with a revamp. It was bigger than it appeared from the outside, and a narrow staircase stretched all the way up to the top floor. It must be a pain to heat, Rob thought, especially with the cost-of-living crisis.

"Does your mother own the property?" asked Jenny.

"Half. My husband and I bought the other half nearly a decade ago. It seemed silly buying our own place when she was rattling around here by herself."

"She didn't want to downsize?" Rob asked, more to make conversation than anything else.

"We suggested it, but she's lived here most of her adult life. First with my father and then with her second husband, Bob. There are too many memories associated with this house for her to move now."

That was sweet, but also quite sad.

"What's your mother's name?" asked Rob.

"Florence." Sally led them through the house and out into a shady courtyard. "She's through here."

Sitting in a rocking chair next to a rambling rosebush was Florence McGregor. Elegant in a flowing forest-green gown, her hair in a neat chignon, she stared vacantly into space. For a moment, Rob thought they'd come in vain. She didn't appear to have the mental capacity to talk to them.

Then he noticed she was smoking a long, slim cigarette, a cut-glass ashtray balanced precariously on the arm beside her.

"Mummy, these police officers would like to talk to you."

Florence blinked and turned her rheumy eyes towards them. Rob thought he could detect the faintest of sparkles there. "Oh, yes?"

Sally smiled. "I'll leave you to it. I've got to get going."

Rob nodded in thanks. "Mrs McGregor." He moved forward so he was standing directly in front of her. Smoke furled between her wrinkled fingers and floated upwards, mingling with the rambling roses. "We need to ask you about your husband, Duncan."

Her thin, pencilled eyebrows shot up. "Why do you want to know about Duncan? He's been dead for over forty years."

Jenny moved to stand beside him. "We traced a number to this address, in Duncan's name. It relates to a crime committed in 2002."

"Ah, that was the year my second husband, Bob, passed away. I was crazy about him. He had a dicky ticker, you know."

"I'm sorry," Jenny said.

Rob frowned. "So were you living alone then?"

She laughed, which turned into a splutter and then into a cough. Once she'd recovered, she said, "Heavens, no. After Bob died, I had to find a way to make ends meet, so I thought to myself, *Florence, what do you have that others want?*"

Jenny raised an eyebrow.

She chortled. "Rooms."

"Excuse me?" Rob was confused.

"This house has plenty of bedrooms, so I rented them out to students."

Jenny grinned. "I see. That was a good idea. How many students did you have?"

"Oh, I don't know, so many youngsters came and went during that time."

The sinking feeling was back.

"Does the name Alan Clayton mean anything to you?" Rob asked.

She repeated it to herself, took another drag of her cigarette, then shook her head. "No, I can't say that it does." Smoke seeped out of her mouth as she talked. "Did he stay here?"

"No, but he may have known someone who did."

"Dearie, I barely knew all the ones who stayed here, let alone who their friends were."

"Didn't you keep records?" Rob tried to hide his frustration.

"Of course, but I've thrown them away. I stopped taking in lodgers when my daughter and her husband moved in ten years ago. There was no need to keep those old record books."

Bugger. Bugger. Bugger. He saw her point, of course, but those books may have contained the name of their killer.

"You don't have anything else from back then?" Jenny tried. "No photographs, no accounts, nothing?"

A slow shake of the head. "You're a couple of weeks too late, I'm afraid. We cleared out all that stuff. Gave it to that young historian who was tracing his relatives."

"What?" Rob's head snapped up.

"Which historian?" Jenny asked.

"Oh, he was such a nice young man. So well-spoken. What was his name again?" She exhaled, squinting as she did so. "Nope, sorry. It's gone."

Rob leaned forward. "Did he leave a business card? Show you some sort of identification?"

"No, I don't think so." She shook her head, confused.

Rob ground his teeth. "Mrs McGregor, it's vital that you remember his name. Was it Felix Hewson, by any chance?"

Her eyes brightened. "Yes. Yes, I think it was. Felix, that's right. Such a nice young man."

* * *

"I knew it!" Rob felt almost buoyant as they walked back to the car. "That's how Hewson found out who the murderer was. He also traced the telephone number to this address. Something in those documents or photographs Florence gave him revealed who the killer was."

"But where are they?" Jenny paused, her hand on the door handle. "You didn't find anything like that in his house."

"Maybe the killer took it with him. Yes! That's it. Somehow, the killer cottoned on to what Hewson was doing and paid him a visit. He stole the damning evidence and killed him."

Jenny gasped. "Before Hewson could tell Humphries what he knew."

They got into the car. "It could have been after," said Rob. "Hewson spoke to Humphries several times in that last week, remember."

"That's why Humphries had to die," said Jenny.

They stared at each other.

"It makes sense," she whispered, her hand on the seat belt.

Rob started the car. "It does."

* * *

"What about Michael Bennett?" Will asked. They'd piled into the incident room, where Rob and Jenny had updated them on the latest findings. "Where does he fit in?"

"I didn't say it was a perfect theory." Rob twiddled the whiteboard marker between his fingers.

"Okay, let's think about this. We know Hewson found out who the killer was," said Jenny. "Maybe he went to Bennett first."

"But they didn't know each other," pointed out Harry.

"Just because we couldn't find a link doesn't mean they didn't know each other." Jenny glanced at Rob.

He sighed. "It's possible. It still doesn't explain why Bennett was the first to die though."

"Let's assume for a moment that they did know each other," Jenny said. "And the killer found out. He could have killed Bennett as a warning to Hewson."

"Pretty stark warning," said Will.

"Then the killer goes after Hewson," Jenny continued. "Hewson tells the killer, probably under duress, that he spoke to Humphries, so the MI5 section chief becomes the next target."

Rob exhaled. "What do we think? Are we completely off base here, or is this within the realm of possibility?"

There was a pause while everybody contemplated it.

Eventually, Harry spoke up. "There's one thing I don't understand. Why the elaborate crime scenes? Why dress the victims up in bondage gear? Why whip them? It's all a bit OTT."

"Perhaps that's to throw us off the scent," said Rob. Harry had a valid point, but he wasn't ready to give up on their newfound theory just yet.

"You mean this may have nothing to do with homophobia?" Will said. "The killer wasn't trying to punish his victims, or to make a statement — he just wants us to think he does?"

Rob threw the marker pen onto the table. "I don't know. That's the only bit that doesn't add up."

If their theory was right, it meant Tony had been wrong, and he'd never known his friend to be wrong about a serial killer before. Ever.

CHAPTER 38

"Guv, Silas Baxter just used a credit card in a pub in Clapham," Jenny called from her desk. "The local CID are heading there now to pick him up."

"Good." He turned to face her. "Do we have a picture of this guy?"

"Only a mugshot." She texted it to his phone.

Rob pulled it up. Slender, dark hair, average height. "He doesn't look anything like the man in the surveillance footage."

"Not in that shot he doesn't," said Jenny. "But picture him with blond hair, a trench coat and a cap."

"I suppose so." Rob tilted his head to the side. He was the right shape and size. With blond hair, it could be him.

* * *

Silas Baxter was picked up and taken to Wandsworth police station, where he was cautioned. By the time Rob and Jenny got there, he'd worked himself up into an indignant rage.

"Why am I here?" he demanded.

"We want to ask you about your whereabouts over the last couple of days," Rob explained.

The ex-con's expression turned dark. "I ain't done nothing wrong. I've just got out of prison, for fuck's sake."

"Then you haven't got anything to worry about."

Silas glared at him.

"Where were you on the evening of Sunday the third of July?"

"I don't know. The pub, probably."

"Are you sure you weren't in Soho?"

Silas frowned. "Why would I have been there?"

"A man was murdered in Soho on Sunday night." He slid a photograph across the table. Michael Bennett in situ.

The ex-con recoiled in shock. "What the—? You think I did that?"

"Did you?" asked Rob.

"Jesus. You ain't pinning that on me! That's sick."

"It's a hate crime," said Rob. "This man was gay. You have a thing against people who identify as gay or transgender, don't you, Silas?" He was baiting him, hoping to get a rise.

It worked. "I don't have anything against them. They can do what the fuck they like."

"That's not what happened outside the bar in Camden, is it?"

"That was five years ago. I've learned from my mistakes."

"That's not what we heard," Rob said.

Silas glared at him. "You heard wrong."

"What about Angelo Reynolds?"

The man scowled. "How d'you know about that?"

"It's in your prison record. You assaulted Angelo while you were inside. You gave him a black eye and a broken rib."

"That guy was a freak," Silas said with a snort. "He was having some sort of hormone therapy to turn him into a woman. Who does that?"

That hadn't been in the report. "Is that why you decided to beat him up?"

"I knocked some sense into him. That's what my father would have done to me if I'd said I wanted to be a girl."

That explained a lot.

"Did he?" Rob asked.

"Did he what?" Silas was momentarily confused.

"Did he beat you because you wanted to be a girl? Or because you were interested in men?"

"Wait — now hang on a minute." Silas stood up. "Who said I was interested in men?"

"Sit down, Silas."

Silas clenched his fists. "I'm not gay, okay, and I'm not a transvestite, or whatever you call it, either. I like women. End of." He sat down again, red in the face.

Rob glanced at Jenny. This guy wasn't their killer. He wasn't smart enough. There was no way Silas could have planned and executed those murders. This was a waste of time.

Jenny gave a tiny nod. She felt the same way.

"Interview terminated at 10.17 p.m."

Silas glanced from Rob to Jenny and back again. "What's happening?"

"It's over, Silas. You're free to go."

"Really?"

Rob was betting life hadn't been kind to Silas. He didn't get many breaks.

"Yeah, you be good now."

Silas was smiling when they left the room.

* * *

"He could have been lying," Mayhew argued, once Rob got back to the office. She'd watched the broadcast on her computer via the live feed.

"I don't think so," Rob countered. "Silas doesn't fit the profile. He's brash and impulsive. The killer is cool and calculated. Silas has a temper. Our killer calmly executes everything according to a plan. I just can't see it. I'm sorry."

She shrugged. "Okay, if you're sure."

"I'm sure."

"So, what now?" She fixed a worried gaze on him. It wasn't often he saw Mayhew at a loss.

"I don't know." He was tired. It had been a long day. "But I'm going home. We'll start afresh tomorrow morning."

Mayhew nodded. "Fair enough."

He knew she was desperate for a result. She'd fended off the Mayor and the Security Service, but now she needed them to deliver.

* * *

"The problem is we have no leads," he told Jo later that night as they lay in bed.

She snuggled up to him. "What does Tony think?"

"I haven't run these latest developments by him yet." To be honest, he'd been putting it off for fear of being shot down. Tony had been adamant, like Jo, that there was a psychological angle to this.

She put her arm over his chest. "It would help if you could find the connection between Hewson and Bennett. That would make your theory more plausible."

"We're looking, but we haven't found anything to link them. Apart from Hewson calling Humphries, there's nothing."

"What about school, university, their early careers?"

"It's possible. We'll have to look again."

"Sounds like you've got some police work to do, DCI Miller."

He couldn't resist giving her a squeeze. "It's obvious you're the brains in this partnership."

She laughed. "As long as we're clear on that."

They were just drifting off to sleep when Rob's watch buzzed on the bedside table. Jo groaned and buried her face in his shoulder.

He reached for it, knocking his glass of water onto the carpet. "Shit." He grabbed his watch and phone before they got wet. "I need a towel or something."

"Answer it." Jo got up, darted into the bathroom and came back with a small hand towel, which she used to mop up the water.

"Hello," said Rob, feeling like the clumsy oaf he was.

"Is that Rob Miller?"

Official. Serious. Too serious.

Rob sat up, fully alert. "Yeah, who wants to know?"

"This is Dr Mason from Charing Cross Hospital. Are you Ronald Miller's next of kin?"

Rob's heart skipped a beat. Had something happened to his father?

"I am."

"Your father has been brought into A&E."

His mind whirled. "Why? Is he okay?"

"I'm afraid not. He's been assaulted. We don't know the extent of the damage yet."

"Is he all right? I mean . . . Can I speak to him?"

Jo stood by the bed, her hand on his shoulder.

"He's unconscious, and he's got a bad bump on the head, along with some other injuries. We're going to take him for some x-rays. Is there any way you can get down here?"

"Yes, of course. I'm on my way. How did you know to call me?"

"There was a photograph of you in his wallet. It had your name and number on the back."

CHAPTER 39

Rob strode into A&E at Charing Cross hospital and was immediately stopped by the duty nurse. "Excuse me, sir. You can't go through there."

The waiting room was filled to capacity, sick and injured people leaning against the walls or sitting on the floor. A drunk man was badmouthing the other receptionist while holding a bloody cloth to his head. Another woman was coughing so hard she had to go outside.

Rob flashed his ID badge and she took a step backwards. "Oh, I'm sorry, officer."

Giving her a friendly nod, Rob marched through the interconnecting door into the bowels of the emergency ward. As was the case in all big hospitals, every cubicle was occupied. Frantic nurses and junior doctors raced around, pens behind ears, clipboards in hands, frazzled expressions on faces.

Suddenly, his job didn't seem quite so frenetic after all. He walked up to the curved reception desk, where an administrator was tapping away at a computer. Behind him a monitor beeped, while the two phones on the desk next to him rang unanswered.

"Excuse me," Rob said. "I'm looking for Ronnie Miller."

The man glanced up. "And you are?"

"I'm his son."

"Can I see some ID?"

Rob showed him his warrant card.

The man didn't react. "Cubicle eight. Down the hall on your left."

Rob drew back the curtains, steeling himself for the worst. It was bad, but not as bad as he'd been expecting. Ronnie was bruised and battered. He had a swollen jaw, a black eye, a crusty wound on his temple and was connected to various machines, but he wasn't in any danger of dying. At least, Rob didn't think so.

A nurse walked in. "Oh, I didn't realise anyone was here. Are you a relative?"

"Yes, I'm his son."

"Your father's been attacked," she said, stating the obvious. "We're preparing him for x-rays now."

"How is he doing?"

"He's a tough old boot, isn't he?" She smiled. "To take a knock like that at his age and keep on ticking."

"That he is."

"He'll have a concussion," she advised, "and possibly some broken bones, but nothing that can't be fixed."

She was very chipper for this late at night, or was it early morning? He'd left his watch by the bed. "Thank you—" his gaze dropped to her nametag — "Bertha."

Another grin. "If you'd like to wait outside, I'll let you know when he's back."

"Sure. No problem."

He took a chair opposite the nurses' station and watched as patients were wheeled in and out, as paramedics signed over their charges to the A&E nurses and went back out into the fray, as doctors appeared, checked over the maimed and wounded, then disappeared again only to come back a short while later. Despite the apparent chaos, it ran like a well-oiled machine.

Twenty minutes turned into forty-five. Rob texted Jo to give her an update and got a thumbs up in reply. She was probably half-asleep. He leaned back and closed his eyes.

"Mr Miller?"

"Huh?" He sat up, dazed. The fluorescent light was overly bright.

"Your father's back."

Bertha's face smiled down at him. "He's conscious now, if you want to have a quick word, although we've given him some strong painkillers."

"Anything broken?" Rob got to his feet.

"I'm afraid so. His jaw is fractured in three places and will need surgery. He's got two broken ribs, which are causing him a lot of discomfort, and a mild concussion."

Bloody hell. "Is that all?" he joked, not very cheerfully.

She smiled at his attempt to be light-hearted. "He's lucky. It could have been a lot worse."

Magnus Olsen. Or rather, his thugs. Rob sighed. Ronnie's gambling addiction was going to get him killed. Sooner or later, they'd realise he couldn't pay them back, and then it would be game over. There'd be no point in letting him live. This was a warning.

"Dad, it's me, Rob. You okay?"

His old man opened one eye. The other was swollen shut. "I know my own son." His words were slurred, like he was drunk, but it was because he couldn't open his mouth properly.

Grumpy as ever. That was a good sign.

"What the hell happened to you? Do you know who did this?"

He shook his head. "Didn't see 'em. Hit me from behind just as I was leaving the pub." Saliva ran out the corner of his mouth. Rob resisted the urge to wipe it away.

"The pub?" He frowned. "Did you get into an argument with anyone?" His father could be cantankerous at times.

Ronnie coughed, then groaned and clutched his side. "Fuck, that hurts."

"You've got two broken ribs," Rob told him. "It's going to hurt for a while."

"Bastards." He tried to sit up but failed and fell back against the pillow.

"Was it more than one guy?"

He shrugged. "Don't know. Got hit on the head, then everything went black. When I woke up, I was in here." He waved a weak arm around.

"Do you think it was Magnus's men? Nod if it's a yes." He could see it hurt his father to talk.

His old man's eyes darkened. He shrugged and winced. "Dunno."

Rob scowled. "This is serious, Dad. If it was his guys that attacked you, you must let me know. We'll file assault charges."

Ronnie stared at him. "I. Don't. Know." He spoke slowly, taking his time with each word. More dribble ran down his chin. "Didn't see 'em."

Rob sat down on the edge of the bed and stretched his neck. Damn, he was tired. Perhaps he was just looking for someone to blame, when really, Ronnie was his own worst enemy. You couldn't expect a leopard to change its spots. Fuck with a loan shark like Magnus, and you get what's coming to you. Still, he couldn't let it go. "Which pub was it?"

"The Black Lion."

He didn't know it, but then Camberwell wasn't and never had been one of his regular haunts. "Who called the paramedics?"

Ronnie shrugged. His good eye was closing now too, so Rob patted him on the arm and let him doze. The painkillers were kicking in.

He put the same question to the ward administrator, who blinked several times, then rifled through a stack of forms on his desk. "Mr Ronald Miller. Here we go. A lady called Angela Dewberry made the 999 call. Pub landlady, apparently."

"Thank you. I'll be back later to see how he's getting on."

"He'll have been admitted by then," the man said. "You'll have to go through the main hospital reception. They'll know which ward he's been taken to."

"Oh, right. Thanks."

The man nodded and went back to his computer screen.

Rob left, sidestepping two paramedics wheeling a young man in on a stretcher. Stab wound. Lower abdomen. His clothing was saturated with blood. It didn't look good.

A small frenzy ensued as nurses and doctors rushed to help. The NHS at its finest.

Rob left them to it.

* * *

"Angela Dewberry?" Rob asked the middle-aged, weathered-looking woman behind the bar. It was late, well after closing, but a few stragglers were still finishing their pints, unwilling to go home and face reality.

"You a copper?" she asked.

He smiled wearily. "What makes you say that?"

"Can smell 'em." Her eyes crinkled. "You here about that old gent? The one who got beaten up outside?"

"That's right. I'm his son."

"Oh." She frowned. "I'm sorry, I thought . . ."

"I'm also a copper." He showed her his warrant card.

She grinned. "Good to know I haven't lost my touch."

"Can you tell me what happened?"

"Not really. There was a commotion outside and some of my regulars went to check it out. As soon as we saw him lying there, we called the emergency services."

"I see. Thanks for that."

"How's he doing?" She leaned forward on the bar.

He grimaced. "Not great, but he'll mend."

She gave a knowing nod. "Fancy a pint? Or a shot of something stronger?" It was the end of the night, and she was winding down.

"Sure, why not?" He wasn't on duty, and after the day he'd had, he needed a drink. "Whisky, please."

"Man after my own heart."

She poured them each a finger and came round to sit beside him.

"Does he come in here often?"

"Ronnie comes in here once or twice a week. He chats to some of the other locals, is always polite to the bar staff and heads home at closing — if a little unsteady on his feet." That savvy look again. Rob was betting Angela had seen it all before, and then some.

"Tonight was the first time I've seen him in any trouble," she added.

"What makes you think he was in trouble? Did something happen during the evening?"

"No, it was much earlier, before he came in. A couple of guys accosted him at the door. They had words. I didn't see much, except it didn't look friendly. Ronnie barged past them, straight to the bar. Ordered tequila. He never drinks tequila. That's how I knew he was rattled."

"How many guys?"

"Two. Mean-looking fellas."

Magnus's men.

"Were these the same guys who beat him up?" Rob asked.

"Now, that I can't tell you. Didn't see the assault. By the time we got outside, it was over. Ronnie was on the ground, out cold. That's when we called the ambulance."

"Nobody saw who beat him up?"

"You can ask, but I don't think so."

"Anybody here from earlier?"

"No, sorry. You'll have to come back. Buck and Dave, they're the two who ran outside. They're in here most nights."

He nodded. "Any CCTV?"

She shook her head. "Not in the pub. We haven't got there yet. You could try the Plough up the street. They have all the latest gadgets."

"Thanks, Angela." Rob downed the whisky. "You've been extremely helpful."

"You're not like most coppers." Her eyes twinkled.

"I'm not on duty."

"Ronnie's son, you say?"

"Yeah."

"I didn't take him as having a detective for a son."

He sighed. "It's a long story."

She patted his arm. "It always is." Getting to her feet, Angela picked up the empties. "You take care now. Hope you catch the bastards who did this."

"I'll certainly try."

Next stop, Leicester Square.

CHAPTER 40

Harry Malhotra met the contact in a secluded spot on Clapham Common shortly before midnight. In a dark hoodie pulled up over his head, weathered jeans and trainers, Harry looked like any other dodgy youth looking to score.

Tall trees cast long shadows across the grass, blocking out the streetlamps. This part of the park was about as far as you could get from the main path, which sliced through the common and bustled with teenagers and partygoers taking a shortcut to Clapham High Street and Northcote Road.

Harry couldn't see the dealer, so he stood under the trees waiting. He hoped the guy wasn't going to stand him up.

"Awright. You Harry?"

Harry spun around. Bloody hell, the geezer had snuck up on him.

"Yeah. Bumper?" Minor drug dealer, reformed addict and confidential informant to SCD9.

"Yeah. Let's get on with it, mate." The dealer's eyes darted around, peering into the shadows, constantly moving. "I don't want people to know I'm talking to the Old Bill."

"Relax. I'm just another customer."

A snort, then a nod of approval. "Yeah, you're better than most. I'll give you that."

Harry prided himself on his ability to blend in. As a kid, he'd been one of six, and if you didn't fit in, you got left out. He did it almost unconsciously, adapting his looks and personality to suit a scene, to become anonymous or to stand out. It had always been his special skill.

"Listen, I'm looking for information. I want to know who's supplying Rohypnol in Soho."

"Roofies?" Bumper's face creased, puzzled. "Prescription drugs are all online now, mate. Nobody buys roofies or GHB on the street anymore."

"You're kidding?"

"Nah, it's not worth the hassle. What's the point getting burned for it when you can do it anonymous, like?"

Harry blinked into the darkness. "But how?"

"Simple, mate. The dealers take the online orders, package the drugs and ship them within twenty-four hours. Door to door, using your friendly neighbourhood postie."

"You're joking."

Bumper shook his head.

Was it really that easy to get your hands on prescription drugs these days? "So how do I go about finding these online dealers?"

"You don't, that's the whole point."

"What if I wanted to buy prescription drugs?"

"Ain't you heard of Google? Might be best to delete your search history afterwards, though, eh?" He chuckled, a deep, hollow sound.

Harry stared at him. "You're serious?"

Bumper gave him a hard look. "That's how it's done these days."

Bloody hell. What was the world coming to? "What about impulse buys?"

"Prescription drugs are a different kettle of fish," Bumper said. "They're not like coke or ecstasy that you buy at a club. These users are full-time addicts. They plan ahead. Make sure they have enough supply."

With a sinking heart, Harry realised this was a dead end. He'd never find the right site or get them to talk to him. And even if he did, there was no way of tracing the shipment. No address. No nothing. The entire process was completely anonymous. *You don't, that's the whole point.*

"Okay, thanks for your help."

Bumper gave a quick nod. "Be seeing ya."

He slunk back into the shadows as quickly as he'd appeared.

* * *

"I have no idea what you're talking about," the Scandinavian loan shark insisted, stony-faced.

Nice try.

"Let's cut the crap," Rob said. The whisky had lit a slow-burning fuse inside him, and he'd had just about enough of Magnus Fucking Olsen and his lies. "I know your thugs spoke to Ronnie earlier this evening." It was yesterday now. "Half the pub saw them."

Magnus shrugged. "So what? He's late on his first payment according to the schedule *you* set up."

Rob grimaced. How he longed to bury his fist in the sanctimonious bastard's smug face. Still, his training had kicked in and he remained cool.

"If you beat him up, he's not going to be able to pay, is he?"

Magnus got to his feet. The men were roughly the same height. "I told you, I didn't send my men to beat him up. They had a chat, that's all."

Bloody liar. Problem was, he couldn't prove it. Yet.

Rob fished in his pocket and pulled out a wad of bills. "Here, this is Ronnie's first payment. You won't be getting another one from me, but this is so you can call off the dogs. I told you if anything happened to Ronnie, I'd come looking for you."

Magnus took the money. "Glad to see you're stepping up, Detective." His face twisted into a grin. "Tell Ronnie we say hi."

His fist itched, and he almost gave in to the urge to retaliate.

Breathe. He's not worth it.

Rob spun around and stalked out. If Magnus had been responsible for his father's assault, he would pay. Rob would make sure of it.

CHAPTER 41

"Sorry about your father," Jenny said.

Rob was late in and feeling rather frazzled. Tanya had called in sick. Apparently her cat had died. This had thrown the tiny household into disarray. Jo had had to call her boss and tell him she needed to work from home. Luckily her operation wasn't at a crucial stage, otherwise she'd never have been able to look after Jack too.

As it was, Rob had fed and settled their son before he'd left the house, and had promised to go home early and take over so she could finish up in peace. It was crazy how one dead cat could have had such a dramatic impact on their lives.

"How's he doing?" asked Harry.

"As good as can be expected." Rob had stopped by the hospital on his way to work, just long enough to make sure his father was okay and hadn't deteriorated overnight. He was still in a lot of pain and morphed up to the eyeballs. Very little sense had come out of his mouth, other than rage towards those who'd done this to him. "Cowardly fuckers," had been the main gist of the slurred conversation. "Couldn't even look me in the eye before they coshed me."

Rob had left as his father had been wheeled into surgery. The doctor had said he'd need a couple of plates in his jaw and would be eating out of a straw for a while. Well, a liquid diet had never been a problem for his old man.

God, when had he become so cynical?

He sat down at his desk. It was only eleven o'clock, but it felt more like two in the afternoon. "What's the latest? Do we need a briefing?"

Harry shrugged. "Not much on my side. My contact told me most prescription drugs are ordered online nowadays. Dealers send it to your home address, no questions asked."

"Really?" Rob raised an eyebrow. "No checks, nothing?"

"Minor checks," said Will, who'd been looking into it. "Name, address, reason for purchase. Nothing you can't get around if you know what to say. It's mainly for their records."

"No prescription?" asked Rob.

"Nope." Will grimaced.

"Bloody hell. Are these sites legal?"

"It's a grey area. It's illegal to sell medicinal drugs to people without a prescription in this country, but that doesn't include websites based abroad. The Medicines and Healthcare Products Regulatory Agency only has jurisdiction over UK sites."

"So these are foreign sites?"

"Mostly, but there's another loophole," Will explained. "For prescription medication, you can just see an online doctor. This means that a quick virtual consultation can make a dodgy transaction legal."

"They do that?"

"Apparently so. Whether you're speaking to a medically qualified doctor or not, who knows. It's what it says on the website. All part of the service."

"What about the drugs themselves?" asked Jenny. "Are they the real deal?"

"There are scams, of course," Will said. "Users run the risk of buying counterfeit products that may be dangerous."

Celeste shuddered. "People must be desperate to take that risk."

"Yep." Will nodded. "Some people will do anything to get their fix."

"Right, so where does this leave us?" asked Rob.

"Nowhere, really," Harry said forlornly. "There are no contact details on the websites, and even if we did manage to speak to someone, they wouldn't divulge their customers' personal information. Even if they could be persuaded to, we don't have any way of identifying the guy we want."

"Shipped to Soho?" said Rob.

"Or not, as the case may be." Will shrugged. "He's not going to use his own address, is he?"

"I suppose not."

"The PO box could be anywhere," Harry agreed. "Who knows how long he's been planning this? There are dozens of online pharmacies and thousands of customers. It'll be like looking for a needle in a haystack."

Rob sighed. "Yeah, okay. Forget it. Our resources are spread thin enough already. We need another way of tracing this guy. Where are we on the victims' backgrounds?"

Celeste perked up. "I've noted everything I can find on all four victims." She swivelled around in her desk chair. "Bennett was in recruitment before he quit to be a househusband. He worked for a firm called Top Class Recruitment. It does a lot of international placements, law enforcement positions, government agencies, that sort of thing."

"Okay, that's interesting," said Rob.

"Felix Hewson was a medical sales rep. He travelled a lot in the early days, when he was living with the very first victim, Alan Clayton, but then he got a managerial role and settled down. He was with that company for fifteen years before moving to GlaxoSmithKline in a sales manager capacity, which was where he was working when he died."

"I'm not sure how that's relevant. But anyway, who's next?"

"Humphries worked for the government all his adult life. Recruited out of Cambridge, he went to work for the NCA before moving to MI5. He moved around in each agency, but his job titles were not always clear-cut. According to LinkedIn, he'd been an analyst, a line manager, a department head and a section chief."

Rob sniffed. "Typical government roles. They tell you absolutely nothing about what the person does."

"I can't find any connection between those three," Celeste said. "Unless you assume that Bennett placed Humphries in a job. That could be. Both the NCA and the Security Service are clients of Top Class Recruitment."

"Is that a fact?" Rob stroked his chin. "What about GlaxoSmithKline?"

"Afraid not. I called and checked."

"What about Alan Clayton?" asked Harry.

"He studied psychology at Surrey University," Celeste explained. "Got a first in behavioural science. His first job was for the Prison Board, where he assessed whether prisoners were fit to stand trial."

"Now that is interesting." Rob frowned. "Remember Judith Walker, the victim in the Box Hill investigation? We initially thought she'd been murdered by a prisoner she was assessing. Someone who held a grudge against her."

"True." Will sat up straight. "Should we look into who he was working with?

"It was twenty years ago," said Jenny. "Will those records still be on file?"

"See what you can find," Rob told Celeste. "I know it's a big ask, but there might be some information out there."

She nodded.

"And call HR at both the NCA and the Security Service. I know they're tight-lipped, but we need them to verify whether Humphries was placed by Bennett. That might be how they knew each other."

"Yes, guv." She swivelled back around and got to work.

"Bingo," she called, a short while later. "Bennett was the agent who placed Humphries at the National Crime Agency. They've confirmed it."

"And we're sure he didn't place Hewson at GSK?"

"No, he'd retired by then."

"Okay, well that's good work. Thanks, Celeste."

She glowed under his praise.

* * *

The surgical operation went well. Ronnie was sitting up, sipping water from a straw, when Rob got back to the hospital. On the way, he'd called Jo to let her know he'd be home soon, but she hadn't picked up. With a live op on the go and a baby to look after, he wasn't surprised.

"We put two plates in his jaw," the surgeon told him when he arrived, "but there's nothing we can do for the broken ribs and concussion. He'll just have to rest."

"Are you keeping him in?"

"One more day," the surgeon said. "Then he can continue to recover at home. Is there someone who can check up on him?"

Rob hesitated. "Yeah, I can."

"Good. He'll be tender for some time, but he should make a full recovery." The surgeon left.

"Do you remember anything from that night?" Rob perched on the end of Ronnie's bed. His father was in a general ward with four other patients, most of whom had the curtains drawn around their beds for a modicum of privacy.

The hospital had a soundtrack all of its own. Beeping monitors, hissing machines, the chatter of nurses and the hushed voices of concerned relatives. It was constant and relentless. Every now and then there was a groan or a yelp as a pain threshold was reached.

"No, I told you, they hit me from behind. Bastards." His voice was less slurred now, although Rob could see it still hurt to form the words.

"Dad, do you think this was Magnus's men?"

A scowl. "Nah. I spoke to them earlier that night. Why would they warn me then beat me up a couple of hours later? Doesn't make sense."

It didn't. And it backed up what the landlady had said.

"Okay, so if we rule out Magnus's guys, who else is there?" Who else had his father pissed off?

"I don't know."

Rob sighed. He was about to say something else when his watch buzzed. He had a call. "Sorry, I'd better take this."

He got up but didn't leave the cubicle. "Tony, hey. Now's not the best time."

"Just calling to find out how the case is going," his friend said.

"We haven't made much progress, to be honest," replied Rob.

"I heard you arrested someone?"

"Oh, yeah." He'd almost forgotten about Silas. "We had to let him go. Wasn't our man."

"That's a bummer."

"Yeah, listen, can I call you back? I'm just at the hospital with my dad."

"Your dad? Shit, what happened?"

"It's a long story. I'll tell you later."

"Sure, no problem. Hope all is well."

"Thanks, mate."

He hung up.

"Who's that?" asked Ronnie.

"Tony Sanderson. My mate, the criminal profiler. You won't remember him."

Ronnie cleared his throat. "I remember Tony. Drove a hot hatch. Peugeot 306 GTi. Flashy car for a student. Studied at Birkbeck, didn't he? Used to hang out with you when you were at the academy."

Rob raised a surprised eyebrow.

Ronnie smirked. "I haven't completely lost the plot, not just yet."

Then again, it was the car he'd remembered.

* * *

Rob tried Jo again. No answer. Never mind, he was about to leave the hospital anyway.

Will rang as he was crossing the road to where he'd left his car. Charing Cross Hospital was on busy Fulham Palace Road, so he'd parked down a side street, his police permit on display. Even so, he'd been issued with a parking fine.

Grunting in annoyance, he snatched it off the windscreen and shoved it in his pocket.

"Guv, remember the vehicle parked behind Compton's Bar in Soho? Well, Control have been trawling through CCTV footage and they've got a blue Ford Fiesta exiting Dean Street into Shaftesbury Avenue on the night of the murder."

He froze, his fingers on the door handle. "What time?"

"Nine twenty-seven," came Will's steady voice.

"It fits."

"Yeah, I know. We've managed to get a partial number plate from the CCTV, but there's a taxi blocking the other half. I'm running it now."

"Okay, I'm heading back to the office. See you soon."

* * *

Rob finally got hold of Jo. "Something's come up. Are you okay for a while longer? I'm sorry, but we might have found our guy."

"I'm good," she said. He could hear by her voice that she was exhausted. A twinge of guilt gripped him.

"You sure?"

"Jack's gone down for a nap, so take your time. I've signed off for the day, anyway."

"What about the op?"

"I've passed it on to someone else to manage," she said. "There's nothing happening at the target's house and there's unlikely to be any further movement today."

"Okay, thanks." It sounded like things were under control. "I'll be home as soon as I can, then I'll make it up to you. I promise."

Her voice softened. "I know you will."

In the background, the doorbell rang. "Sorry, Rob. I've got to go. There's someone at the door. Go catch this guy."

"I intend to."

CHAPTER 42

Rob strode into the squad room. "Any lead on the reg number?"

"I've got a list of 130 registered new blue Ford Fiestas with the four characters LE61." Will handed Rob a sheet of paper.

"Sounds manageable." Rob ran his eyes over the names. Nothing stood out. "Anything flag?" he asked Will.

"Nope. I'm running the names against the National Database to see if anyone's got previous, but so far nothing."

"Good start." He paused, tapping his finger against the back of the paper. "One of these owners is our killer."

"We could remove the women," said Harry.

Jenny was already shaking her head. "The killer could have borrowed his wife's car, his mother's car. In fact, he's unlikely to use his own, don't you think?"

"True, sorry." Harry pouted. "Wasn't thinking."

"We'll go through all of them," Rob said. "Let's divide them up and call every single person on this list and find out where their car was on the night of the Soho killing."

Nods all round. With five of them, it wouldn't take longer than a couple of hours. They got to work.

A short time later, there was a gasp from the vicinity of Celeste's desk.

"Celeste, you got something?" Rob asked.

"Not about the vehicle, but it could be important."

"What is it?"

Her cheeks were flushed. "Remember Felix Hewson said Alan Clayton was going for some big job and that's why he wouldn't have killed himself?"

"Vaguely." The retired DCI had said something along those lines.

"Well, guess what? The big job was for the National Crime Agency." She sat back, her eyes gleaming.

Rob stared at her. "The same place Humphries worked?"

She nodded. "If Clayton hadn't died, they'd have worked at the same government agency."

"Where Bennett placed Humphries?"

"Yep."

There was a pause.

"Did he place Clayton too?" Rob asked, his voice breathy. Could this be the link between them?

"I'll get back onto HR and check."

Rob waited while she made the call.

"Yes. That's right. Okay, I'll hold." She nibbled on her lip.

Rob found he was holding his breath.

"Oh, yes? Perfect. Thank you." She hung up.

Rob raised an eyebrow.

"Michael Bennett placed them both."

"What does it mean?" asked Jenny, who'd overheard the conversation.

"Clayton, Bennett and Humphries all have a link to the National Crime Agency." Rob got up and started pacing. His brain worked better when he was moving. "That could be where they met."

"But what about Hewson?" asked Jenny.

"I don't know. Maybe being Clayton's partner was enough."

"It's possible." Will turned around. "They were living together at the time."

"Did Humphries and Clayton work in the same department? I mean would they have if Clayton had lived?"

"No." Celeste shook her head, making her curls bounce. "Humphries was an agent, while Clayton had a job as a behavioural scientist. He was a psychologist."

Rob stopped pacing. "He was what?"

"A behavioural scientist." Celeste looked up at him.

"Guv?" asked Jenny.

"I . . . I just had a thought."

"Yeah?" They all waited expectantly.

"No, it can't be." He clawed a hand through his hair.

"What?" Celeste asked, glancing worriedly at the others.

"Show me that list of car owners," he rasped.

Jenny reached across her desk to get the printout, then handed it to him. His eyes scrolled down the list.

"Guv, you've gone white." Jenny was staring at him.

"Shit." He prodded a name on the list.

Jenny grabbed it from him. "What? What have you seen?"

He grabbed his jacket and backpack. "I've got to go."

He dashed out of the room, down the stairs, through the lobby and to the car. A million neurotransmitters were firing in his brain.

It's registered to a residence in Marylebone.
The big job was for the National Crime Agency.
He was a psychologist.
They were living together at the time.
There's someone at the door.

Jesus, no.

Rob screeched out of the car park, tyres spinning as they fought for traction. Siren blaring, he roared down Upper Richmond, swerving into the opposite lane to overtake. His car wasn't made for high-speed driving, but he kept his foot glued to the accelerator all the way to Richmond.

Hold it together. You could be wrong.

Except he knew he wasn't.

He studied at Birkbeck, didn't he?
She said it made me look younger.

Everything was adding up. Rob felt sick. Nausea rose, threatening to choke him. The journey seemed to take for ever, but he finally swung into his road. Seconds later, he ramped the pavement outside his house. A black BMW was parked outside.

He went cold. He was too late.

"Jo!" He jumped out of the car and fumbled over the key in the lock. "Jo, are you okay?"

He pushed open the door and almost fell inside. The house was deathly quiet. No Trigger. No baby crying. No Jo.

His heart flipped. *Christ, please let him not have hurt them.*

He raced down the hallway, calling Jo's name. He got a whimper in response.

Heart in his throat, he threw open the door.

A familiar voice said, "Hello, Rob."

Jo sat on a wooden chair, bound and gagged. Her eyes were huge, terrified.

Rob came to a halt, breathing hard. He stared at the man holding a knife to his partner's throat.

"Hello, Tony."

CHAPTER 43

"Don't hurt them," he begged.

His old friend gazed at him through haunted eyes. "I'm truly sorry it's come to this." He sighed and shook his head. "Why couldn't you have charged Silas?"

"Silas?" Then he got it. "You wanted us to find Silas. You sent us in his direction."

Tony smirked. "It was my last-ditch effort to save you. To keep you from discovering the truth."

"Because I didn't fall for your homophobic psycho theory?"

"I hoped you would. I went to great lengths to make it look like a serial killer was at work. Right down to killing Humphries on his anniversary."

Rob frowned. "A serial killer *was* at work."

He snorted. "Touché."

"How did you know it was his anniversary?"

"A lucky coincidence. I was going to kill him earlier. I was right outside his house, waiting for him to get home, but then I heard him on the phone telling his wife he'd taken the day off for their anniversary, so I decided to wait. It couldn't have been more perfect." He let out a soft laugh.

The man was truly diabolical.

"What about my father?" he asked, coldly. "Did you beat him up too?"

"I was hoping it would distract you from the investigation." He shrugged. "But you weren't to be swayed."

Rob clenched his fists. "I'll get you for that."

"No, you won't. I'm afraid you've run out of chances."

Rob suddenly realised how quiet the house was. "Where's Jack?" he asked, his heart pounding. "You haven't hurt him, have you?"

"Don't worry. He's asleep upstairs. I've shut your dog in the room with him in case you're wondering. I'm not a monster."

Relief flooded his body. So much so that his legs gave way. He put a hand out to steady himself. As to whether Tony was a monster or not, that was debatable.

"How did you figure it out?" Tony asked, almost conversationally.

"When we were talking about Humphries, you said, 'With his job, you can understand why he would have kept it secret.' It suddenly struck me that I'd never told you what Humphries' job was. You couldn't have known."

Tony tutted. "How silly of me."

"I don't understand why," said Rob. "Why did you do it? Bennett, Hewson, Humphries. Why did they all have to die?"

"Because they *knew*." His voice dropped to a hoarse whisper. "They knew about Alan."

Rob stared at the man he'd called a friend for over fifteen years and thought how little he really knew about him. His rise to fame had been astronomical. Working with law enforcement, training with the FBI Behavioural Science Unit, writing *Mind Games*, the book that catapulted him to success, sent him around the world.

Then it clicked. "You killed Alan to get the job at the National Crime Agency, didn't you?"

Tony smirked. "I knew you'd figure it out. Too clever for your own good."

"But why?" Taking a life was unfathomable, taking four was insane.

"I needed that job." Tony's gaze drifted to a place beyond Rob, a place in the past. "It launched my career. The first time a national law enforcement agency had worked with a behavioural scientist — whoever got that job would be a pioneer in their field. It had to be me."

"But Alan Clayton got the position."

"Just." Tony's expression darkened.

"So you killed him to put him out of the running?" He shook his head. "Who does that?"

"A psychopath does that, Rob." Tony looked almost exasperated. "I've known I was different ever since I was a little boy. I didn't react to things the way other kids did. I didn't experience . . . emotions like them."

Rob was beginning to understand. "You lacked empathy?"

"Exactly. Do you know what that's like? Not being able to feel anything?"

He could only imagine.

"It's like being dead inside."

Rob studied him, wondering what he'd do next. Jo's eyes were filled with unshed tears. She was usually so strong, so brave. Now she feared for her son's life besides her own. It made her vulnerable. He longed to go to her, to tell her it was going to be all right, but he couldn't.

"It has its advantages, though." Tony snorted. "No remorse. It was a simple matter of making Alan's death look like a suicide."

"That's why you dressed him up in the bondage gear. You didn't just want to get him out of the picture, you wanted to destroy his reputation too."

He scoffed. "The agency rang me immediately to offer me the position. You see, it worked."

"Except his partner, Felix Hewson, never believed it."

Tony scowled. "Felix was a problem, but luckily the police didn't listen to him, so he gave up. No further action needed."

"Until now."

Tony sighed. The blade glistened at Jo's throat. "I didn't want to go there. Unlike some serial killers, I wasn't on a murderous rampage. I take no pleasure in killing."

"No remorse either."

A shrug.

Rob wanted to keep him talking as long as possible. The team might just make the same connection and send someone round to his house. Maybe. He could hope.

"But you went there anyway. You lured Michael Bennett to the bar in Soho. You drugged him, just like you did Alan years before."

Tony's gaze clouded over. "You have done your homework."

"We've got you on CCTV."

Tony looked worried for a second, then he shook his head. "If you had, you'd have picked me up days ago."

He was right. But Rob wasn't done. "You used your daughter's car, the Ford Fiesta, to take him back to the apartment in the square, which you'd rented through a shell company. Then you brutally raped and strangled him."

"Very good." His eyes were hard. "I'm impressed you found that flat."

Rob wasn't about to tell him how he'd found it. Let him wonder. "Why did you kill Humphries?"

"I didn't want to. Humphries was a good man. We worked together at the NCA. He was my boss for a time. Unfortunately, Hewson rang him and told him what he'd discovered."

"About the boarding house in Marylebone."

"Yes, that was a stroke of bad luck. Hewson was like a terrier, he just wouldn't let it go."

"Hewson traced that phone number back to you, didn't he? He investigated your past and realised you'd worked at the NCA. That was the connection. Is that what happened?"

Tony gave a stiff nod. "He spoke to Michael Bennett. Bennett had told Humphries I was in the running, and that when Alan died, I got the job."

"And Bennett told you this?"

"Yes, I forced it out of him before I killed him."

Jo grimaced and turned her head. The blade pressed at the skin of her throat.

"What now?" Rob asked, his gaze on the knife. "Where do we go from here?"

"Unfortunately, this is the end of the line for you, Rob. I can't let you live. Either of you." The tears in Jo's eyes overflowed and ran down her cheeks.

Do something, she begged wordlessly.

But what? If Rob charged him, Tony would slit Jo's throat.

As if reading his mind, Tony said, "Don't do anything rash, Rob. I know you, my friend. You're thinking how you can stop me. Well, you can't. It's too late."

"Please don't hurt them," he pleaded. "Jesus, Tony. This is my family."

"I'm sorry, Rob. Truly." But there was no apology in his gaze. He really didn't have any feelings. How had he never picked up on that before?

"They'll know it's you," Rob tried. "My team, they'll figure it out. They're only one step behind me."

"No they won't, because they can't prove anything. I helped on the case. There's no way anyone but you has figured it out."

"You're wrong," he insisted. "There's your old telephone number."

"Circumstantial." He sniffed. "How many lodgers did the batty old doll have staying there?"

Rob felt a weight descend. Tony was right. It wouldn't stand up in court. There was no forensic evidence.

"We have your daughter's car on CCTV."

"Regrettable, but not insurmountable. She has a friend who lives in Soho. She'll testify she was visiting him at the time. There's not a shred of Bennett's DNA in that car. I've had it valeted." He shook his head. "No, I'm afraid this is going to be a double suicide. Stressed detective kills his family and then himself."

Jo's eyes widened.

A siren could be heard in the distance. Was it his imagination or was it getting louder? "It's them," Rob hissed, taking a chance. "It's over, Tony. Don't do this."

A flash of annoyance. "You're bluffing. That's not for me."

Rob had never prayed so hard in his life. The sirens got closer, shriller. They were coming up his street.

"If you leave now, you can still get away," Rob said, attempting to bribe him with a chance at freedom. Anything to save his family.

"I'm sorry, I can't."

Rob saw the look in Tony's eyes and knew it was now or never. He bolted forward. "No!"

But he was too late. The blade sliced across Jo's throat seconds before Rob barrelled into Tony. They sprawled across the kitchen floor. The knife rose again, but Rob twisted away. It nicked his leg but he barely felt it.

"Trigger!" Rob screamed.

Upstairs there was scuffling and an angry bark. Seconds later, paws could be heard on the stairs, and a furry blur burst into the kitchen. Teeth bared, he went straight for Tony.

Instead of having another go at Rob, Tony jerked back, scrambled to his feet and kicked out at Trigger, who had him by the arm. The dog growled ferociously, hair bristling down his back. Tony backed into the garden, Trigger still attached. With one final kick, he shoved the dog off and slammed the sliding door.

Rob lunged towards Jo, who was as white as the kitchen tiles. Blood was gushing from her throat onto the floor. So much blood. He put his hands over the gaping wound and tried to keep it closed, tried to stem the flow.

"Please don't die," he rasped, while Trigger went mad, pawing at the glass door.

The front door burst open. Seconds later, Jenny and Harry ran into the kitchen.

"Oh my God!" Jenny fell to her knees beside Jo. "Call an ambulance!"

Harry already had his phone out.

The rest was a blur. Someone opened the sliding door and Trigger bolted out after Tony. More uniformed officers raced in, then out again. Rob kept his hands glued to Jo's throat to stop the blood.

"You're not going to die." Tears ran down his cheeks. "I'm not going to let you die."

The paramedics rushed in and took over. Jenny gently pulled him away. "She's in good hands, Rob. They've got her now."

The ground seemed to tilt, and he felt himself falling. Jenny and Harry helped him into the lounge. More voices, but he couldn't hear them over the roaring in his ears. The only thing that penetrated it was Jack's crying. He blinked, and realised his face was wet.

"He's fine." Jenny's voice. "Rob, Jack is fine."

But not Jo.

CHAPTER 44

Five weeks later...

Rob sat on the hospital bed and clutched Jo's hand. He couldn't seem to let it go. After the surgery she'd had a tracheostomy tube inserted, which had only just been removed. She was able to talk properly and eat unaided for the first time in over a month.

Her voice was different. Hoarse and breathy. The doctor said it was because of her paralysed vocal cords. She'd been incredibly lucky.

"You saved her life," the surgeon had told him afterwards, not that it meant anything at the time. He'd been demented with guilt. Apparently, because Tony had pulled her head back before slicing her throat, the major blood vessels had been pushed to the back of her neck, so they hadn't been severed.

He shook his head. "I don't know how I didn't see it."

"None of us did," Jo reassured him. "Not me. Not even his wife."

He arched an eyebrow. "Kim came to see you?"

Jo nodded. "She was beside herself. I asked if she knew that Tony was a psychopath, and she told me she had suspected there was something not quite right. He had this ability to focus for hours and put everything else aside, even his family. They weren't happy, you know."

Rob exhaled. "The worst part is that he was helping us with our investigation. He must have been laughing at me the whole time. I feel like such an idiot."

"You weren't to know."

"Still, I suggested bringing him in. It was my idea to hire him." He scoffed. "Mayhew is livid." As superintendent, she'd also taken a hit.

"How long do you have off?" Jo asked.

He'd taken compassionate leave after Jo had been hurt, but he suspected he'd have been suspended in any case. He'd made a big mistake and was going to pay for it. "As long as I want. Galbraith has taken over my active cases."

She gave his hand a squeeze. "Tell me again how Trigger caught Tony. I love this story."

He managed a small grin. He'd told her once before, but she'd been too out of it to remember all the details.

"It's quite astounding really. He tracked Tony across the golf course, through Old Deer Park and down to the river towpath. A passer-by called the emergency services when they discovered him attacking Tony. They tried everything, even throwing water at him, to get him to release Tony, but he wouldn't let go. It took a police dog handler to get him off."

"Bless." Tears sprang to Jo's eyes. She'd been much more emotional lately, understandably so. Holding Jack for the first time after her surgery had made her cry.

"Tanya's been unbelievable," Rob told her. "She's come every day to help, even though I'm at home. I think she feels bad about letting us down."

"It wasn't her fault. I can't believe Tony went so far as to kill her cat to get her away from the house." Jo shook her head. "But I guess that shouldn't surprise me, knowing he's a psychopath."

"The doctor says you can come home in a couple of days."

Her face lit up. "I can't wait. I miss him so much."

"He misses you too." Although he brought Jack to the hospital to visit her, it wasn't the same as being at home with him. "We both do."

"When's the trial?" Jo asked.

"In a couple of weeks. Jenny interrogated him. I watched the recording, it gave me shivers. He confessed to everything, even renting the apartment in Soho. He talked about it as if he was giving a lecture. No hint of emotion."

"Did he admit to running you off the road?" she asked.

"No, that's one thing he didn't admit to." Neither did he admit to entering the garden the night Trigger had woken Rob up growling. That meant someone else was keeping tabs on him, and someone else had tried to run him down.

Cranshaw.

Except now wasn't the time to tell Jo about that. It could wait until she was stronger. Then he'd have to fill her in. If their lives were at risk, she had a right to know. Never again would he leave her unprepared.

The nurse asked him to leave shortly after that. Jo needed to rest, and they had to do a series of tests before allowing her home. He couldn't wait.

That afternoon, Rob took Trigger for a walk along the river. Tanya was at home with Jack. It was his nap time, and the babysitter had kicked Rob and Trigger out to clean the house. It was a humid, overcast day, the sun constantly darting behind the clouds as if it couldn't make its mind up whether to shine or not.

Trigger bounded along next to him, his tail wagging furiously. Thankfully, there didn't appear to be any lasting effects on him from the trauma. Rob wished he could say the same about himself.

What had happened to Jo would haunt him for the rest of his life. That look in Tony's eyes before he'd slashed her throat. Rob had known it was going to happen and there was nothing he could do to stop it. He'd never felt so powerless in his life.

He kept thinking what he could have done differently. If only he'd seen it sooner. Tony had been manipulating him from the start, trying to dictate the course of the investigation.

He muttered to himself, then shook his head. Nothing sprang to mind. It was Celeste connecting the dots to the National Crime Agency that had given him the first real clue. She was a gem, that girl. He must let Mayhew know she'd cracked the case. Although they'd all done their bit.

Harry had discovered their first lead, the blue car and the blond man. He scoffed. That's why Tony had a brush cut when he'd first seen him. He'd had to grow his hair long for the facade, then chop it all off again to avert suspicion. Another clue he'd missed.

Will had figured out that Hewson and Humphries had known each other and traced the old phone number to the house in Marylebone. Jenny had put it all together and come to his rescue. She'd saved his life, and Jo's. Her and Trigger.

He felt his eyes prickle and blinked angrily. He had to pull himself together. Somehow, he had to get over this.

Kew Bridge loomed ahead, its arches casting dark shadows onto the shimmering silver surface of the river. The tide was coming in, surging around the foundations as the waterline rose.

Rob was always fascinated by how quickly the tide came in. He'd known people who'd parked beside the river only to return from their walk to find their car had vanished, swept away by the current. That's why this section of the Thames was called the Tideway, he supposed.

"Trigger!" he called, as the Lab rushed into the undergrowth at the side of the towpath. A fat rat had ambled across their path, then darted into the foliage. "Leave it alone."

Chagrined, Trigger emerged, a leaf stuck behind his ear.

Why couldn't he be like Trigger? Easily distracted, the drama of the last month already forgotten. He would never be like that. He'd never forget.

"It's how we survive," he muttered to the Lab, who rubbed his leg.

And he'd need all his senses to be firing on high alert for the next few months. Cranshaw was gunning for him, and there was no way he was going to let that fucker win.

He was tired of turning a blind eye. There'd been too many coincidences, too many close calls. If the OCG thought they could keep trafficking underage girls and unaccompanied minors into this country and corrupting the police force, they could think again. He was coming for them.

No more Mr Nice Guy.

THE END

ALSO BY BIBA PEARCE

DETECTIVE ROB MILLER MYSTERIES
Book 1: THE THAMES PATH KILLER
Book 2: THE WEST LONDON MURDERS
Book 3: THE BISLEY WOOD MURDERS
Book 4: THE BOX HILL KILLER
Book 5: THE SOUTH BANK MURDERS
Book 6: THE SOHO KILLER

Thank you for reading this book.

If you enjoyed it please leave feedback on Amazon or Goodreads, and if there is anything we missed or you have a question about, then please get in touch. We appreciate you choosing our book.

Founded in 2014 in Shoreditch, London, we at Joffe Books pride ourselves on our history of innovative publishing. We were thrilled to be shortlisted for Independent Publisher of the Year at the British Book Awards.

www.joffebooks.com

We're very grateful to eagle-eyed readers who take the time to contact us. Please send any errors you find to corrections@joffebooks.com. We'll get them fixed ASAP.